The story, all names, characters, and incidents portrayed in this production are fictitious. No identification with actual persons (living or deceased) is intended or should be inferred.

First paperback edition: May 2025

Book cover by DreamStudio AI

ISBN   978-1-9680273-7-7 (5x8 paperback)

The Survivor's Compound

Part II
The Tattoo Artist

M.P. Hendy

Table of Contents

Chapter 14

The Houston Salvage

David was performing a radio check as everyone got into their positions. Lily, fully decked out in her tactical attire, was already wearing her helmet, thermal imager mounted. "All right, all players, give me a SITREP and radio check!" "This is Red Beast, I'm green on propane, green on ammo, two pax, and Seth brought sandwiches." Romeo one, this is Whiskey four, can we bring something more apocalyptic next time? Like beef jerky?"

"Romeo one, this is Whiskey two, I'm green on fuel, five pax and I'd like to add, you look delicious in that gettup." "Whiskey two, I'm sitting right next to you. You don't have to announce it on the radio, and please, let go of my dick." "But Master, you just announced it on the radio too, plus I'm horny!" "Whiskey two, it's important for us to learn from each other's mistakes." "Romeo X-ray, this is Papa Yankee, if you're monitoring this, we are literally two rows back, watching this bullshit happen from the back seat." "Daddy, if you don't stop fucking around, I'm going to march my pregnant ass down to that garage and claw your eyes out."

David sighed, pinching the bridge of his nose. "Okay, people, settle down. Red Beast, Papa Yankee, Whiskey Two, copy all that. Let's try to maintain some semblance of professionalism, alright? Jessica, darling, I appreciate the sentiment, but save the eye-clawing threats for when they're actually warranted. Lucipurr needs you to stay calm." He could practically feel Jessica's glare through the radio. "Romeo X-ray… out."

He turned to Jennifer, who was smirking behind the wheel of the Transit. "You find this amusing, don't you?" "Master, you know I live for the chaos," she purred, adjusting her night vision goggles. "Besides, someone has to keep you on your toes. Discipline is great, but a little bit of chaos keeps things interesting." Lily, perched in the gunner's seat, fiddled with her thermal scope. "Daddy, are we going to see any bad guys tonight? I've been practicing my headshots." "It's possible, sweetheart," David replied, adjusting her helmet. "But we're aiming for a quick in-and-out. No unnecessary risks. But yes, if we do see any bad guys, you're authorized to deliver some lead induced freedom."

He checked his watch. 2000 hours. "Alright, people, let's roll. Aidan, you take the lead. Maintain a safe distance. Let's try and keep it quiet but be ready for anything." The Beast roared to life, the modified engine a symphony of controlled aggression. The Transit followed close behind, its headlights extinguished, relying solely on night vision and Brian's drone for guidance.

As they pulled onto the deserted highway, the world transformed into a stark, monochrome landscape through the lens of their night vision. Abandoned cars littered the roadside, ghostly reminders of the world that had ceased to exist just two weeks prior. "Drone online," Josh's voice crackled over the radio. "All clear ahead for approximately five kilometers. Minimal heat signatures." "Copy that, Lima Bravo," David replied. "Maintain overwatch."

The journey through Austin was eerie. The once-bustling city was now a graveyard of metal and concrete, silent save for the hum of their vehicles and the chirping of crickets. They passed darkened skyscrapers looming like skeletal giants against the night sky. Inside the Beast, Aidan navigated the treacherous roads with ease. Elena studied the digital map on a tablet. "Aidan, take the next exit. There's a detour marked on the route. There's a large pileup further down the highway." "Copy that, Elena," Aidan replied, smoothly maneuvering the Beast onto the exit ramp. Seth, ever vigilant, scanned the surroundings with his thermal optics, his hand resting on the grip of his rifle.

Back in the van, Parker and Eric shared war stories, their voices low and serious. Josh, glued to the drone's feed, nervously chewed on his lip. "Romeo One, I'm picking up a heat signature about one kilometer ahead, off the main road. Looks like a small group, maybe five or six individuals." "Copy that," David replied, his tone hardening. "Standby for engagement protocol." He looked at Lily, who was eagerly awaiting instructions. "Lily, get ready to paint the target with the infra-red laser. Jennifer, prepare to stop the vehicle."

As they cautiously approached the location, David could see the individuals through his night vision. They were huddled around a campfire, their faces illuminated by the flickering flames. They looked weary and desperate. "David," Josh's voice trembled slightly. "They appear to be civilians. Possibly a family." David hesitated. He had prepared for raiders, for looters, for a fight. Not for a family trying to escape the city. "Romeo One to all units," he announced.

"Stand down. We're not here to hurt anyone. We'll engage with them a bit, then continue our mission."

The Beast rumbled to a gentle stop a safe distance from the campfire. Jennifer cut the engine, enveloping the scene in relative silence, a stark contrast to the city's recent cacophony. David watched the family through his night vision goggles. They were as Josh described: weary, disheveled, and radiating an aura of desperate hope and simmering fear. Stepping out of the van, David adjusted his posture, projecting a calm authority. Lily, ever mirroring her father's movements, shadowed him, her hand hovering near her sidearm. "Evening," David called out, his voice neutral but carrying across the distance. "We saw your fire. Everything alright?"

The man, the one who looked like he'd spent his life wrestling asphalt, slowly rose to his feet, his wife close behind. Their hands instinctively went to their children. The older daughter, sporting a half-finished sleeve of what looked like biker-themed tattoos, remained seated, observing David with a cool, assessing gaze. "We're fine," the man said, his voice raspy. "Just trying to get out of Austin." "Heading anywhere specific?" David asked, keeping his tone conversational. He needed information, a read on their character.

Were they resourceful? Trouble? Or just… lost sheep? "Nowhere specific," the woman answered, her voice laced with a hint of despair. "Just… away. Austin's gone to hell. No power, no water, no food. People are… changing." "Changing how?" Elena's voice chimed in. She emerged from the Beast, her notepad and pen in hand. Always the meticulous recorder of information. "The second blackout hit, and everything just went crazy," the man exhaled. "The supermarkets were emptied in hours. Then the looting started. The smell… the smell of shit and rotting food… you can't imagine. The cops just disappeared. It's every man for himself."

The tattooed girl finally spoke, her voice surprisingly soft. "The gangs are moving in. Claiming territory. Janet saw… things. People doing… things they shouldn't. That's when we decided to leave." David nodded slowly. This was consistent with what he remembered. The initial chaos was giving way to an even more frightening form of societal breakdown. "So, you have no destination in mind?" David pressed. "No," the wife admitted, her eyes brimming with unshed tears. "We don't know where to go. Anywhere is better than here."

David turned slightly, his gaze sweeping over his team. He saw the compassion in Jennifer's eyes, the analytical glint in Elena's, and the unwavering loyalty in Lily's stance. Could they help? His mind raced. Assimilating them presented logistical and social challenges. Plus, David didn't know if they could be trusted, but he could always use the extra help. And he couldn't lie, the young woman might make a good addition to their rabble.

David turned his back to the campfire, effectively muting the family's hopeful gazes. "Jennifer, Elena, Lily, a word." He gestured towards the van, the universal signal for a private conference. Once inside, the air hung thick with unspoken questions. Jennifer spoke first. "Master, we can't just leave them there. They're terrified, especially the children." "I know," David replied, his voice clipped. "But sentimentality will get us killed. We need to assess the risks. Elena, what's your read? You always see more than you let on."

Elena tapped her pen against her notepad. "The dad's a decent man, hardworking, but easily overwhelmed. The mother is strong, resourceful, but her priorities are her kids, as they should be. The teenager… she is interesting. Cynical, observant, but loyal to the others. The little ones are just scared, but they were raised well." Lily, who had been silently observing the family, spoke. "The teenager kept watch while the adults talked. She's got an eye for detail, like you, Daddy. She noticed me watching her, and she didn't flinch."

David nodded. "That's what I saw too. She's got potential. But potential can be a double-edged sword." He turned to Jennifer. "Can you gauge their… willingness to integrate?" Jennifer frowned. "Integration isn't the right word, David. They're desperate. They'll agree to anything to survive. We need to be clear about what we expect, what we offer. And we need to be prepared for… complications." "Complications are a given," David said dryly. "The question is, can we mitigate them? My gut is telling me they are good people, and can be trusted, but I need to make sure. We'll need to do some basic tests."

Outside, the man shifted uncomfortably, watching David and his group huddled in the van. His wife squeezed his hand, her gaze filled with apprehension. The teenager, however, remained impassive, her eyes narrowed, calculating. After a few minutes, the team emerged from the van. David approached the man, his expression unreadable. "We can offer you a temporary solution. We're heading to Houston to pick up some supplies. You can come with us. We'll provide food and protection for the night. After that... we'll see."

Relief washed over the man's face. "Anything, sir. We're just grateful." "Don't call me sir," David said sharply. "I'm David. And don't think this is a charity case. We expect our weight to be carried. Everyone contributes." He turned to the teenager. "You seem like you can handle yourself. We might have some use for you." The girl raised an eyebrow, a flicker of amusement in her eyes. "I'm always up for a challenge, David." "Good," David said. "Then let's get moving. We'll talk more on the road."

As they packed their meager belongings into the back of the Ford Transit, David watched them closely. He saw the exhaustion in their movements, the fear in their eyes, but also the faint glimmer of hope. He knew this was a gamble, but sometimes, a gamble was all you had. "David, I'm Mark. This is my wife, Janet. And these are our kids, Beth, and Lori. The teenager is Kris, our friend's little girl." Mark offered his hand, his grip firm despite his weariness. David shook it. "Welcome to the caravan, Mark. Let's see if we can get you all somewhere safe."

Back inside the packed Ford Transit, the atmosphere was thick with unspoken questions. Mark and Janet tentatively munched on the sandwiches Josh had provided, their eyes wide as they took in the tactical vests, the holstered weapons, and the casual competence radiating from everyone in the vehicle. Lori, the youngest, was asleep in Janet's lap, while Beth stared blankly at the back of the seat in front of her. Kris, was another story entirely. Kris, perched near the back, looked over Josh's shoulder, glued to the tablet he was using to pilot the drone circling overhead. It was clear to Kris that this wasn't just some hobby. Then she noticed the weapons. Everyone had one. Even the blonde in the driver's seat had a pistol tucked into her side holster.

"So, Mark," David began, breaking the silence. "Before all... this," he gestured vaguely at the wrecked world outside, "what did you do?" Mark swallowed, seemingly caught off guard by the question. "Road construction, mostly. Paving, repairs... that sort of thing." He rubbed his stubbled chin. "Not much use for that now, I suppose." Janet chimed in, "And I was a teacher. Fourth grade. Though, I doubt those kids are doing much learning these days." She sighed, a wave of sadness washing over her face.

David filed that away. Road construction meant some understanding of logistics and infrastructure, however basic. A teacher meant some level of patience and organizational skills. Not useless, not by a long shot. "Kris," David directed, turning his attention to the young woman. "You seemed pretty interested in the drone. What's your story?"

Kris met his gaze without flinching, a small, almost imperceptible smile playing on her lips. "Before the world went sideways?" she asked, tilting her head slightly. "I was a tattoo artist. Custom work, mostly. Pretty detail oriented." David's mind clicked. Detail-oriented, artistic, and observant. Someone who could remain calm under pressure, judging by how she'd handled the chaos back at the campfire. Potential. He liked potential.

A few hours passed, the landscape outside the Beast slowly transforming from open highway to the outskirts of Houston. The abandoned cars became more frequent, clustered together like metal carcasses picked clean by vultures. Then, they saw it. A roadblock. Or rather, what looked like a horrific accident scene. Two cars were tangled together at an awkward angle, blocking the road. A small group of people, some visibly injured, were waving frantically, calling for help. It looked desperate, chaotic, almost… staged. "Hold up," David ordered, his voice calm but firm. He already had a bad feeling. "Josh, drone up. Check for anything suspicious."

Josh, without a word, tapped away at the tablet. A moment later, a live feed from the drone appeared on the screen. The image panned across the scene, revealing the injured people, the wreckage… and then, hidden away behind the cars alongside the road, glinting in the fading light, the unmistakable shapes of weapons. "Ambush," Josh stated flatly, his voice devoid of emotion. "Definitely an ambush."

David's eyes narrowed. He turned to Jennifer, his voice low. "Stay here. Watch our backs. If things go south, get Mark's family to safety. I'm going to take a closer look." Jennifer nodded, her expression serious. "Be careful, Master." He turned to Lily and Seth. "Stay behind me guys, I might need some muscle."

Lily slipped out of the gunner's seat, grabbing her carbine. Josh quickly took her place, scanning the scene with the 338 mounted on the roof. Seth, his face set in a determined expression, followed close behind. Both of them moved with an unsettling proficiency. "Mark," David said, turning back to the startled man. "Stay in the van. Keep your family safe. Don't be a hero."

David, Lily, and Seth approached the staged accident, their movements a study in controlled purpose. The "injured" cried out louder, their pleas for help sounding increasingly hollow. David stopped a few feet away, his gaze sweeping over the scene, taking in every detail. Seth, standing slightly behind him, sniffed the air. "Bullshit," Seth announced, his voice surprisingly deep for a fourteen-year-old. "Smells like motor oil and desperation, but no blood. And their acting sucks."

David chuckled, a low, rumbling sound. "Indeed. You'd think with the world ending, people would at least put some effort into their scams." He raised his voice, addressing the group. "Alright, people, let's cut the crap. I've seen better acting in a kindergarten play. Clear the road. Now." A murmur rippled through the crowd. Some of the 'injured' looked at each other nervously. A few, the more hardened ones, tensed, their hands twitching towards hidden pockets and makeshift weapons. One particularly gaunt man, sporting a dirty bandage wrapped around his head, stepped forward, attempting a pathetic limp. "Please, mister," he whined, his voice raspy. "We're hurt bad. We just need some help..."

David cut him off with a dismissive wave. "Save it. I'm not an idiot. I can see the guns hidden behind those cars. I suggest you re-evaluate your life choices and pick a new hobby. Maybe knitting. Or interpretive dance. Anything other than highway robbery." A young woman with matted hair and a wild look in her eyes spat on the ground. "We need what you got! We're surviving here!" David winced. "Surviving by preying on others?" David countered, his voice hardening. "That's not survival. That's parasitism. And parasites get exterminated."

The woman's eyes flashed. She reached behind her back, drawing a rusty pipe. "You think you're so tough?" David actually smiled. "Ah, you see, I was hoping someone would be this stupid." His smile widened, becoming almost predatory. "Desperation is boring. Hostility? Now that's something I can work with."

Back in the van, Kris watched with wide eyes. "He's... enjoying this?" Jennifer smiled. "Master hates it when people use compassion as a weapon. After all, we picked you up, didn't we?" The rusty pipe clattered to the asphalt. David hadn't even seemed to move, yet somehow, the woman was weaponless, disoriented, and staring at him with dawning horror. "One down," David said, his voice conversational. "Who's next?" A hush fell over the group. The bravado had evaporated, replaced by a palpable fear. They had expected an easy mark, a soft target. Instead, they'd found a predator.

That's when the head of the man, trying to flank David, exploded in a shower of blood and bone. The sudden, shocking violence silenced the remaining would-be attackers. All eyes turned to the Ford Transit, where a plume of smoke wafted off the barrel of a rifle.

David was impressed. Josh had acted decisively, eliminating the immediate threat with brutal efficiency. He shot the man on the right, and Elena shot the man on the left. Lily looked back at Josh, a flicker of heated admiration in her eyes. David made a mental note to commend the young man later, before Lynn could try to coddle him.

But the moment of stunned silence was fleeting. The remaining members of the ambush party, fueled by desperation and a primal urge to survive, surged forward. A ragged chorus of shouts and curses filled the air. Some brandished knives, others swung pipes and clubs, while a few desperately fired handguns, the bullets whining harmlessly off the armored plating of Aidan's Red Beast, as it swerved around to help provide cover. David sighed, a sound that was more annoyance than fear. "Alright," he muttered. "Let's get this over with."

He drew his wakizashi, the polished steel gleaming in the dim light. Lily, her face alight with excitement, unsheathed her own sword, a gift from her father that she wielded with surprising skill. Seth, his expression grim and focused, pulled his knife, a wicked-looking blade he'd sharpened himself. The three moved as one, a ballet of controlled aggression. David, with his decades of experience, was the focal point, a whirlwind of deadly precision. His blade danced, deflecting steel weapons, parrying thrusts, and cutting through their adversaries with lethal efficiency.

Lily, younger and more impetuous, fought with a raw, untamed energy. Her attacks were fast and furious, a whirlwind of steel that kept her opponents constantly on the defensive. The bandits were shocked to see that a teenage girl could be so dangerous, because they certainly didn't see it coming. Seth, despite his youth, was a miniature version of his father, cold and calculating. He moved with a quiet grace, his knife a silent killer, finding the gaps in his opponents' defenses with unnerving accuracy.

As the three fought off the attackers, Elena, perched on the hood of the Red Beast, and Josh, from his vantage point in the Ford Transit, continued to pick off the outliers with their rifles. Each shot was precise, lethal, eliminating threats before they could get too close. David, Lily, and Seth seemed unfazed by the gunfire, moving through the chaos as if the whizzing bullets didn't exist. They were a force of nature, an unstoppable tide of steel and fury.

Back in the van, Mark and Janet watched the scene unfold with mounting horror. Their children huddled around them, wide-eyed and terrified. "What... what is happening?" Janet whispered, her voice trembling. Mark, his face pale, could only shake his head. He had thought they were being rescued, taken to a safe haven. Now, they were caught in the middle of a brutal firefight. Kris, however, was staring at David and his family with something akin to fascination.

Mark, like many others, had been ready to accept their fate, to become just another statistic in the post-apocalyptic wasteland. But these people, this strange, deadly family, were fighting back. And they were winning. "He's terrifying," he breathed, his eyes fixed on David as he effortlessly dispatched another attacker. Jennifer, sitting in the front, smiled knowingly. "Master hates bullies. He always protects the weak."

The fight was brutal and short. Within minutes, the ambush party was broken, scattered, and defeated. Some lay dead on the asphalt, others limped away into the darkness, their dreams of easy plunder scattered, along with some of their limbs. David stood amidst the carnage, his wakizashi dripping with blood. He flicked the blade, splashing a stream of blood against the door of a nearby abandoned sedan, then sheathed the blade with a sharp click, his expression unreadable. "Clear the road," he said, his voice flat and devoid of emotion. "Let's move."

Parker and Kyle, weapons drawn, cautiously emerged from the van. They surveyed the scene, a mixture of horror and awe etched on their faces. They had seen combat, but this…this was different. Parker turned to Kyle. "At least we're on the same side," he said with a faint smile. Parker and Eric began dragging the bodies to the side of the road, their movements methodical and grim. But then Lily and Seth moved forward. Without a word, they grabbed the nearest corpse, one in the throes of death, and tossed it effortlessly over the barrier, the body landing with a sickening thud in the ditch below. They moved onto the next, and the next, until the bodies were a macabre pile on the side of the road. Mark and Janet gasped. Kris, however, continued to watch with rapt interest.

Next, Lily and Seth approached the abandoned car blocking the road, a rusted hulk of metal and broken glass. With a grunt, they each gripped a side of the vehicle and, with seemingly minimal effort, lifted it clear of the road. The car screeched and scraped as it was dragged aside, leaving gouges in the asphalt. The casual display of strength was unnerving. These were not ordinary people. As they walked back to the vehicles, Lily and Seth were nonchalant, even chit chatting. Their expressions betraying no hint of the violence that had just transpired. They might as well have been removing a fallen tree branch from the road.

David, unfazed by the carnage, turned to Mark. "Sorry about the delay, Mark. Things tend to get a little…kinetic out here." He offered a reassuring smile, which, given the circumstances, felt a little like a serial killer offering a lollipop, but Mark managed a weak nod, nonetheless. With the road cleared, Aidan revved the Red Beast, its throaty rumble a stark contrast to the unnerving silence that followed the ambush. Jennifer followed closely behind, David issuing directions. They drove for another hour, the landscape slowly transitioning from abandoned subdivisions to industrial parks, a monument to a world that was rapidly dissolving.

Finally, David pointed to a sprawling complex behind a chain-link fence topped with razor wire. "That's it. Surplus stockyard. Should be something useful in there." The gates were padlocked, but Aidan, with a practiced flick of his wrist, had them open in seconds. The yard was a chaotic jumble of forgotten machinery, abandoned containers, and piles of scrap metal.

"Alright," David announced, clapping his hands together. "Aidan, you know what we need. Start sniffing around for sheet metal. Specifically, the good stuff. Elena, keep him company, make sure he doesn't get distracted by anything shiny." Aidan, already halfway to a towering stack of corrugated iron, grinned. "Distracted? Me? Never!" Elena simply rolled her eyes and followed him, her rifle slung casually across her front.

"Parker, Eric, Josh, and Lily." David gestured towards Aidan's muscle car. "We need to find a truck.

Something big, something reliable, and preferably something that hasn't been completely cannibalized for parts." Lily, practically vibrating with excitement, bounced on the balls of her feet. "Can I drive, Daddy?" David chuckled. "Of course, sweetheart. Parker and Eric, you two are the muscle, so go find us a beast."

As Lily, Josh, Parker, and Eric piled into the Red Beast, Kris watched them go, her expression unreadable. She turned to David, who was studying a map of the stockyard. "Mr. David?" she asked tentatively. David looked up, his expression softening slightly. "Just David, Kris." "David," she corrected, a faint blush rising on her cheeks. She hesitated for a moment, then plunged in. "What…what was that all about back there? On the road? And…and Lily and Seth…they just…how can they do that?"

David sighed internally. He knew this question was coming. "They're gifted, Kris. It seems to be…genetic." He shrugged, as if discussing their eye color. Kris's eyes widened. "Gifted?" David only nodded. Jennifer, who had been listening from nearby, chuckled. "Gifted is an understatement, Master. They are forces of nature." She ruffled Kris's hair playfully. "Don't worry, you'll get used to it. We all do…eventually." Kris looked from David to Jennifer, clearly still processing everything. "But…the way you called him…" she hesitated, "Master?"

Jennifer's smile widened as she stepped closer to Kris, lowering her voice. "Oh, that? That's a whole different story. I'm David's property. His willing slave, for life." She winked, leaving Kris completely dumbfounded. David rolled his eyes, but a hint of amusement flickered across his face.

"Jennifer, please don't corrupt the poor girl." He turned back to Kris. "She enjoys theatrics." Jennifer laughed. "Theatrics with a heaping helping of truth! But seriously, Kris, don't let it scare you. We're all…happy here."

Later, Kris watched Aidan and Seth effortlessly maneuvering massive sheets of steel, stacking them with a precision and speed that defied logic. Seth casually tossed a particularly unwieldy piece, and Aidan, without breaking a sweat, caught it one-handed, redirecting its momentum with a grunt of effort. Kris was even more impressed than before. She began to think in a way unknown to her. If her future children had any hope of thriving, of surviving in this new, brutal world, they needed to be like David's. Or…a daring, reckless thought sparked in her mind…they needed to be David's children.

Chapter 15

The Children of David

The thought of bearing David's children. It was audacious, bordering on insane, but it took root with surprising tenacity. David was strong, intelligent, capable, and he clearly knew how to prepare his children for anything. It was survival of the fittest, and Kris wanted her family to be on the winning side. Driven by this newfound resolve, Kris searched for Elena. She found her leaning against the doorway of the warehouse, watching Aidan and Seth work. "Elena?" Kris asked hesitantly. Elena looked up, her eyes sharp and assessing. "Kris, right? What can I do for you?" Kris took a deep breath. "I…I was wondering about David. About his children." Elena raised an eyebrow, intrigued. "What about them?" "How many does he have?" Kris asked. "I've only met Aidan, Lily, and Seth. Are they all…exceptional? Or is his…'gift' random?"

Elena considered the question for a moment. "David has a large family," she said carefully. "He has two daughters, four sons, and of course there's another on the way. They are all…unique. And yes, they are all exceptional in their own ways. It's not random, not exactly. They all seem to inherit…something from David. A strength, a resilience, a knack for survival." Kris nodded slowly, absorbing the information. "So, it's… consistent? They're all like that?" "Yes," Elena confirmed. "They are all capable of things most people can only dream of. They've been taught, trained, and prepared for anything. David made sure of it."

Kris's mind raced. Six children. All exceptional. All inheriting some part of David's incredible abilities. It was a staggering thought. "And… Jennifer?" Kris ventured, her cheeks flushing slightly. "Is she also gifted?" Elena laughed. "No, Jennifer's not exceptional, none of his women are. I'm certainly not. But that doesn't mean we're incapable. We all have our specialties and our talents, even Jennifer."

Kris just realized she only considered Jennifer as David's partner. The thought embarrassed her, it felt naive. "Are you…with David as well?" Kris asked, the question hanging in the air. Elena's expression softened, a small smile playing on her lips. "Yes, I am. We all are. Tiffany, Jennifer, Summer, Taylor, Nicole, Kayla, Tanya, Jessica… and me. We're a…family." She said the last word with a hint of amusement.

Kris's jaw dropped slightly. It was all so…unbelievable. "And your children?" she dared to ask. "Are they…" Elena's eyes twinkled with amusement. "I don't have any children, Kris. I'm everyone's favorite aunt. But if I did, and David was the father, you can bet they would tear through the world." Kris was reeling. This… this was more complicated, and more fascinating than she could have imagined. "I… I don't even know what to say," she stammered, completely overwhelmed.

Kris, still absorbing the bombshell Elena had dropped, stumbled slightly as she made her way back towards David. The enormity of it all pressed down on her — the tactical genius, the super-powered children, and the… the harem. It was like a movie, a bizarre fever dream she hadn't woken up from yet.

As if on cue to further shatter her perception of reality, a colossal vehicle rumbled into view, dwarfing everything around it. It was an Oshkosh M1070 HET, a beast of a machine designed to haul tanks. And from the cab, emerged Eric and Parker, looking slightly grimy but undeniably triumphant. Lily and Josh pulled up immediately after in Aidan's beast.

Parker hopped down, a grin splitting his face. "We got it running, David! Little rough around the edges, but she's a beast." He gestured towards Josh and Lily. "These two worked miracles. Though, fair warning, almost none of the electronics are functioning." David simply waved a hand dismissively. "Night vision. We all have it." He wasn't concerned about the lack of fancy gadgets. "Aidan will have a blast fixing it up."

Kris watched, dumbfounded, as David smoothly transitioned back into command mode. The realization that this was his normal was almost too much to process. She could barely keep up. "Alright, everyone," David announced, his voice cutting through the air with authority. "Let's get those metal plates loaded onto the back of this beauty. Kyle, find some heavy-duty ratchet straps. We don't want any surprises on the way back."

The group sprang into action, a well-oiled machine moving with practiced efficiency. Even Mark was helping, though he looked utterly bewildered, glancing between the mountain of metal and the tank-hauling behemoth. As Kris watched Mark struggle with a particularly unwieldy plate, she couldn't help but feel a pang of guilt. They had been plucked from a desperate situation and thrust into… this. A family consisting of super-humans, polyamorous relationships, and logistical operations involving military-grade vehicles.

She approached David, who was directing the loading with his usual calm precision. "David," she began hesitantly, "Mark's family… they don't know anything about all this. About you, about…" She gestured vaguely around, unable to articulate the sheer weirdness of it all. David paused, turning to face her. His gaze was direct, assessing. "They're safe. That's what matters. They're with us now, and we take care of our own." His words were simple, but they carried a weight of conviction that was strangely comforting. He wasn't offering platitudes; he was stating a fact.

The loading finished, the M1070 looking like a metallic hedgehog bristling with jagged edges. Parker and Eric climbed into the cab, the engine roaring to life with a guttural growl. David began issuing instructions with his characteristic efficiency. "Aidan, Elena, take point again. Seth, overwatch from the HET. Jennifer, we're behind them with the van, Lily will do overwatch. He paused, his eyes sweeping over the group. "Our next stop is fuel. We need diesel, and this beast gets thirsty."

The convoy rumbled to life, Aidan's beast leading the way, followed by the hulking M1070, and Jennifer's van bringing up the rear. Seth, perched atop the truck bed, scanned the horizon with the 300 win mag, a silent sentinel. Inside the van, Mark and his family clung to their seats, their faces a mixture of fear and awe. "So," David said, turning to Mark, "how are you holding up?" Mark swallowed hard, his eyes wide. "Honestly? I feel like I've wandered into a movie. Or maybe a very strange dream." David chuckled.

As they drove, Josh was fiddling with a handheld device. "David, I'm picking up a large concentration of generator power about twenty miles north, it's at a Buc-ee's truck stop." "Good. I'm sure they have fuel. But I also know there's a good chance the place is being controlled by someone." David said. "Either way we get fuel and snacks" Lily added from the gunner's seat.

As they approached the Buc-ee's, the scene confirmed their suspicions. Armed men patrolled the perimeter, their weapons glinting from the generator powered lights. The parking lot, normally a bustling hub of activity, was now eerily silent, save for the hum of the generator powering the building.

David turned to the group in the van. "Alright," he said, his voice calm but firm, "here's the plan. Aidan and Elena will take the front entrance, creating a diversion. Seth will provide sniper cover from the HET. Jennifer, Lily, you're with me. We'll flank them from the side. Josh, keep the drone in the air, give us intel. Parker, Eric, secure the perimeter. Mark, you and your family stay put. This shouldn't take long." Mark's face paled even further. "Stay put?" he squeaked. "But... but we don't even have guns!" David smiled reassuringly. "Don't worry, Mark. You won't need them. Just trust us. We've got this."

The team sprang into action with well-rehearsed precision. Aidan's car roared forward, tires squealing as he careened towards the main entrance, Elena perched in the passenger seat, firing shots toward the guards. The guards, startled by the sudden attack, scrambled for cover, their attention focused on the approaching vehicle. Seth, true to his word, had already found a sniper's nest on top of the HET. With a crack of his rifle, the first guard fell, his body crumpling silently to the ground. The remaining guards, now thoroughly panicked, began firing blindly in Aidan's direction.

Taking advantage of the chaos, David, Jennifer, and Lily moved swiftly along the side of the building, hugging the shadows. They reached a side entrance and, as Jennifer pulled the door open, David and Lily slipped in. Inside, more guards were frantically trying to organize a defense. "Hi, Fellas" Lily said before opening fire with her M4, followed by Jennifer and David.

The ensuing firefight was short and brutal. David moved with lightning speed, his movements a blur of lethal efficiency. Jennifer, a skilled marksman, picked off targets with deadly accuracy. Lily, grinning with exhilaration, danced through the chaos, her M4 spitting bullets. Within minutes, the remaining guards lay dead or wounded. Parker and Eric, having secured the perimeter, moved inside to provide assistance. Josh, guiding the drone, provided real-time intel, alerting them to any remaining threats. Soon, the Buc-ee's was under their control.

David surveyed the scene, his expression grim. "Alright," he said, "clear the bodies, secure the area. Aidan, Elena, check for any survivors. Jennifer, see if you can find the manager. I want to know how much fuel they have. Seth, find a mop or something, I don't want to traumatize the kids." As the team began their tasks, David approached the van, where Mark and his family were huddled together, their faces pale with shock. He opened the door, his expression gentle. "It's over," he said. "It's clear now. Come on, let's get you some refreshments. You've earned it."

Mark, still trembling, slowly emerged from the van, followed by his wife and daughters. Kris, however, hung back, her eyes fixed on David. "You're incredible," she said, her voice barely a whisper. "All of you. How do you do it?" David smiled. "Practice," he said. "And a lot of coffee. Now come on, let's get some snacks. I hear Buc-ee's has the best beaver nuggets in Texas."

Aidan, meanwhile, was outside, already halfway inside of a battered-looking generator abandoned near the fuel pumps. He popped the access panel open, a tangle of wires staring back at him. He began expertly connecting cables, muttering to himself. "What are you doing?" Mark asked, cautiously approaching him. He felt ridiculously out of his depth, a suburban dad suddenly thrust into a Mad Max movie. "Wiring the generator to the fuel pumps," Aidan replied, his voice matter of fact, devoid of any drama. He didn't even look up. "We need to fill up the HET." "But… how?" Mark stammered, gesturing feebly at the complex machinery. "They're all… computerized. And the power's out."

Aidan finally straightened up, a wide grin spreading across his face, mirroring David's own brand of unsettling charm. "It's all about knowing the right circuits," he said, winking. "And a little bit of reverse engineering." He went back to work, his movements fluid and confident, a stark contrast to Mark's own fumbling attempts to understand what was happening.

Within minutes, the pumps were humming to life, the rumble of the generator a defiant roar in the sudden quiet. The massive Oshkosh M1070 HET, a vehicle that looked like it belonged on a battlefield, began guzzling diesel, its fuel tanks swallowing gallons with alarming speed.

As the tanks filled, David emerged from the store, a brown paper bag tucked under his arm, a satisfied look on his face. "Alright, people," he announced, his voice carrying over the noise of the pumps. "Time to move out. Next stop, La Porte. We need to find some UHMWPE." A chorus of groans erupted from the assembled group. Jennifer pinched his arm, a playful scowl on her face. "What happened to you calling it by its full name? Ultra-High Molecular Weight Polyethylene? You're normally such a stickler."

David shrugged, his eyes momentarily losing their characteristic twinkle. "It's just not the same without Jessica here," he said quietly, then clapped his hands together, effectively shaking off the momentary melancholy. "Alright, let's load up! Beaver nuggets for everyone!" He started walking back toward the van, tossing the paper bag to Kris, who caught it with surprising dexterity.

The drive to La Porte was tense. Mark and his family were crammed into the back of the van, the silence punctuated only by the occasional nervous cough and the drone of the HET lumbering along behind them. "So," Janet said tentatively, breaking the silence. "Ultra-High Molecular Weight... what was it?" "Polyethylene," Kris supplied, popping a beaver nugget into her mouth. "It's a type of plastic. Super strong. They use it for armor, apparently." "Armor?" Mark repeated, his voice rising in pitch. "As in… bulletproof vests?" "Among other things," Kris said, her eyes gleaming with a newfound excitement. "I think they're planning on building something… bigger."

David, overhearing the conversation, chuckled. "You're a quick study, Kris," he said, glancing at her in the rearview mirror. "Maybe you'll fit right in." The closer they got to La Porte, the more chaotic the scene became. Abandoned cars littered the highway, their occupants long gone. Looted storefronts gaped open, their shelves stripped bare. The air hung thick with the smell of smoke and desperation. "Alright, people, eyes peeled," David commanded, his voice sharp and focused. "Aidan, take point. Elena, you're on lookout. Seth, Lily, you know the drill."

Mark watched in stunned silence as the group sprang into action, their movements coordinated and efficient. Aidan accelerated ahead in his Red Beast, scouting the road. Elena scanned the rooftops with her rifle, her gaze unwavering. As they pulled into a deserted industrial park on the outskirts of La Porte, David pointed to a sprawling warehouse. "That's our target," he announced. "A plastics manufacturer. Let's see what we can find."

The warehouse was a scene of utter devastation. Shelves lay overturned, boxes were ripped open, and the air was thick with the scent of spilled chemicals. But amidst the chaos, stacks of UHMWPE sheets, still neatly palletized, stood untouched, seemingly forgotten in the frenzy of looting. "Jackpot," David said, a predatory gleam in his eyes. "Alright, let's load it up!" Mark, still trying to process the sheer efficiency and preparedness of David's team, ventured a question. "Why… why would they leave all this plastic behind? Everything else is trashed."

David didn't break his focus as he directed the loading efforts. "Most people are thinking short-term. Food, water, maybe some weapons. They wouldn't know what to do with Ultra-High Molecular Weight Polyethylene. It's not exactly Twinkies." Jennifer, hoisting a surprisingly large sheet of the plastic with effortless ease, added, "Most folks are just trying to survive the day. We're planning for the long haul."

The sun was starting to peek over the horizon, casting long shadows across the industrial park. Lori and Beth were fast asleep in the back of the van, oblivious to the chaos around them. The M1070 HET, already a behemoth of a vehicle, was quickly filling with the UHMWPE sheets. Seth and Lily worked with a practiced ease, using a forklift they'd discovered in surprisingly good condition to load the heavier pallets. With the M1070 groaning under its heavy load, Aidan maneuvered his Red Beast alongside the van. "Alright, everyone ready?" David called out. "Let's head back before we attract any unwanted attention."

Just before pulling out of the industrial park, Aidan positioned his Red Beast next to a massive propane tank located near the warehouse. With a few quick adjustments and the help of Josh over the radio, Aidan attached a hose and began siphoning propane into the van's modified fuel tanks. He then repeated the process with his own car. Mark, bewildered, watched the operation. "Propane? Why are you filling up with propane? Don't you need gasoline?"

David chuckled, a low rumble in his chest. "Gasoline's a liability now, Mark. Hard to find, goes bad quickly, and attracts the wrong kind of attention. Remember that EMP?" "The… the what?" Mark stammered. "Electromagnetic pulse, it's what caused the blackout," Elena interjected, not unkindly. "Fried most modern electronics, including the fuel pumps at gas stations. Gasoline is difficult to pump. Besides, most gasoline car computers are fried and won't run. Propane is a simpler system. Less to go wrong. And we've modified our vehicles to run on it."

David clapped Mark on the shoulder. "Necessity is the mother of invention, my friend. We've been preparing for scenarios like this for a long time."

Lily said from the gunner seat, her voice teasingly sweet, "I think the girl likes us." "Which girl, Sweetheart?" David responded. "Kris. She keeps looking at you and Seth." "She's observant, Lily," David said. "That's a good thing. We need more observant people."

As they continued, David decided to stop by some tattoo shops. He pulled Into the parking lot of a boarded-up strip mall. "We're gonna stop for a minute," David announced to everyone in the van. "I need to pick up some supplies." Mark looked around, confused. "Supplies? What kind of supplies?" David grinned. "Tattoo supplies." He stepped out of the van, and Lily followed close behind. "Stay here. Seth, keep an eye on things from the truck."

Inside the first tattoo shop, the scene was grim. Overturned furniture, shattered glass, and a lingering smell of stale beer painted a picture of desperate looting. David, unfazed, began to methodically sift through the debris. He knew what he was looking for: sterile needles, various inks, sanitizing solutions, and stencils. Lily, ever his little shadow, helped him gather the supplies, her delicate fingers surprisingly adept at sorting through the mess. "Daddy, look!" Lily exclaimed, holding up a near-empty bottle of vibrant purple ink. "Can we get this?" David chuckled. "Of course, Sweetheart. Purple is always a good choice." He imagined Summer, her platinum curls a stark contrast to the bold color, and smiled.

They moved on to another shop, then another, amassing a small arsenal of tattooing equipment. David was meticulous, checking expiration dates and ensuring everything was still usable. As they left the last shop, Lily skipped ahead, humming a tuneless melody. Back in the van, Kris's eyes lit up as David and Lily loaded the boxes of supplies. "You're a tattoo artist?" she asked, her voice filled with excitement. David smiled. "No, you are, remember?"

As they pulled back onto the highway, Kris leaned forward again. "So, about those tattoos…" she began, a playful glint in her eyes. Janet elbowed her gently. "Kris!" David, catching the exchange in his rearview mirror, simply grinned. "Don't worry, Janet. We'll tell you all about it. It's… a family tradition. A way of honoring the people who matter most to us." Jennifer, seeing an opportunity to tease Mark's family and show off, leaned forward and flashed a part of her tattoo toward the back of the van. Right on her shoulder blade, visible for a fleeting moment, were the words, "Property of David Ranado" written in his distinctive handwriting. Mark, Janet, and their younger daughters stared, speechless, at the sight. David shook his head slightly, a hint of exasperation in his expression. "Jennifer," he chided gently, "a little discretion, please." Jennifer simply winked. "Where's the fun in that, Master?" she purred.

David slowed the van, signaling a left turn onto the dirt road leading to the valley where his ranch was nestled. Aidan, a respectable distance behind in the Red Beast, mimicked the signal. Mark and his family were stirring in the back, finally waking up from their uneasy naps. "Almost there," David announced, his voice calm and reassuring. He glanced in the rearview mirror, catching Kris's bright, inquisitive eyes. She was a sharp one, that girl. He could see the wheels turning in her head. He'd have to be careful what he said around her; she wouldn't miss a thing.

The rumble of the M1070 faded as Eric expertly parked it next to the work shed, its massive tires crunching on the gravel. Relief washed over David as he stepped out of the van, Lily practically glued to his side as Josh held her hand. It had been a long, messy, and occasionally hilarious sixteen hours. He could already smell the familiar scent of Summer's baking wafting from the main house, a promise of warmth and normalcy.

Mark, his family, and Kris, still wide-eyed from the events of the past day, gaped at the ranch. The white plantation-style house, gleaming under the Texas sun, looked like something out of a movie, an impression only amplified by the imposing fortifications subtly integrated into its design. Janet, clutching Beth tightly, whispered something to Mark, who nodded in agreement, their faces a mixture of awe and gratitude.

As David led them towards the house, a wave of warmth enveloped him. Tiffany, Summer, Nicole, Taylor, Jessica, Kayla, and Tanya spilled out onto the porch, their faces alight with concern and then pure joy. The air crackled with affection as the women rushed forward, enveloping David in a group hug, their voices a chorus of welcomes.

"Welcome to our little slice of sanity, Mark, Janet," David said, his voice laced with genuine warmth as he disentangled himself from the embrace. He gestured towards his wives, each radiating a unique charm. "This is Tiffany, Summer, Nicole, Taylor, Jessica, Kayla, and Tanya. They keep this place running, and me grounded, most of the time." Mark and Janet exchanged bewildered glances, a silent conversation passing between them. David chuckled, accustomed to the initial reactions. "Yeah, it's a bit of a crowd. But we make it work."

While David introduced Mark and Janet, Aidan and Elena pulled into the driveway, parking neatly in the garage. Alissa, having clearly missed her husband, launched herself at Aidan, pulling him into a passionate kiss that made Elena whistle appreciatively.

David turned his attention to Kris, who stood slightly apart, her eyes darting around with a mixture of curiosity and apprehension. "Kris, come meet the rest of the family." He led her towards a small gathering of younger faces. "This is Grace, my youngest daughter and Seth's twin sister, and these two are Brian and Junior. They are both Jennifer's sons. And this lovely lady is Seo-Yeon, Brian's wife. Her sister Tanya, is over there," he said, gesturing to the hoard of wives.

As David's wives tended to the rest of the family, David pulled Mark and Kris aside. "I want you two to come with me. I'm going to give you the tour." The first stop was the work shed, where Kyle, Scott, Parker and Eric were already working to unload the HET. "Hey guys, get Junior and Brian out here to help you," David said, his voice cutting through the sounds of metal clanging. Kyle nodded before running toward the house.

"That was Kyle, Kayla's younger brother. He's a gunsmith and a good firearms instructor. He even taught Junior the trade," David said, leading them inside. Mark marveled at the size of the workspace. Everything they could need was here. Kris, not one to miss the details, pointed at the stairs. "Where does that go?" she asked. David smiled. "That's the generator room. We'll look at that later," he answered, urging them along.

On the other side of the property was the shooting range. "You'll be here often," David said, gesturing to the shooting area. "Everybody learns to shoot, and everyone must be armed. Especially nowadays." Next, David walked them to the barn. "Miniature cows?" Mark asked, genuinely bewildered. He'd seen a lot of strange things in the last few days, and this certainly made the list.

David chuckled. "Easier to manage, eat less, and still produce enough milk for us. Plus, they're adorable." He pointed to the goats, who were engaging in a playful headbutting contest, then to the chickens clucking contentedly in their coop. "Sustainability is key." Kris was fascinated, taking it all in with a sharp eye. She saw the logic, the planning, the sheer practicality of it all. David wasn't just surviving; he was thriving, creating a miniature world where his family could not only exist but flourish.

After returning to the work shed, David led Mark and Kris down the concrete stairs into the generator room. The air changed immediately, dropping a few degrees and carrying the low hum of machinery. Eight massive generators, each the size of a small car, sat in neat rows, their engines idling smoothly. The room was brightly lit by industrial lights, reflecting off the painted concrete walls.

Mark stared, impressed. "This is… incredible. How long will this keep the power on?" "Indefinitely, with proper maintenance and fuel," David replied matter-of-factly. "These run on propane, so fuel isn't too much of a problem. Plus, most of the ranch runs on solar anyway." Kris nodded, absorbing the information. "And the ventilation?" "Extensive. Filters everything before it exhausts. Brian monitors it, along with the hydroponics." David gestured towards a complex array of pipes and vents running along the ceiling. " redundancy is always good."

Mark eyed the heavy steel door set into the far wall. "What's behind that?" David gave a slight smile. "That's where you'll be staying, at least for now. Below us are the apartment bunkers. Come on, let's get you settled." He punched a code into a keypad beside the door, and with a hydraulic hiss, it swung inward, revealing another set of concrete stairs descending further into the earth. Kris, ever observant, noticed the layers of security. Keypads, heavy doors, redundancies upon redundancies. It spoke volumes about David's preparedness.

Chapter 16

A New Family Plan

As they descended, the air grew noticeably cooler. The harsh industrial lighting of the generator room gave way to a softer, more diffused glow. The concrete walls were painted a pale, calming blue, and the hum of the generators was muffled to a low thrum. They reached a long corridor lined with identical doors. David stopped before one and swiped a keycard. The door clicked open, revealing a surprisingly spacious apartment. "648 square feet," David stated, as if reading her mind. "One master bedroom, two smaller bedrooms, kitchenette, common room, and a bathroom. Fully stocked with essentials. Three artificial windows."

Mark and Kris stepped inside, their mouths agape. The apartment was far more comfortable than anything they had imagined. The furniture was simple but functional, the kitchenette was stocked with non-perishable food items, and the bedrooms were neatly made with fresh linens. "LCD screen windows?" Kris asked, approaching one of the screens set into the wall.

David nodded. "They project whatever image and sounds you want. Nature scenes, cityscapes, even just a blank blue sky. Keeps things from feeling too claustrophobic." He tapped a control panel, and the screens flickered to life, displaying a peaceful forest scene, complete with the gentle sounds of birdsong and rustling leaves. "They can even show you any live image from any one of the cameras around the property. So you can watch the kids. Or watch the perimeter," he said, smiling.

Mark walked over to a shelf stocked with books and games. "You've thought of everything, haven't you?" "Tried to," David replied, a hint of a smile playing on his lips. "We've got enough supplies down here to last for years. And if you need anything else, don't hesitate to ask. Kayla and Tanya keep track of everything. So they'll be here to stock up on your perishables later."

Kris, meanwhile, was taking in the details. The cleanliness, the order, the sheer level of preparation. It was all a testament to David's meticulous nature. And then there were the LCD windows. They were 3 by 5ft, projecting nature scenes, complete with environmental sounds, wind and lights, used in place of windows. "This is incredible, David," Kris said sincerely. "Thank you." "Don't mention it," David replied. "We're all in this together now." He paused. "There's another level of apartments below this one."

As David watched them, Kris approached him. "David, can I ask you something?" He turned his head, his expression open and patient. "Of course." "I've been thinking... about everything you've built here, and about your family," Kris began, choosing her words carefully. "Your children... they're extraordinary. The way they fought back in Houston, the way they moved that car..." David remained silent, listening intently. "I want my children to have that kind of strength, that kind of skill," Kris continued, her voice gaining confidence. "I want them to be prepared for whatever comes next. And I think the best way for that to happen... is for them to be part of your family." "So," Kris began, her voice a low hum, "about that… about my future children." She traced a finger along the rim of the door trim, her gaze unwavering. "I mean, seeing your kids… Aidan, Lily, even little Seth… it's… impressive. They're not just strong and smart; they're exceptional."

David nodded slowly, his eyes mirroring the cool composure of the scene in the window. "They are. It's… a family trait." He didn't elaborate, and Kris didn't expect him to. She knew better than to press for unnecessary details; this was a man who dealt in facts, not flowery explanations. "And that," Kris continued, her voice barely above a whisper, "that's not something you can teach. It's genetic, right? It's… inherent." She leaned forward, her boldness astonishing even to herself. "I want that for my children. I want them to be as… resilient… as capable… as yours."

A beat of silence hung heavy in the air. Mark shifted uncomfortably, his eyes darting between Kris and David. He'd known Kris was fascinated, almost obsessed, with the family, but this… this was a level up. "I understand your ambition," David finally responded, his voice calm and even. "But this is a rather… unconventional approach to family planning, wouldn't you say?" He paused, letting the remark hang in the air like a carefully placed landmine.

Kris didn't flinch. "I'm proposing to become one of your wives, David." The words hung in the quiet room, bold and unapologetic. Mark choked on his saliva. David raised an eyebrow, a flicker of amusement in his eyes. "Well, that certainly streamlines the process." His expression remained unreadable, a mask of practiced calm. "And what makes you think I would agree?"

"Because," Kris said, her voice gaining strength, "I can contribute. I'm adaptable. I'm a quick learner, and I already know you have a system in place, a way of life that works. I want to be a part of that, for me, yes, but more importantly for the future of my lineage." She smiled, a genuine, unwavering smile that held a surprising amount of confidence. "And besides," she added, "I think I already know why your wives love you so much." Mark's jaw hung slack; he was utterly speechless. David, however, seemed to find this amusing. He chuckled, a low, rumbling sound. "You're remarkably forward, Kris. I appreciate your directness."

"So," David retorted. "You want to become one of my wives to ensure your children inherit...certain qualities." He paused, letting the implication hang heavy. "Essentially, you're proposing a strategic breeding program." Kris, surprisingly unfazed by his blunt assessment, nodded eagerly. "Precisely." David chuckled again. "And you believe that's all genetic?" "Primarily, yes," Kris replied confidently. "Though obviously, environment plays a part. But the core...the inherent resilience, the tactical prowess...that's hereditary. I want that for my children."

David leaned back, considering. He wasn't necessarily averse to the idea, he had, after all, accumulated quite a collection of wives over the years. Yet, this was...different. A calculated attempt to leverage his family's unique circumstances for purely pragmatic reasons instead of the usual emotional ties. He found it strangely fascinating.

"Kris," he said, his tone shifting slightly, "you don't need to become my wife to access those benefits."

Mark sputtered, clearly relieved by this statement. However, Kris's eyes widened in surprise. David continued, "My children receive extensive training. Survival skills, combat training, strategic thinking...it's a comprehensive program, not just something magically passed down in the genes. Your children could receive this training without you becoming my wife."

Kris shook her head, her dark eyes unwavering. "But marriage," she insisted, "offers unparalleled access. Individualized attention. My children wouldn't just be part of a program; they'd have you, specifically, as a mentor, a father figure, dedicated to their development." She paused. "It's not just about the genes, David. It's about… security. Stability. You've created that here. I want that for my children."

David leaned back, the amusement fading slightly as he truly considered her words. He admired her candor, her clear-headed assessment of the situation, a stark contrast to the priorities of many before the blackout. "Kris, I want you to understand that if we were to become husband and wife, it would mean complete submission and ownership under my authority. I would be your master, and you would be my devoted wife," David explained, searching for any signs of uncertainty in her eyes. Kris, however, remained resolute. She had witnessed the strong, stable, and protective community David had built and knew that she wanted a similar future for her children. She saw hope and safety in this new world, and she was determined to be a part of it.

"Kris, I think my son David Junior might be a better fit for you. He's closer to your age and carries the same genetic benefits. What do you think?" David asked, carefully gauging her reaction. Kris thought for a moment, considering David Junior's qualities and how they might complement her own. She knew that either way, she wanted to be a part of this community, and she was willing to explore any possibilities that would lead her there. "I think that could work, David. I'm open to getting to know him better," she replied, a small smile playing on her lips.

David, pleased with her response, decided to give Kris some space to consider her options. He suggested that she choose where she wanted to live, as Mark and Janet's apartment would soon become too crowded. "Kris, you can have your own apartment here in the bunker, neighboring your friends, or you can live in a guest room under the main house. The bedrooms upstairs in the main house are reserved for me, my young children and my wives. The apartments are private, and you'll be close to everyone else, but you'll be on your own for the most part. The guest rooms in the main house have easier access to other amenities, and my family is right upstairs," David explained, leaving the decision up to her. Kris weighed her options, considering the pros and cons of each choice. She ultimately decided that living in an apartment would be best for her, as it would allow her the privacy and independence she desired.

Later that same afternoon, David gathered Kris and Mark's family back at the house. "Kayla, Tanya, could you both take some produce and milk down to Mark and Kris's apartment," he said, his voice carrying a note of gentle authority. "I'm going to give them a tour of the main compound." Kayla nodded. "Of course, sir. We'll get right on it." Tanya smiled reassuringly at Janet. "We'll make sure you have everything you need."

With Kayla and Tanya attending to the provisions, David turned his attention back to Mark and his family. "Now," he announced, ready to see the rest of the house?" He led them down to the garage, vast and organized. "David, is this garage reinforced?" Mark asked, noticing the walls and impressively robust garage door. "Yes, it is. And these," David gestured to the doors to his right, "lead to the guest rooms I told you about. Although, one of the rooms has been converted into a classroom, while another serves as an aide station that Andrea runs."

Mark and his family admired the size of the space, it was certainly bigger than any garage they had ever seen. "That lift over there is for moving heavy machinery and supplies further down," David said, noticing Mark's gaze. "If you'll follow me, we have more to cover," he said, gesturing to the other staircase.

He descended first, the others following close behind, their faces a mixture of apprehension and curiosity. As they reached the bottom of the stairs, they stepped into the storage bunker, a vast space that dwarfed anything they had imagined. As far as they could see, were rows and rows of pallets, shelves and supplies that seemed to go on forever. "This is our long term storage. We have enough freeze dried, semi perishable and emergency rations to feed a full complex for at least twenty years."

Mark ran his hands over the secured pallets, reaching to the ceiling. "Are these the same rations I saw in the apartment hallway?" Mark asked, noticing the contents. David nodded. "Our ranch and hydroponics subsidize our food supply with fresh meat, dairy and vegetables. We also have medical supplies, tools, spare parts and materials for the house." A look of realization washed over Marks face. "David, how long have you been preparing for this? I mean, this isn't just a coincidence. This is calculated." "We've been preparing for a long time," David said, his tone matter of fact. "But that's a story for another time."

Next, David led them to the recreational bunker. The centerpiece was the massive swimming pool, its surface shimmering under artificial lights. "We believe in staying active," David said, "even when the world outside is falling apart. Morale is essential in maintaining peace. Plus, it gives us a little something more to fight for." Kris stared at the pool, her jaw practically on the floor. "You have a pool? Underground?"

David chuckled. "Indeed. And a spa, and a sauna, and enough exercise equipment to make even the most dedicated fitness fanatic weep with joy. Tanya and Seo-Yeon work mostly from here, but privileges are limited to contributing community members."

Finally, they reached the maintenance bunker, a sprawling complex filled with generators, hydrothermal pumps, and a surprisingly verdant hydroponics greenhouse. "This is where we keep the lights on," David explained, pointing to the rows of generators. "And this," he added, gesturing towards the greenhouse, "is where we grow our own food. We're not entirely reliant on the supplies in the storage bunker." Mark, his mind reeling from the sheer scale of it all, finally found his voice. "What about fuel?" he asked. "And water?"

David smiled reassuringly. "We have enough fuel to last at least twenty five years, as I said. And as for water, we have two wells, a massive water reserve and a sophisticated filtration system. We can produce virtually unlimited clean water. We also have plenty of spare generators and solar panels to replace anything that might fail."

He paused, letting the information sink in. "We could all live here, comfortably and sustainably, for the next 25 years without ever needing to leave the ranch." Kris tilted her head and considered him. "So," she said, her voice laced with curiosity, "if you have all this, if you never have to leave… why were you going to Houston yesterday?" David's smile widened, a hint of mischief dancing in his eyes. "Ah," he said, "that's because I have bigger plans than just waiting out the apocalypse." He paused for effect, then continued. "Plus, if we hadn't gone to Houston, we would never have found you."

He clapped Mark on the shoulder. "Besides, sometimes," he added with a wink, "you have to take a little risk to reap a big reward." David waited a moment before continuing. "Does anyone want to see the fuel and water reserves?" Kris, immediately raised her hand, while Mark, looked to his wife for confirmation. "Is it safe?" Janet asked. David nodded his head. "It can be a bit intimidating, but it's perfectly safe." Mark and Janet looked at each other before shrugging their shoulders. Kris, on the other hand, seemed genuinely curious.

David led the family to the far side of the bunker, just beyond the generators. "These hatches here are for maintenance, but sometimes the kids like to sneak in here for a little mischief," he said with a wry smile. David opened the left hatch, it's pressure sealed door hissed as it swung open. "These doors can be opened from either side, but in the event of an unlikely breach, the area can be completely sealed off," David explained, crawling into the concrete tube.

David opened the second hatch, before stepping inside the next bunker. Kris, then Mark and his family following after. "This is huge, David," Kris exclaimed, looking around at the massive space. "Yup, almost a quarter of a million gallons of water down here. All of which are fed by the well pumps," David explained, circling the array of water silos. "The water is kept in a perpetual state of motion, which helps keep the water fresh."

After leaving the water reserve bunker, David opened the other hatch. "This can start to feel claustrophobic, so if you want to wait outside, it's cool," he said as he crawled into the tube. Illuminated only by a headlamp, he crawled the fifty feet to the next bunker. After opening the next hatch, he stepped into a colossal space, filled with massive steel tanks that seemed to reach the sixteen foot ceilings.

The room was filled only by the low humming of pumps and the light woosh of the displacement valves. "There are eight tanks in this bunker, each one containing nearly fifty thousand gallons of liquid propane." Kris immediately began climbing one of the service ladders. "This bunker is bigger than your whole house!" she exclaimed. "Yup, you could easily fit the whole house in here with room to spare," he said, casually.

Mark marveled at the sheer scale of the operation. "David, how long did it take you to build this?" he asked, admiring the detail and enormity of it all. "We started about eighteen years ago, but it took about three years of total work time to get it all done." David pointed to another hatch on the other wall. "That one leads to the petroleum tanks, but it's pretty much the same as this, only smaller. How about we go up?" David gestured to a ladder to the right.

As the family climbed the ladder, it eventually narrowed into a tight concrete tube, only two feet around. After opening another hatch, David crawled out, followed by Mark, his younger daughters, his wife, then Kris. "We're inside the barn?" Kris asked, petting one of the miniature cows. David nodded. "There's also a service hatch that leads to the stairwell going down to the apartment bunker on the opposite side of the Propane reserve. This whole compound is connected," David said, smiling.

He led Mark, Janet, Kris, Lori, and Beth back through the labyrinthine hallways of the apartment bunker. Mark was still reeling, trying to process the sheer scale of David's preparedness. Janet was quieter, her brow furrowed in thought as she mentally inventoried her own skills and how they might contribute. The kids, Lori and Beth, were mostly oblivious, excited by the sheer novelty of their surroundings. Kris, however, was practically buzzing. The tattoo artist who, just hours ago, had been skeptical and sarcastic, was now radiating genuine interest.

Back in their designated apartment, David surveyed the scene, his gaze meeting Mark's. "Now, I want to be clear about something. This isn't a labor camp. We don't chain people to treadmills and force them to churn butter for the glory of the collective." A slight smile tugged at his lips. "There are chores. Everyone contributes. We have a schedule, a division of labor. Security, maintenance, cleaning, education – it all needs to be done."

He turned to Janet, "And as a teacher, your skills will be invaluable. We have several children here, including my own, who are still of schooling age." Then, his attention shifted to Kris. "And you, Kris, your artistic talent is a commodity. We need art. We need beauty. We need things to remind us that even in the face of… well, this…" he gestured vaguely, "…there's still joy to be found. Plus, everyone always wants tattoos." Kris smirked, her earlier awe replaced by a confident swagger. "So, I'm basically the house artist? Sounds good to me."

David chuckled. "Basically. But it's more than just aesthetics. It's about finding your place, your strength, your purpose. We offer training in a variety of areas; self-defense, first aid, weapons handling, gardening, mechanics, pretty much anything you can think of, we have someone here that knows something. Find something that interests you, something you're good at, and dive in. Contribute, and you'll not only survive but thrive."

He looked around the apartment, taking in Mark's family. "We're not just surviving here, Mark. We're building a future. A better future, hopefully. But it takes everyone pulling their weight, everyone finding their purpose. And remember," he added with a wink, "I'm always available for… guidance." He paused, his gaze lingering on Kris for a moment. "In all areas." Kris smiled. "I bet you are, Master David," she responded, coquettishly.

David, unfazed by the sudden shift in address smiled brightly, enjoying the light jab. "Jennifer would be proud." He grinned then looked back at Mark, "We also have family meetings every Friday. That way you all are kept in the loop on everything that's happening. They can be a little… chaotic, but they're important,"

He clapped his hands together again. "Alright, I'll leave you to it. If you need anything, anything at all, don't hesitate to ask. Summer and Tiffany will be by shortly to check on you and answer any questions. Welcome to the ranch." With a final nod, David turned and exited the apartment, leaving Kris, Mark and his family to their own thoughts.

As soon as the door clicked shut, Kris turned to Janet, her eyes wide. "Okay, wow. This place is amazing! Did you see that pool? And the art studio potential? This is way better than dad's basement!" Mark, still trying to grapple with the implications of everything he'd seen, sighed. "It's a lot to take in, Kris. A lot. We need to figure out what we can do to help, to earn our keep." Janet nodded in agreement. "I'm happy to help with the children. I miss teaching. And I'm sure there are other ways I can contribute. Organization, record-keeping… Whatever needs doing."

Kris flopped dramatically onto the couch. "I'm thinking I might take that weapons training class? See what else they have to offer." Lori, finally finding her voice, piped up. "Can we go swimming? Please? Can we, can we?" Janet smiled, a genuine smile for the first time since the blackout. "We'll see, sweetie. First, we need to unpack and get settled. And then, maybe, just maybe, we'll check out that pool."

As Kris looked around the apartment, a question popped into her mind. "Janet, do you think David will care if I start a tattoo on someone immediately?" Janet looked at Kris, then sighed. "I'm sure someone around here has a tattoo gun for you to use, Kris." Kris smiled. "Actually, David picked up a whole studio for me on the way back from La Porte," she reminded her. Janet nodded, suddenly remembering. "I think I'll convert one of my bedrooms into a tattoo studio, and the other into an office, or an art room," she said, standing up to leave.

As David walked into the house, he plopped down onto the couch, the worn leather groaning in protest. David sighed contentedly. Even amidst the apocalypse, life, of a sort, went on. "Long day," he murmured, his voice raspy with exhaustion. Jennifer instantly abandoned her jigsaw puzzle – a particularly challenging depiction of a field of sunflowers that had occupied her for the better part of the afternoon – and knelt beside him, resting her hand on his knee. "You did good, Master," she purred, her blonde bob swaying gently.

"They seem to be settling in alright," David replied, his gaze sweeping over the familiar scene. Tiffany sat at the dining table, surrounded by notebooks and pens, meticulously organizing supplies. Taylor was perched on the arm of a nearby chair, idly cleaning her pistol. Summer and Elena were engaged in a silent battle of wits over a game of chess, their expressions inscrutable. He closed his eyes for a moment, letting the quiet murmur of his wives and the warmth of Jennifer's touch soothe his frayed nerves.

"Janet seems like a good woman," Tiffany declared, glancing up from her notebook. "We could definitely use her help with the younger kids. And she's a teacher, so that will help Seth and Grace." "And Mark seems solid," Taylor added. "Said he's handy with tools. Scott can put him to work right away. Plus, Janet mentioned he can cook."

David nodded. "Everyone has something to offer. It's just a matter of finding where they fit best." He paused, a thoughtful expression crossing his face. "Kris, though… she's got a spark. She might be a good match for Little David." The thought amused him, the image of the intense, almost unnervingly focused Little David paired with the bold, flamboyant Kris. It was either going to be a disaster or a stroke of genius. Probably both.

A ripple of amusement spread through the room. Jennifer chuckled, her eyes sparkling with mischief. "I think Kris has her sights set a little higher than Little David, Master. I think she would like to be your tenth wife." David sighed deeply. "I'm aware, she already proposed. Said something about the lineage of her future children." He pinched the bridge of his nose. "She presented a rather… compelling argument."

"She's been quite vocal about her admiration," Elena said wryly, without looking up from her book – a well-worn copy of Machiavelli's The Prince. "Apparently, she appreciates a man with a plan." Summer snorted softly. "She called him 'apocalypse daddy' when she thought no one was listening."

"Apocalypse Daddy?" David repeated, a mixture of amusement and concern coloring his tone. He looked around, his eyes searching. "Where's Jessica? Don't let Jessica hear her say that. She'll claw her eyes out." The thought of the petite but fiercely protective Jessica going toe-to-toe with the taller, more physically imposing Kris was both terrifying and hilarious. He loved his wives, but their capacity for drama sometimes rivaled the apocalypse itself.

"She's in bed resting," a voice chirped, and David turned to see Tanya entering the living room, her long black hair cascading down her back. "She wasn't feeling well this afternoon." David's face softened with concern. "How is she? Is Luci keeping her company?" "She seems to have a little morning, err, afternoon sickness," Tanya replied with a knowing smile. "And Luci hasn't left her side. That cat's got a sixth sense, I swear."

David relaxed slightly. Luci was fiercely protective of her mistress, and seemed to possess an uncanny ability to detect when Jessica needed comforting. "Good. Make sure she gets plenty of rest. And keep Kris away from her for the time being." He then ran a mental checklist. "Where's Aidan, Josh, Lily, and Seth, are they all right?"

Tiffany looked up from her notes. "Aidan, Josh, Lily, and Seth are all sleeping. Exhausted from the supply run last night. Those kids never get tired of that stuff." "That's good. They earned it." David paused, frowning slightly. "What about Brian? And Junior? Are they off tinkering with something explosive again?"

Jennifer chuckled. "Brian is probably in the hydroponics lab, convincing the tomatoes to grow faster through sheer force of will. And Little David… well, he's probably training. Or helping Kyle in the shed. I try not to ask too many questions." "What about you two?" David asked, turning his attention back to Jennifer and Elena. "Why aren't you sleeping? You were out there too."

Jennifer shrugged. "We took a nap when we got back. We're good, Master. Besides," she added with a playful glint in her eye, "someone has to keep you company." Elena smirked. "And make sure you don't start strategizing about world domination again. You get a little manic when you're tired." David chuckled, knowing she was only half-joking. His mind was always racing, always analyzing, always planning.

Chapter 17

The Family Tapestry

In Kris's newly renovated tattoo studio, the air buzzed with the whir of her tattoo machine. Kris, the perpetually curious tattoo artist, was hard at work on Little David's arm. "You sure about this, David?" she asked, her brow furrowed in concentration as she guided the needle. "This is... intense."

Little David didn't flinch. "Yup. Four Horsemen. Seemed appropriate." He suppressed a grin, knowing Kris was a sucker for anything dark and dramatic. Kris smiled. "It's not the four horsemen I was talking about, it's the likenesses. I understand you being war and your father being conquest, but why Aidan and Brian?" she asked. David thought a moment. "Because Brian is a farmer and he who can provide something, can deny it. So, Famine seemed appropriate. Then Aidan, he was the first of us to kill, so he's death, plus I like that his horse is red with flames."

"I'm only doing the outline today, I want you to come back each week until it's done, should only take about four passes," she said as she wiped away the excess ink from his arm. "So, dad thinks we should be a couple," David said, matter of factly. Kris jerked, drawing blood from David's arm. "You can't just say things like that out of the blue. Not when I have a tattoo gun in my hand," she scolded.

David smiled. "It's cool, it doesn't bother me. But seriously, are you really just trying to get access to the family recipe? You seem kind of… young to be thinking about such things." Kris smiled faintly. "I've always had a thing for older guys. You see a lot of that in my line of work. Plus, before I dropped out, I was a psychology major, and your dad is an enigma. I've never seen anyone who can be so detached and yet so caring at the same time," she said, her voice trailing off.

Little David didn't respond. He was use to this perspective. He, fortunately or unfortunately, didn't think the same way. His motivation was fueled by pride, not some longing for connection. As far as he was concerned, if his offspring could benefit from his unique condition, they would make fine Soldiers, the vanguard of the Renado family.

Downstairs, in the main house, David found Josh sitting on the back porch swing, staring out at the valley. Lily was curled up beside him, her hand resting on his knee. Despite being married, they still looked like kids playing house. "Rough night?" David asked gently, sitting on the opposite swing. Josh sighed, running a hand through his already disheveled hair. "It's just… different, you know?"

David nodded his head. "Killing for the first time tends to do that. Honestly, it wasn't until a month after everything went to hell before I first killed someone. Then, it was him or me." Josh furrowed his eyebrows, but didn't look up. "I thought you were a Soldier and a contractor before? You mean you never killed anybody then?" David shook his head. "Not that I was aware of. Serving in the Army and working as a protection officer doesn't guarantee a kill. In fact, it's always best if nobody dies."

Josh chuckled. "I honestly didn't expect that. Especially since you do it so well." David steepled his fingers, the gesture strangely formal. "Josh. It's normal to feel guilty after taking a life. Have you ever heard of Sergeant York? Alvin York was a Medal of Honor recipient during World War 1, and he was a conscientious objector. Do you know what that is?" Josh thought for a moment. "That's where you refuse to kill people?"

David nodded. "Essentially, but it's a little more complicated than that. Anyway, Alvin York made a decision that every person he killed, wasn't a life he took, but a potential life saved. A death he prevented." "David, are you telling me to consider the lives saved?" he asked, finally meeting David's gaze. "Kind of," David admitted. "It's not like we're picking off people for target practice, but consider this. For every fifty people you meet, maybe one will live. Now, you can let them kill themselves, or you can thin the crowd. Help the good ones live. It's ugly, Josh, I know. But evil men flourish when good men do nothing."

David paused, letting his words sink in. He knew Josh wasn't a simple farm boy, not anymore. He was a protector, a killer, and he was grappling with the weight of that. "Look, I see it in you, Josh. You're trying to hold onto your humanity. That's good. That's essential. Don't let the world turn you into a monster. But don't be naive either. Be strong, be smart, be compassionate, but be prepared to do what needs to be done."

David softened his tone. "And Josh? Leverage Lily. She's your anchor. Love her shamelessly, playfully, and joyfully. You need as many happy memories as possible to outweigh the bad ones. Don't let the darkness win." Josh smiled slightly, glancing at Lily. The affection in his eyes was clear. He took her hand, squeezing it gently. "I am pretty lucky, aren't I?"

As the silence started to build, a question hung in the air, unasked but palpable. Finally, Josh blurted out, "David, is… is that why you have nine wives?" David sputtered, coffee threatening to exit through his nose. He grabbed a napkin, dabbing at the corners of his mouth, a faint blush creeping up his neck. He looked at Josh and Lily, both staring at him with a mixture of curiosity and… well, Lily's expression was mostly adoration, thankfully. "That... that is a vastly oversimplified and intensely personal question, Josh. And frankly, none of your business."

Josh, now feeling like he had the advantage, grinned. "Okay, okay, fair enough. But how often... I mean, with nine wives and all… you're so busy! Surely you don't have... relations, every day? Especially not with nine women?" He had David now. Josh thought he'd checkmated the man. There was no way David could be so dedicated to his wives while running a ranch and keeping everyone safe.

David sighed, running a hand over his head. "Josh, seriously… we were talking about moral quandaries and the weight of responsibility. This is a rather abrupt and frankly, inappropriate, turn in the conversation." He shot a pleading look at Lily, hoping she would shut this down. Lily, however, was not going to let this go. She leaned forward, her eyes sparkling with mischief. "Oh, come on, Dad! You can't just leave us hanging like that! It's a perfectly reasonable question. Josh is just curious about the logistics! It's not like we're asking for details!"

David groaned inwardly. Autistic or not, he knew when he was being ganged up on. "Alright, alright," he conceded, "but this stays between us. And no spreading rumors around the ranch. Understood?" "Understood!" Josh and Lily chorused, grinning at each other. David hesitated, then glanced around as if checking for eavesdroppers. "The frequency of intimacy between my wives and myself… is a private matter."

Before he could attempt another sidestep, Summer walked onto the porch, carrying a tray laden with sandwiches and chips. "Lunch is served!" she announced cheerfully. She placed the tray on the table, a knowing smile playing on her lips as she took in the scene. "What are you all talking about?" "David's… intimate schedule," Lily offered innocently. Summer raised an eyebrow, instantly catching on. "Oh? His schedule, huh? Well, let's just say David manages to fit everything in. He's remarkably efficient, you know." She winked at Josh. "On average, I'd say he manages… twice a week, maybe?"

Josh's eyes widened. Twice a week! He mentally calculated. Nine wives, two times a week… that meant each wife had to wait at least four to five weeks between… encounters. He smirked, he'd won the argument. David was definitely stretched thin. "Wow, that's… less than I expected." Just then, Nicole strolled onto the porch, her expression thoughtful. "Summer, did you decide who's making dinner tonight? I was thinking of trying that new Thai recipe, but Tanya might have something special planned." She paused, noticing the slightly awkward atmosphere. "What's going on?"

Summer glanced at David, a mischievous look in her eye. "We were just discussing David's amazing time-management skills." Nicole's brow furrowed. "Time-management? What does that have to do with dinner?" She looked at Josh, then Lily, and finally settled her gaze on David, who was clearly trying to disappear into the porch swing. "It turns out David doesn't have enough time for each of his wives," Josh offered smugly.

A quiet chuckle started behind him. Nicole tilted her head, her eyes narrowing slightly as she pieced together the conversation. "Oh, I see. I think maybe once a week, sometimes twice when he isn't busy. David groaned internally. He loved his wives, truly, but their collective intelligence and tendency for playful chaos could sometimes be… overwhelming. He had known this was coming, but had hoped for a few more hours of peace to prepare himself.

Jessica waddled onto the porch, "Anyone mention sandwiches? I'm eating for two, you know," she announced, grabbing a plate and piling it high. She caught the tail end of the conversation and raised an eyebrow. "David doesn't have enough time? For what, exactly?" Summer, unable to resist the urge to stir the pot further, filled her in. "Josh here was under the impression that David's… romantic schedule… was, shall we say, rather sparse."

Jessica snorted, nearly choking on a chip. "Sparse? Honey, you have no idea." She turned to Josh, a look of amused pity on her face. "Okay, let me break it down for you. On average, David has sex with each of us probably a few times per week. But that's just an average."

She paused for dramatic effect, popping a chip into her mouth. "Nicole and Tanya? They prefer once a week, maybe. They're more about the cuddles and deep conversations. Jennifer and I, on the other hand… well, let's just say we like it almost daily. And then there's Tiffany, Summer, Elena, Kayla, and Taylor… they're all somewhere in between, averaging two or three times a week, per person."

David winced, the porch swing creaking in protest as he shifted uncomfortably. He could feel Josh's bewildered stare burning a hole in the side of his head. Jessica's "explanation", while technically accurate, had somehow managed to make the situation even more absurd. And not that it mattered now, but the chatter had even attracted Tiffany and Jennifer.

Josh, a young man teetering on the edge of adulthood and used to a simpler, more straightforward world, looked utterly flabbergasted. He sputtered, "But… but how? How do you even… schedule that?" His eyes darted around, landing on each of David's wives in turn, a mixture of awe and incredulity etched on his face.

Nicole took pity on the boy. "It's not as complicated as it sounds, Josh. Everyone is usually doing different things. Tiffany is busy with the ranch. Kayla is usually in the supply bunker. Tanya is usually in the spa. Summer is typically in the house. Elena is… doing what Elena does. Jennifer is usually in hydroponics, Jessica is chasing Luci… so there are seldom any scheduling conflicts. Besides," she added with a wink, "we're all pretty understanding, and we have each other."

A wave of murmurs and nods rippled through the assembled women, a silent agreement to Nicole's assessment.

But Josh wasn't buying it. "But... the choice? How does David choose who gets... you know... when?" He gestured vaguely, his face a mask of confusion.

A slow, predatory smile spread across Jennifer's face. "Oh, honey, that's the best part. With David, nowhere is safe. Anywhere is fair game. You might be folding laundry, tending the chickens, or even just minding your own business, and bam! He decides now is the time, and there goes your panties."

A chorus of laughter erupted from the women, many of them recounting similar stories of David's unpredictable and often hilarious romantic ambushes. David buried his face in his hands. This was exactly what he had been afraid of. He knew his wives loved to tease, but he hadn't expected them to lay it on quite so thick, especially in front of Josh. He straightened up, cleared his throat, and attempted to salvage the situation. "Okay, okay, that's enough," he said, trying to sound authoritative. "It's not as chaotic as it sounds. Most of the time." He shot a pointed look at Jennifer, who merely grinned back at him.

"The truth is," David continued, "I try to be attentive to everyone's needs and desires. If they come to me, I try not to deny them, and if I feel like I haven't been as close as I should be, I'll take the initiative. It also helps that they keep things running for me, so I'm not doing everything. Plus sometimes, I like being the wrench in their plans," He said, a sadistic grin spreading on his face. "Now, if you'll excuse me," he said, as he quickly stood to leave. Concerned he might be upset, Jessica called out. "Daddy, where are you going?" David paused momentarily. "To fuck Taylor!" he yelled back.

Meanwhile in the garage, Aidan stared at the half-assembled Detroit Diesel, a Frankenstein of gleaming original parts and salvaged components, a testament to his meticulous work. The massive engine filled much of the space, its sheer size a constant reminder of the beast it was meant to power.

The dual compound turbo conversion was ambitious, even for him. Taking a naturally aspired diesel engine and forcing air into it wasn't a new concept, but doing it with propane and adding a second set of turbochargers to eliminate any chance of lag? That was pushing the boundaries of what the old workhorse was designed to handle. He knew the risks. One wrong calculation, one faulty weld, and the whole thing could eat itself, turning his efforts into a destructive, albeit spectacular, lesson in failure.

He ran a gloved hand over the smooth metal of the existing turbochargers, mounted low on the engine block. They were Garretts, his favorite and obviously a replacement from whenever this engine was last rebuilt. Good quality, but he needed two more. Two more to ensure the propane would ignite with the ferocity he envisioned, unleashing a torrent of power that would make the M1070 a force to be reckoned with.

Austin. The name echoed in his mind. He knew of a shop that stocked Garretts, especially for engines like this one. It was a risky run, but the reward was worth it. He'd have to broach the subject with David. Convincing him to risk a trip to Austin for something as "frivolous" as turbochargers wouldn't be easy. He tossed his wrench onto the workbench, the clang echoing in the confined space. "Dad!" he yelled, his voice booming over the sound of the air compressor. "We need to talk about Austin!"

Nearby, Brian hunched over a tangled mess of wires and circuit boards. The original power distribution center for the M1070 was a dinosaur, a convoluted system of relays and fuses that looked like it was designed by a committee of engineers who hated each other. His goal was to streamline it, to modernize it, to make it as efficient and reliable as possible.

The new schematic, a product of late nights mulling over the old schematic from the original manual and a comprehensive understanding in electronics. It incorporated solid-state relays, digital control modules, and a sophisticated cooling system. It would not only improve the performance of existing systems but also allow them to easily incorporate new ones, like the enhanced cooling system and proximity monitors used in newer vehicles.

He soldered a wire with meticulous precision, his brow furrowed in concentration. He had to get this right. The power distribution center was the nerve center of the entire vehicle. If it failed, everything failed.

Out in the work shed, the air was thick with the smell of epoxy and the metallic tang of freshly cut steel. Eric wiped sweat from his brow with the back of his hand. "Damn, this stuff is sticky," he muttered, adjusting the respirator on his face. Parker simply grunted in response, expertly wielding a heat gun to smooth a section of UHMWPE onto Elena's car. "It's cool shit though, maybe I should do one for myself." Scott chuckled as he bolted a pre-molded steel plate against the firewall. "This car... it's going to be a tank," he finally said, his voice low. "I just hope it's enough."

Mark, the strongman of the group, wrestled with a particularly large sheet of UHMWPE, grunting with effort. "Enough or not, we're doing everything we can," he declared, his voice muffled by his respirator. "David and the others are counting on us." The instructions left by David, Aidan, and Brian were indeed straightforward, but the execution was grueling. The UHMWPE was tough and unforgiving, the steel plates heavy and cumbersome. Every cut, every weld, every bolt had to be perfect. Because once it was on there, it wasn't coming off easily.

Across the shed, the heavy duty armor plating for the HET was taking shape. The layered steel and UHMWPE, gleaming under the fluorescent lights, looked formidable. The plan was for range testing tomorrow. Hopefully it would stop whatever they threw at it.

Just then, the sound of footsteps echoed outside the shed, followed by the appearance of Tiffany in the doorway. "Hey guys, how's it going?" she asked, her eyes scanning the shed with interest. Eric and Parker exchanged a look, before Eric replied, "It's going, Tiffany. We're just trying to get this armor plating sorted out." Tiffany nodded, her eyes lighting up with excitement. "I can see that. I brought some lunch, thought you guys might be getting hungry."

As they finished their lunch, the men returned to work, their spirits high and their focus renewed. They knew that they had a long day ahead of them, but they were determined to get the job done. And as they worked, they couldn't help but feel a sense of pride and purpose.

Later that same afternoon, Kyle, lean and wiry, knocked on Mark's apartment door. Mark opened the door cautiously. "Yes? Oh, hey Kyle," he said, relaxing his shoulders. "Mark, David wants to see you and Janet at the main house before dinner," he responded, his voice low. Mark exchanged a glance with his wife, Janet. A knot of apprehension tightened in Mark's stomach. What could David possibly want?

Meanwhile, Taylor, petite and kind, materialized as if summoned, a picture of calm amidst Mark and Janet's rising anxiety. "I'll look after Lori and Beth while you go," she offered, her voice gentle but firm. The twins, Lori and Beth, were blissfully unaware of the undercurrent of tension.

Kyle moved on, his footsteps echoing faintly through the corridor. He knocked on Kris's door, her apartment just next door from Mark and Janet's. "Kris," he said, "David wants to see you at the main house before dinner." Kris, sensing an opportunity, quickly changed into a cute, but surprisingly practical outfit. A fitted black top, jeans, and sturdy boots. She was ready for anything.

A short while later, Mark and Janet stepped onto the wrap-around porch of David's house. They paused, surprised to see Kris already there, perched on a chair, looking impeccably dressed as if for a date, an almost comical contrast to her surroundings. She'd gone for a slightly more elegant approach than her typical attire. David opened the door, his gaze sharp and intelligent. "Come in," he said, his voice calm and clear.

Inside, the living room was surprisingly warm and inviting. The scent of woodsmoke mingled subtly with the clean scent of cleaning products. Leather armchairs sat around a large area rug, and the muted sunlight shown in through the French doors, surrounding the room. On a table lay three AR-15 rifles and three Glock 19 handguns. David gestured towards the weapons. "These are yours to keep," he said, his voice lacking any hint of aggression. "Kyle or Junior can modify them to your specifications."

Mark and Janet exchanged glances, then looked at Kris. She looked back at them. The guns were immaculate, their weight feeling substantial but reassuring in her hands. David's words hung in the air, a simple statement that spoke volumes about their changing reality. This was their reality now, and these weapons would become as common of an accessory as a wristwatch.

Mark, ever the cautious one, voiced his concern. "David," he began, a hint of nervousness in his tone, "about the guns... Lori and Beth... are they going to be safe with them in the apartment?" He gestured vaguely towards the formidable-looking weapons laid out on the table. Janet, ever supportive of her husband's anxieties, nodded in agreement, her eyes wide.

David, sensing their apprehension, smiled faintly. "Safety is paramount," he stated, his voice calm and reassuring. "Each apartment has a secure wall cabinet near the entrance, easily accessible but hidden from casual view. It can hold four sets of weapons—rifles, handguns, and ammunition—all secured. They're not as secure as a safe, but good enough to keep small children out."

He paused, then continued, addressing their specific worry about their younger daughters. "Lori and Beth will receive weapons familiarization, but it'll be age-appropriate and phased. We'll start with basic safety, proper handling, and respect for firearms. Think of it like driver's ed, but with guns. It's not about turning them into soldiers, but about responsible preparedness. This isn't just about self-defense; it's about understanding the tools we have at our disposal."

Mark and Janet visibly relaxed, the tension leaving their shoulders. "That makes sense, David," Janet said, her voice now laced with gratitude. "We appreciate you thinking everything through." Mark nodded firmly, "Yeah, thanks. Driver's ed with guns, I like that analogy." He gave David a respectful nod. "We'll leave you to it, then. We've got some settling in to do." Janet smiled warmly at Kris, then followed Mark out of the house, their concerns seemingly alleviated.

Once they were gone, David turned his attention fully to Kris. "So," he began, his voice gentle, "you're looking... different. Not that you don't normally look great, you do. You look like you're ready for date night rather than, you know, wielding a tattoo gun."

Kris started fidgeting with the hem of her shirt. "Well, yeah," she responded, her voice soft. "When you asked me to come up here... I just thought..." She trailed off, avoiding eye contact.

David's brow furrowed slightly, and he stepped closer, careful to maintain a respectful distance. "Thought what, Kris? That I was finally going to whisk you away for a romantic evening?" He chuckled softly, trying to lighten the mood. "Maybe," she mumbled, still looking at the floor. "I mean... you know how I feel, and... well, a girl can dream, right?" "Kris," he said gently, "I would never tell you to stop dreaming." He paused, searching for the right words. "How about this? Nicole is trying out a new Thai recipe tonight. Why don't you join us for dinner? We'd all love to have you."

Kris's eyes widened slightly, a mixture of determination and relief washing over her face. "Really? You mean… with everyone?" "Absolutely," David confirmed, his smile genuine. "It would be great to have you. Plus," he added with a playful wink, "you can give us your expert opinion on Nicole's cooking. She's been slaving away all afternoon."

A smile finally blossomed on Kris's face. It wasn't the romantic evening she had perhaps hoped for, but it was an invitation, an inclusion into David's life, and for now, that was enough. "Okay," she said, her voice lighter. "Dinner sounds… perfect." She quickly straightened up. "I'll go freshen up."

As Kris headed toward the bathroom, David turned and headed into the kitchen, a slight spring in his step. He could hear the familiar sounds of meal time emanating from the doorway – the clatter of pots and pans, the murmur of voices blending together in a harmonious symphony.

Inside, the kitchen was a hive of activity. Nicole, her brow furrowed in concentration, stirred a bubbling pot on the stove, the fragrant aroma of lemongrass and chilies filling the air. Seo-Yeon and Tanya chopped vegetables and prepared dipping sauces. While Jennifer and Jessica carefully laid out the silverware and napkins. "Evening, ladies," David announced, his presence immediately drawing their attention. "Hey, honey," Jennifer greeted him with a smile, tilting her head for a quick kiss. "Everything alright?" "Everything's fine," David assured her. "I invited Kris to join us for dinner. She's just freshening up."

A collective murmur rippled through the kitchen. Nicole paused in her stirring; her eyebrows raised in surprise. "Kris? That's… nice." She glanced at Jennifer, a silent question passing between them. Jennifer shrugged, a hint of amusement in her eyes. "More the merrier, right? Besides," she added with a playful smirk, "she can help clean up."

Kris returned to the kitchen, a touch of lipstick and a forced smile enhancing her features. The atmosphere was warm and inviting, not at all what she was expecting in a house with so many people. David led her to the table. It was a long, sturdy oak table, easily seating a dozen people. Tiffany sat at one end, her eyes twinkling with a mixture of warmth and amusement as she surveyed the scene. David never took the "head" spot; it wasn't his style. Something that genuinely surprised Kris.

Kris's eyes darted around the room, taking in the sheer efficiency of the operation. Tanya, graceful and serene, brought David his plate, leaning down to press a sweet kiss to his cheek. Kayla followed close behind with a glass of water, offering her own affectionate peck. It was a well-oiled machine, a dance perfected over years of shared life.

Then, there was a flurry of activity. Josh and Lily, hand in hand, piled plates high with food, waving a quick goodbye as they headed to Lynn's apartment. Brian and Seo-Yeon, followed by a younger, more pragmatic version of David, disappeared down the stairs leading to the lower levels, presumably to share their meal with Aidan and Alissa.

The whole scene was a testament to David's ability to cultivate a sense of community and family, Kris found herself genuinely impressed. As she sat down, a question bubbled up. "How… how long have you all been with David?" she asked. Summer raised an eyebrow. "Just with him, or as his wife? There's a bit of a difference, you know."

A fresh wave of determination crossed Kris's face. "Both, I guess," she mumbled, fiddling with her napkin. David chuckled, which eased some of her tension. "Alright, let's do this systematically. And in order, so we don't get confused." He paused, thinking for a moment. "Summer has known me the longest – thirty-eight years, since we were kids, really. But Tiffany was the first to marry me, that was twenty-seven years ago, six years after we met." Tiffany smiled, reaching out to squeeze David's hand. "Took him long enough too,"

Jennifer piped up next. "Well, I have known him over thirty-one years and married for twenty-two years. Tiffany, Summer and I actually went with him to prom," she said, winking at Kris. Then it was Elena's turn. "I've known David for just over twenty-two years, been with him for Twenty years, give or take." Taylor then said, "I've known David since I was eighteen, and been with him for almost sixteen years. Nicole and I were actually roommates in training together."

Nicole took over, "Yeah, we've known David for over seventeen years, and we've been together for almost fifteen years, plus Seth and Grace are mine". Jessica giggled. "I've known David since I was sixteen, even though I dreamed about him since I was thirteen. However, we've been together for eleven years. Kayla smiled warmly, "I've known David for twelve years, and Jessica and I pretty much came in together." Tanya, beaming, chimed in, "I've known David for three years. And we've been together for almost two."

All eyes turned to Kris, who felt a bit like she was under a spotlight. She swallowed nervously. It was a lot of information to process, a complex tapestry of relationships woven together by one very unusual man. She smiled shakily. "Wow," she managed, at a loss for anything more profound. "That's… quite the commitment."

Chapter 18

The Depths of Devotion

"Alright," David began, his voice calm. "Let's get started. Brian, give us the good news." Brian straightened up, a slight smile lighting his face. "The network antenna is online. We have cell service, but it's limited to a ten-mile radius. Enough to cover the ranch and the immediate surrounding area."

A ripple of relieved murmurs went around the table. Summer leaned forward; her brow furrowed. "Can we encrypt the signal? I'd hate for any unwanted ears to pick up our conversations." "That seems kind of presumptuous, considering the state of things," Brian replied, "But the network is locked to our IMSI and IMEI combination." David nodded. "Excellent work, Brian. That will significantly improve our internal communications. No more yelling across the valley." He glanced at Jessica. "How are you feeling, Baby?"

Jessica, whose usual sass was currently softened by pregnancy, offered a small smile. "Good, Daddy. A little tired, but good. Luci seems to like all the extra attention." She playfully rubbed the cat's head. "She's probably convinced she's running the place." "She definitely thinks she does," Kayla quipped, earning a chuckle from the table.

David continued, "Parker, Eric, Scott. The M1070?" Parker cleared his throat. "Ready to roll, David. We've christened her, The Behemoth. Appropriate, I think."

"Appropriate," David agreed, picturing the armored behemoth lumbering across the landscape. "That beast can haul anything we need it to."

Which brings us to the next item, ammunition. We're not exactly running low. But we could always use more especially .223 and 9mm. The next scavenging run will be to Dallas." A collective groan rippled through the room. Dallas was a mess, a festering wound on the Texan landscape.

"Dallas?" Elena asked, wincing. "Isn't there anywhere closer? Less… chaotic?" David sighed, his gaze hardening slightly. "I wish there was, Elena. But Dallas has the largest concentration of ammunition depots and manufacturers in Texas. And we can't rely on gun shops and outfitters for this one, plus we need to replenish our supplies if we want to maintain our training tempo." He paused, his gaze softening as it drifted towards the younger members of their family. "Junior," he said. "You'll be leading the security detail. Take Kris with you."

David Jr, nodded seriously, excitement shining in his eyes, betraying his eagerness to put his training into practice. Kris, sitting beside him, smiled. She'd made no secret of her… admiration for David, and even though David considered little David a better match for Kris, she seemed to consider his son a stepping stone to David himself. He continued, "Lily, as usual, you're paired with Josh."

The meeting continued, covering everything from hydroponics yields to the mini-cows. He touched on security protocols, confirming that the training regimen would remain unchanged, and emphasizing the need for constant vigilance.

They couldn't afford to be complacent, not with the world as it was.

Finally, David broached a more personal subject. "Alissa, you had something you wanted to share?" Alissa took a deep breath, her cheeks flushed. "Aidan and I... we're trying to start a family." A chorus of congratulations erupted from around the table. Tiffany, especially, seemed thrilled. "Oh, Alissa, that's wonderful news! We'd love to have another little one running around."

Jessica, never one to shy away from the risqué, leaned forward. "Aidan, congratulations! Looks like you've got a free pass to raw dog your wife!" David chuckled, a persistent rumble that almost couldn't stop. "Baby, those are bold words coming from the pregonator," he quipped, exchanging an amused glance with Tanya, who was busy making sure everyone had enough fresh fruit.

Elena steered the conversation back to a celebratory track. "We should definitely celebrate tonight. I volunteer to make twice-stuffed potatoes for dinner." Jennifer, who started giggling at the 'stuffed' part, added. "And we should make cream pies for dessert." The table immediately erupted in laughter at the innuendo. Jessica, still riding the wave of amusement, added. "Actually, there's a recipe for eggplant tacos I've been wanting to try."

David raised an eyebrow, a small smile playing on his lips. "Alissa gets to choose the menu, of course. It's her celebration." Jennifer grinned. "Oh, I bet Alissa will just want a very specific type of sausage." This sent another wave of laughter rippling through the room. Alissa, blushing furiously but laughing along, playfully swatted Aidan's arm. He just grinned back, clearly enjoying the attention.

The cacophony of laughter and suggestive culinary ideas finally subsided, leaving a warm, convivial atmosphere in the main house. David, still faintly grinning, watched as everyone dispersed, each heading towards their morning tasks. The talk of babies and, let's be honest, the blatant innuendo, lingered in the air.

Kris hovered at the edge of the table during breakfast, mechanically stacking plates while she listened. Tanya glanced at her, eyebrows lifted, but Kris couldn't meet her gaze. Every clink of china magnified the words she'd heard: Alissa and Aidan trying to conceive, racing against an unforgiving world. A tight knot formed in her stomach. Babies... hope or burden? She couldn't stop thinking about it.

When the last dish was whisked away, Kris slipped downstairs to the garage bunker. Her friend, Janet, presided over the makeshift schoolroom, where the hum of the HVAC and children's soft chatter felt like balm, and yet only reminded Kris of how hollow she felt.

Inside, Grace stood before Lori and Beth, chalk in hand, unraveling a tangled string of equations. Taylor knelt beside Lori, guiding her trembling fingers across the page. Across the room, Seth captivated Mike and Bonnie with stories of vanished empires, Janet filling in dates and cultural details. Kris leaned against the doorway, awash in envy and unease. How could children so young carry such fierce brilliance?

Janet caught her eye and offered a warm smile. "They're extraordinary, aren't they?" Kris cleared her throat. "They are." She watched Grace's steady calm, so assured, so complete. A spark of determination burned inside of her. Jessica, bulging with pregnancy last night, had seemed luminous. Kris bit her lip. What she craved wasn't just a child; it was a claim, a place under David's protective shadow. "Grace's lessons actually… spark something," Taylor said with a grin. "They want to learn." Kris answered with a brittle nod. Her mind churned: I want that too. I want his attention, his strength, his power.

Later, she found Janet in the hallway and forced her voice low. "Janet, can we talk? Alone?" Janet's face softened. She closed the classroom door. "Of course, sweetie." Kris drew in a long breath. "I want a baby." Janet's surprised blink reverberated like thunder. "With David." Janet smiled, her fingers touching her lips. "That's wonderful news Kris. I always knew you two would make a good couple…" "No," Kris interrupted. "Not with his son. With him."

Janet's hand flew to her chest. "David? You…" "Yes," Kris cut in, too loudly. "I know what you're thinking. He's older, has like, a million wives, but… he's perfect. He leads, protects, provides. We need kids for the future. I want to bring one into the world with him." "But Kris…" Janet ran a hand through her hair. "David Jr. is your age, single, and you two…" "David Jr. is only interested in breeding soldiers." Kris's voice trembled. "I want more than that. I want a partner."

Janet pinched the bridge of her nose. "You'd be one of many wives, honey. The logistics…" "I know!" Kris hissed. "I keep wishing… I could be one of them! Tanya, Summer, Jessica, they all have him, and they're content, they're safe." She sat on the floor, tears pricking. "It's not just about survival. It's that feeling. That belonging."

When the first tear slipped free, Kris clasped her hands over her face. "I just… want to be his. I want to cook for him, give him blowjobs, be… be used by him." Janet sagged against the wall, silent and stunned. Kris's voice cracked. "What's wrong with me?" Janet knelt beside her, lifting her chin. "Nothing's wrong, sweetheart. You're frightened by how strong your feelings are."

Kris trembled. "I feel like I'm losing control." Janet hugged her fiercely. "Let's take this slow. Talk it out. There are people who understand." Kris pulled back. "You mean Tanya, Kayla, or Jessica?" Janet nodded. "I'm sure they've lived it." Kris shuddered. "They'd think I'm insane." Janet's eyes were kind. "Maybe they'll surprise you."

Kris left Janet and wandered the ranch. Compulsion drew her to the work shed. Inside, Little David was hunched over a disassembled rifle. She leaned against the doorway. "Hey." He glanced up. "Kris. You look like shit." She managed a wry half-smile. "Can we talk?" He set aside the barrel. "Always."

Kris sat next to him. "I… I think I'm obsessed with your dad." She said, unapologetically. David Jr. tilted his head, expression calm. "Obsession?" "A bit. Fascination?" She retorted. "I told Janet I wanted to be his wife." He didn't flinch. He stood and came to her, placing a steady hand on her shoulder. "Kris, you wouldn't be the first. Plus, you're allow to have these feelings."

She looked at him. "You're not… judging?" He gave a small, sad smile. "Your feelings are yours. My father is… magnetic. People are drawn to him. But you have to distinguish admiration from something deeper." Tears welled again. "I can't tell the difference." He pulled her into a firm, brotherly hug. "You will. I promise." She trembled. "I feel like I'm losing my mind."

He released her gently. "You're not. You're human. And you have a choice." He picked up a wrench. "Talk to his wives. Kayla, Mom, even Jessica. They understand the pull he has… and the sacrifices." Kris nodded. "Okay." He gave her a reassuring smile before returning to the rifle. The shed fell silent except for metal on metal.

Instead of venturing into the lion's den, Kris opted for a slightly less intimidating approach. She sought out Lily. The past month she had formed an unlikely bond with her. They connected over shared frustrations with the apocalypse, a mutual love for bad jokes, and a surprising number of late-night conversations fueled by contraband soda and nervous energy.

Finding Lily practicing knife throwing in the back yard with Josh, Kris hesitated for a moment. Josh, noticing her, gave her a small wave and a reassuring smile. He seemed to radiate an aura of burgeoning competence that had grown exponentially in recent weeks. Lily grinned and effortlessly hurled another knife, hitting the bullseye with a satisfying thwack.

"Hey, Kris! What's up?" Lily asked, wiping her brow with the back of her hand. "Come try!" Kris forced a smile. "Hey, guys. Actually, Lily, could I talk to you for a sec?

Alone?" She glanced apologetically at Josh. Josh simply nodded. "I'll go get some water. Want anything, Lily?" Lily shook her head. "Nope, I'm good. Thanks, babe." As Josh walked away, Lily turned her attention to Kris, her expression softening with concern. "Everything okay? You look... stressed." Kris sighed. "I... I need to talk about something. It's... complicated."

They moved to the front porch, settling onto the swing. The rhythmic creaking seemed to amplify the silence that stretched between them. Kris swallowed. She could taste the dust in her mouth. "I...shit. I think I'm totally screwed up, Lily." Lily didn't laugh. She just waited. Kris closed her eyes and took a deep breath. "It's about David." Her voice hitched. She peeked up, saw Lily's unblinking calm, and pressed on. "Even though he's...way older, and he's got like... a dozen wives, I can't stop thinking about him. I feel like I'm drowning and I need him to pull me out."

Lily's eyebrows rose. She folded her arms. "So, you're... in love with my dad. And it feels all wrong?" Kris nodded. "Incredibly wrong. Mortifying. He's your dad... Hell, I could be your sister..." "A slightly younger sister," Lily supplied, lips twitching into a smile.

Kris buried her face in her hands. "Worse. I'm supposed to be this independent badass, and...all I want is to be controlled by him, used by him, owned by him. To have his babies." Lily sat back, weighing Kris's confession. Finally, she said, "Okay. I get it." Kris jerked her head up. "You do?" "Look, I've only ever known Josh," Lily explained. "So, I don't know how my dad feels about his wives. I do know he loves Jessica, we've all known that. And she struggled the way you are now, most of them have."

Kris felt something harden in her chest. A spark. "I want that. I want to belong… even if it's chaotic." She fidgeted with the hem of her shirt. "I just…I was so worried you'd think I was completely weird. Especially since…well, you know, I tried to get close with little David. But he's just not interested in…romance."

Lily sighed, searching for the right words. "Look, you aren't going to be my dad's true love, he's already got that. However, that doesn't mean there isn't room. All of David's wives have one thing in common, just one." Kris leaned forward, a determined look in her eye. "Submission. Absolute servitude, surrender, even slavery." Kris wrung her hands. She understood what this meant, but to what extent?

Lily's eyes glinted. "Hey, you want to see something funny?" "Depends," Kris said. "Is it exploding pumpkins?" Lily shook her head. "No, but you might get a kick out of it." She hopped off the swing, tugging Kris by the hand toward the house's side door.

They went back down to the classroom in the garage. Seth sat by the window, knees hugged to his chest as he sketched a rifle mechanism in a worn notebook. His tongue peeked from the corner of his mouth in concentration. "Just watch and see what happens," Lily whispered.

Seth looked up, calm as dawn. "Lily. Kris. What's up?" Lily perched on a desk, close enough for Seth's pencil to scratch wood. "Kris was asking about relationships. Maybe marriage. We thought you might have…" She waved a hand at Kris. "Interesting insights." Kris smiled. "Yeah. Like, do you plan to get married?"

Seth set his pencil down and tapped the notebook's page. "Eventually. I value companionship and raising children, but it would be unfair to marry someone who doesn't fully grasp the commitment. Immaturity is a problem." Kris blinked. "But you're fourteen." "Precisely," Seth said with a sly grin. "I'm ready; she's not."

"So," Kris pressed, unable to resist, "who is this paragon of future marital bliss you're waiting for?" Seth didn't hesitate. He turned his gaze towards Bonnie, who was currently arguing with Mike about the proper way to clean a paintbrush. He just straight up pointed at her. "I will marry her," he stated, his voice devoid of any childish bashfulness. "Bonnie. She's eleven, but I'm willing to wait."

Bonnie's jaw dropped, brush slipping from her fingers. Her eyes widened as she met Seth's gaze. Her mouth opened and closed like a fish, rendering her speechless. Lily burst out laughing. "Well, Bonnie, there you have it! You've been proposed to! Better start planning the wedding!" Bonnie, still stunned, managed a squeaky, "But...but I'm only eleven!" "See? Immaturity," Seth said dryly, turning back to his sketchbook.

Bonnie steeled her resolve, face flushed. "I… I love you too, Seth," she blurted, words tumbling out in a rush. The brush clattered to the floor, forgotten. Lily's giggles reached a fever pitch. Kris's jaw dropped. The air in the classroom crackled with awkward teenage-adjacent energy. Seth, however, remained as composed as a seasoned diplomat. He nodded once, a small, almost imperceptible dip of his head.

"Good. Now, finish cleaning the brushes. You have a long way to go before you're ready to be a wife."

Bonnie, momentarily stunned into silence, just stared. The pronouncement, delivered with the seriousness of a Supreme Court ruling, seemed to deflate all the romantic bravado she'd just mustered. Her shoulders slumped slightly, and she bent to retrieve the escaped brush. Kris, recovered from her initial shock, choked back a laugh. She eyed Lily, who was practically doubled over, clutching her stomach with mirth.

Lily, still snorting, managed to regain her composure. "Good call. I think I pulled a giggle muscle." She winked at Bonnie, who was now scrubbing furiously at the sink, a mixture of paint and embarrassment swirling down the drain.

As they exited the classroom, leaving Seth and Bonnie to their… domestic pre-bliss, Kris couldn't help but wonder if she'd just witnessed the most awkward, yet strangely efficient, declaration of love in history. "So," Kris said when they were safely in the hallway, "that was… something."

Lily wiped a tear from her eye. "Told you it was funny. Seth's got this whole… spreadsheet in his head about relationships. I'm pretty sure he has compatibility ratings for everyone in the valley." "A spreadsheet?" Kris echoed, incredulous. "He's fourteen!" "Yeah, but he's Seth," Lily said, as if that explained everything. "He's been planning his life since he was, like, five."

Lily's laughter subsided, replaced by a knowing glint in her eyes. "Speaking of Dad… You really want to break through that fortress of his, don't you?" Kris flushed. "I… I just want to understand him. Maybe… maybe be someone he can… rely on." Lily sobered. "Then listen to me, Kris. You have to talk to his wives. They're the key. And the only way to really win Dad over is to genuinely submit to him. Not for some grand plan, not to get something in return, but because you want to. Because you recognize his strength, his dedication, his… everything. He can smell insincerity a mile away, and he doesn't tolerate betrayal." She paused, a thoughtful expression on her face. "It's not easy. But if you're serious, that's the path."

With a final wink, Lily turned and headed towards the armory, leaving Kris. She started up the stairs, the scent of simmering something delicious drawing her towards the kitchen. As she rounded the corner, the scene that greeted her made her stop dead in her tracks. David stood behind Summer, his arms wrapped around her waist, his face buried in the crook of her neck. Summer leaned back into him, a contented sigh escaping her lips. It was an intimate, unguarded moment.

Kris felt a wave of heat rush to her cheeks. She was intruding. She should leave. But before she could retreat, David straightened, turning his head towards her. His expression was open, unperturbed. "Kris," he said, his voice warm and welcoming. "Perfect timing. Summer's been helping me with the tiramisu. Would you like to try a sample?" Kris stammered, "Oh, no. I wouldn't want to interrupt." David chuckled. "Nonsense. You're not interrupting. And I always appreciate a second opinion. Come, tell me what you think."

Against her better judgment, Kris approached the counter. David, with a gentle hand, scooped a spoonful of creamy custard from a bowl and held it out to her. The aroma of coffee and cocoa filled the air. "Open," he commanded gently. Kris hesitated. His eyes held a genuine invitation. His hand strategically placed under the spoon. She opened her mouth, and as he carefully placed the spoonful on her tongue. His fingers brushed against her chin, sending a jolt of electricity through her.

The custard was heavenly, rich and smooth, a perfect balance of sweet and bitter. She closed her eyes for a moment, savoring the taste. Then the words that followed. "Good," he murmured, his tone laced with approval. Kris felt a strange sensation wash over her, a dizzying lightness that made her head spin. The kitchen seemed to fade around the edges, and all she could focus on was David's gaze, warm and intense. Her eyes glossed over as the sounds around her began to fade.

Suddenly, Summer's hand touched her arm, jolting her back to reality. "Kris? Are you alright?" Summer asked, her brow furrowed with concern. Kris blinked, struggling to regain her composure. The world seemed to snap back into focus, sharp and clear. Shame washed over her. What had just happened? She couldn't meet David's eyes. Lowering her head, all she could do was mumble. "Thank you, David."

Then, she turned and fled, stumbling out of the kitchen and down the hallway, her heart pounding in her chest. She needed to get to her security detail, to little David, to… anywhere but here. Kris burst through the door of the work shed, her breath coming in ragged gasps. The smell of gun oil and solvents, usually comforting, now felt suffocating.

Little David, perched on a high stool meticulously cleaning his disassembled AR-15, didn't even look up.

His movements were precise, economical, a miniature mirror of his father's efficiency. "Kris," he said, his voice calm and even. "You're here. I was beginning to wonder if I'd have to single-handedly defend the perimeter today." Kris managed a weak smile. "Sorry, I'm late. Something… something came up."

Little David finally glanced up, his sharp, intelligent eyes assessing her. He saw the flushed cheeks, the slightly unfocused gaze. "You're not late," he corrected, returning to his task. "Patrol isn't for another fifteen minutes. Plenty of time to get your gear. Take your time."

His nonchalant tone was strangely reassuring. Kris appreciated his lack of prodding. "David?" she asked, her voice unsteady. He paused, his hand hovering over a small brush. "Yeah?" "Do you… do you ever just… feel things?" she stammered, hating how vague and ridiculous she sounded.

He considered her for a moment, his expression unreadable. "Feelings are biological responses to stimuli," he stated matter-of-factly. "Of course, I feel things. But if you're asking if I ever experience overwhelming emotional responses that interfere with logical decision-making? Then the answer is no, not usually."

Kris sighed. Of course, he answered literally. What was she expecting? Still, she pressed on. "No, it's not that exactly. It's… it's like… my body reacted before my brain could process what was happening." David finally set down his brush. He swiveled on the stool to face her fully, his young face suddenly serious. "With dad?" he asked, his tone neutral.

The question surprised her. How did he know? A shiver ran down her spine. Had it been that obvious? Could he tell? "Yes," she admitted, her voice barely audible. She suddenly felt incredibly vulnerable, like a bug pinned under a microscope. "I don't understand it. I'm comfortable talking about him with you, but… when he… when he does certain things… it's like… my control disappears."

David nodded slowly, as if he understood perfectly. "It's his presence," he explained, his voice measured. "His… effect. It's more pronounced on some people than others. His will is… strong." Kris frowned. "But why? I'm not… I don't… I didn't consciously choose to submit." "Submitting to dad isn't always a conscious choice," David said. "Sometimes, it's a natural response. You know he wants what's best for everyone. He looks out for us." He paused, then added, almost as an afterthought, "And he's very good at what he does."

Kris felt a blush creep up her neck again. She didn't need a reminder of how good David was. She knew it intimately, even if she didn't want to admit it. "But it's… unnerving," she confessed. "To feel so out of control. I'm supposed to be part of your security detail. I can't be effective if I'm… melting into a puddle because he said 'good.'"

David chuckled, a sound she wasn't expecting. "Don't worry, Kris. Dad wouldn't let anything happen to you. He's aware of his… influence. He wouldn't consciously put you in a position where you'd be compromised." He hopped off the stool, grabbing a can of pressurized air to blow the dust off the rifle parts. "Besides," he added, "You're tougher than you think. Now go get your armor. We have a job to do."

Kris took a deep breath, trying to regain her composure. Maybe David was right. Maybe she was overreacting. Maybe it was just a temporary glitch in her system. She needed to focus on her duty, on contributing, on fitting in. She nodded, a newfound resolve hardening her gaze. "You're right. Thanks, David." She turned and headed towards the door, her steps now firm and purposeful.

As she descended the stairs, she couldn't shake the feeling that she was missing something. David's explanation, while logical and reassuring, didn't quite satisfy her. There was something more, something deeper, that she couldn't quite grasp. She reached her apartment, a small but comfortable space. As she donned her body armor, she couldn't help but replay the scene in the kitchen. David's warm smile, his gentle touch, his low, approving voice. The memory sent another shiver down her spine, a mixture of embarrassment and a strange, undeniable thrill.

She was still trying to puzzle it out when she heard David calling from the top of the stairs. "Kris! Let's go! The post-apocalyptic world isn't going to protect itself." Kris took one last deep breath, steeling her resolve. Whatever was going on with David, whatever effect he had on her, she wouldn't let it compromise her mission. She climbed back up the stairs, her rifle held firmly in her hands. Little David was waiting for her, his own weapon slung across his back. He gave her a sharp, appraising look. "Ready?" he asked, his eyes filled with a seriousness. Kris nodded, her gaze unwavering. "Ready."

Chapter 19

The Dallas Factory Raid

"Everyone ready?" David's voice, usually a calm baritone, was amplified by the unusual urgency he felt. He trusted his people, trusted their training, but Dallas was a wild card. Tiffany shouldered her M4, the weapon looking almost perfect in her capable hands. Her Colt Python gleamed at her hip. Yet even after the world had turned to shit, she still carried the same maternal grace that she had grown into. She winked at him. "Always, love. Just say the word."

Beside her, Kris stood, an inconceivable smile playing on her lips. "Thank you again, Tiffany," she gushed, latching onto Tiffany's arm. "I really appreciate you talking David into letting me come." Tiffany chuckled, patting Kris's hand. "He's a softie, deep down. Besides, it's good to get out sometimes, and you could use the experience."

David carefully strapped on his wakizashi, his favorite close combat weapon. As he turned, his eyes met Tiffany's, a silent conversation passing between them. He reached out, cupping her face, and leaned in for a kiss. It wasn't a quick peck; it was deep, lingering, a taste of defiance against the uncertainty of the road ahead. Kris watched, eyes wide, a slight blush spreading on her cheeks. She hadn't expected such raw affection. They're tactical geniuses and hopelessly romantic at the same time, she thought, utterly fascinated.

Lynn bustled forward, laden with insulated bags. "Here, David, I packed extra meals for everyone. You never know what you'll find out there," she said, looking to Kris. David gave her a nod, a small smile playing on his lips. "Thank you, Lynn. We appreciate it." As Lynn turned to go back upstairs, she looked at Tiffany. "Don't let him get into too much trouble."

"Aidan, Summer," David addressed as he grabbed his coffee cup, "you're in charge while we're gone. Any issues, you know what to do." Aidan, standing beside Alissa, gave a curt nod. Beside him, Summer gave a reassuring smile as she reached for him. "Be careful out there. We need you back in one piece," she said as she kissed him, pulling herself into his embrace.

Parker, little David and Kyle climbed into the behemoth, growling like a slumbering beast. Parker, with the help of Brian, managed to outfit the HET with all the comforts of a long-distance rig, while Little David helped design the tactical widgets. Kyle sat in one of the rear seats, shelving his rifle, as Parker and little David took the driver's seat and passenger seat, respectively. Meanwhile, Tiffany, David, Grace, Kris and Scott piled into the Ford Transit, each one armed and armored.

After saying his last goodbyes, David noticed the entire community seemed to have a determined look. Everyone owned their part and he knew deep down that they believed in what they were doing. "Alright," he announced, his voice clear and strong. "Let's go get some bullets, bitches." As Tiffany started the Transit, Kris leaned forward, her voice a quiet whisper. "David, I have a question."

David turned his attention to her, his expression neutral. "Yes, Kris?" "You... you called Tiffany 'love'. Do you call all your wives that?" David blinked, a flicker of amusement in his eyes. "Sometimes," he admitted. "It depends on the situation, and the person. Each of my wives are different, and each has different needs and preferences." Kris nodded slowly, processing this information. "Tiffany isn't just one of my wives. She's one of my core supporters and the house's matriarch," he added.

The garage door rumbled open, and David patted Tiffany's knee, his touch both possessive and reassuring. "Ready?" Tiffany grinned, her eyes sparkling. "Born ready, darling." As the two vehicles rolled out of the compound, Jessica watched from the bedroom window. She hated telling him goodbye. Even though she knew these moments had to happen, in order to experience those emotional 'welcome home' moments.

Inside the Transit, Kris continued to pepper Tiffany with questions. "Tiffany," her voice a mix of genuine interest and barely concealed envy. "What's it like? Being the... matriarch?" Tiffany chuckled, glancing at David before answering. "It's... a lot. It means I get to help David make decisions, keep the house running, and generally be a pain in everyone's ass," she said with a wink. "But seriously, it's always about supporting David, especially when he isn't there. My biggest job is keeping the peace." David smiled, appreciating Tiffany's pragmatic assessment. "A woman's mind is no place for a man," he added. "So, when there are issues, I may not understand, she intercedes on my behalf."

"Do you ever... argue?" Kris persisted, leaning forward. "Like, about decisions for the group?" Tiffany considered the question. "Of course, we argue. We're all adults, and many of us have strong personalities. But it's never about jealousy or anything petty like that. It's about figuring out the best course of action for everyone. David always listens to our opinions, and ultimately, he makes the final call. We trust him."

David reached over and squeezed Tiffany's hand. "I don't always have the answers, but I'm still responsible for the outcome. So, I rely on their input to know what's best for everyone." Kris giggled, then turned her attention to David, her eyes wide with a mixture of awe and curiosity. "David... do you ever feel overwhelmed? Having so many wives, so many people depending on you?"

David paused, considering the question seriously. Overwhelmed wasn't exactly the word he'd use. More like… intensely managed. He wasn't overwhelmed because he had built a system, a family, that anticipated his needs and supported each other. "Overwhelmed implies a lack of control," David began, his voice calm and measured. "And while I am not always in control, I lead. There's a significant difference."

Kris tilted her head, clearly intrigued. Scott, sitting quietly by the window, seemed equally interested in David's explanation. Grace, however, was engrossed in a drawing, oblivious to the conversation. "I don't feel overwhelmed because my wives pretty much take care of everything," David continued. "And, perhaps more importantly, they take care of each other. I just take care of them and make the big decisions."

He paused, a thoughtful expression on his face. "Leading isn't about absolute control; it's about trust. I trust them to handle the day-to-day, the emotional support, the… well, the things that men aren't particularly good at." Kris leaned forward even more, her eyes sparkling. "Like what?"

David chuckled. "Like remembering birthdays. Or shoe sizes. Or the precise shade of lavender that Summer likes for her bath bombs. That's not to say that men can't remember those things, but our brains are generally wired for different tasks. We are problem solvers and protectors."

He gestured expressively. "I'm designed to figure out the optimal route to Dallas, calculate the amount of ammunition we need, and ensure everyone gets home safely. With so many women in my life, I rely on each of them to help me remember the little things. Tanya, for instance, knows exactly what skincare products each of the wives prefer. Summer knows everyone's allergies and sensitivities. Elena knows who can shoot. You get the idea"

Tiffany laughed. "He makes it sound so… organized." "It is organized," David insisted, a hint of mock offense in his voice. "Chaos is inefficient. And inefficiency leads to…" "Death," Scott finished the sentence for him, his voice flat. David nodded approvingly. "Precisely. Inefficiency leads to death. Now, Kris, to answer your initial question, do I ever feel the weight of responsibility? Absolutely. But overwhelmed? No. Because I have built a team, a family, that allows me to focus on what I do best." He paused, a mischievous glint in his eyes. "Besides, if I ever did start to feel overwhelmed, I have nine incredibly capable women who would… persuade me otherwise.”

“I don’t get it,” Kris said. “Your kids, they’re all monogamous. Aidan, Brian, Lily… they all have one partner. But you, you have… nine wives.” She raised an eyebrow, her eyes sparkling with intrigue. David chuckled. “Ah, Kris, you want to know the secret to my success, don’t you?” He leaned back in his seat, a self-satisfied smile spreading across his face. Tiffany, seated behind the wheel, snorted. “It’s not a secret, Kris. David just likes to think he’s a puzzle wrapped in a mystery, inside an enigma.” David shot her a mock-offended glance. “Hey, I’m a complex and interesting individual, thank you very much.” Kris laughed, her eyes never leaving David’s face. “I think what I’m trying to understand is how you ended up with multiple wives. You are traditional, aren’t you?”

David’s expression turned somber, his eyes clouding over for a moment. “Yes, I was monogamous. And it didn’t work out. Multiple times.” He paused, collecting his thoughts. “Abandonment, loss, death. After that, I didn’t want anything to do with relationships. I’d been hurt too many times, lost people I cared about... I just didn’t want to go through that again.” Kris studied David’s face, her expression soft.

“But then,” David continued, “I met Tiffany, Jennifer and Summer. They were all drawn to me, each for their own reasons. And after a while, I realized I needed them. I needed a team, a support system. I realized that I couldn’t do it alone.” As he spoke, his eyes seemed to glaze over, lost in thought. “I grew to love them, each one individually and collectively. And then, of course, there were the others... Elena, Nicole, Taylor, Kayla, and Tanya. They all needed me in some way, and my need to take care of them, only made all of us stronger."

Kris's gaze never wavered, her eyes drinking in every word. "And you just... allowed it to happen? You didn't try to stop it?" David's smile returned. "You see, I'm a man, Kris. I have urges, desires. Besides," his face turning serious. "If you could help someone. If that person needed you, and deep down, you genuinely cared for them. Would you throw them out, knowing they might not survive?"

The question hung in the air as Kris shifted in her seat, her brow furrowed. "Survive what? What do you mean?" Before David could answer, Scott chimed in. "He's just saying he's a good guy, Kris. You know, takes care of people." He offered a reassuring smile, but Kris wasn't buying it. She knew there was something more to David's words, something hidden beneath the surface.

"But it's more than that, isn't it?" Kris pressed, her voice barely a whisper. "You knew this was coming, didn't you? The blackout, the chaos... you knew this was going to happen." Tiffany glanced at David, a flicker of concern in her eyes. She knew how perceptive Kris could be, how easily she could unravel a carefully constructed facade. David, however, remained calm, his gaze fixed on the road ahead.

"Of course, I knew," David said matter-of-factly. "Anyone with half a brain could see the writing on the wall. The world was heading for disaster, and I wanted to be prepared." "Prepared? You built a fortress, David! A very specific one at that. You've got an armory that could arm a small country! This isn't just being prepared, this is very... specific," Kris exclaimed. "You don't just build all of this because you think there might be a blackout. What did you know that we didn't?" David sighed, running a hand on the back of his neck. "Kris, you're smart. You're observant. You see things that other people miss. That's what I like about you."

Tiffany took the reins, sensing David's reluctance to delve into the specifics. She turned to Kris, her expression gentle. "Okay, Kris, think of David like… a player in a video game. A really, really good player. He played through the game once, saw all the traps, knew all the boss fight weaknesses. Then… he got to start over. But this time, he kept his experience."

Kris stared at Tiffany. "You're saying… he's… reset?" "Essentially, yes," Tiffany confirmed. "He remembers the future. He knows what's coming." Kris's brain whirred, trying to reconcile this information with the David she thought she knew. "So, he's like… he hit a save point? Only he got to keep his XP and stats when he respawned?" Scott, who had been listening intently, chuckled. "Pretty much. Except the 'game' is real life, and the 'respawn' was… well, a bit more complicated."

Then, Kris had a thought. "Wait a minute… is that why he has so many wives?" Grace and Scott exchanged a look, a silent conversation passing between them. Tiffany chuckled. "No, Kris. None of us knew. We all fell for him… before we knew. Before the blackout. It was a privilege we earned, learning the truth."

"What about his kids?" Kris asked, her curiosity piqued. "Aidan, Brian, Little David… they all seem… different. Like they're playing on a higher difficulty setting than the rest of us." David, who had been silent for a moment, spoke up. "It's the same, Kris. Only the XP and stats are… gifted. They are given to someone that has never played before." Tiffany interjected. "It's like they started the game with a level twenty character."

"Okay," Kris finally said, drawing the word out like taffy. She turned to Grace, the youngest member of the vehicle, who was calmly sketching in a notebook illuminated by a small book light. "Grace, you're… what, fourteen? And you understand all this 'reset' stuff?" Grace looked up. "Of course. Daddy explained it. It's not that complicated." "Not complicated?!" Kris sputtered. "The fate of the world rests on your dad's shoulders, and you say it's not complicated?"

Grace shrugged, returning to her drawing. "Not the fate of the world, but we do have a responsibility. The world will heal once it purges the weak." Kris gaped. "The weak? You're talking about billions of people!" "Unfortunate," Grace said, without a hint of malice. "But necessary. Once the planet heals, we'll be responsible for rebuilding. Making sure we don't make the same mistakes."

Scott, observing everything with rapt interest, cleared his throat. "The girl's got a point, Kris. If this is going to happen anyway, might as well rebuild it the right way from the start." "But… to hear it from a fourteen-year-old…" Kris trailed off, shaking her head. "It's unsettling." "She and Seth have learned all the unspoken languages," Tiffany chimed in, coming in from left field. "Sign language, Braille, Morse code. They can read lips, they know when people are lying. They're… prepared, in a way the rest of us aren't." Kris felt a shiver run down her spine. "Unspoken languages? Why?"

"Daddy says it's important to communicate," Grace answered, looking up again. "Plus, why reinvent the wheel?"

David leaned forward slightly. "Grace understands that the world will heal, and that they have to 'carry' the knowledge of the past to the future. Society also shouldn't forget its past mistakes, Kris. Otherwise, it's destined to repeat them." "So, what am I supposed to do?" Kris asked, her voice laced with a hint of desperation. "I make tattoos. How is that going to help rebuild society?" Grace closed her notebook and turned her full attention to Kris. "No skill is too small. You can create beautiful art. Art can inspire. It can heal. But what's really important is compassion, and purpose. Why do you want to be here, with us? Why do you want to be a part of this community?"

Before Kris could formulate a response, the radio crackled to life. It was Parker, his voice tight. "Behemoth to Transit, we've got a roadblock ahead. Looks like some scavengers trying their luck." Tiffany's eyes narrowed. "Acknowledged. Behemoth, take the lead. Show them what you've got." She glanced at David, a silent question in her eyes. He nodded, a faint smile playing on his lips. "Remember, no unnecessary casualties," he said, his voice calm but firm. "Just clear the path."

Tiffany gripped the steering wheel, then expertly maneuvered the Transit to the side, allowing the Behemoth to surge ahead. The monstrous vehicle, a behemoth of steel and propane-fueled fury, roared down the highway, its crash bars gleaming in the headlights. A few tense moments ticked by. Then, a series of loud crashes echoed over the radio. Parker's voice, now laced with a hint of amusement, returned.

"Roadblock… neutralized. Those guys scattered like cockroaches. I don't think they'll be bothering anyone again anytime soon." "Good work, Parker," Tiffany replied, her voice crisp and professional. "Transit taking the lead again. Let's keep moving."

As the Behemoth slowed, allowing the Transit to pull ahead, Scott leaned forward, a grin spreading across his face. "Well, that was anticlimactic. I was expecting a bit more of a show." The Transit resumed its position at the head of the convoy, the highway stretching before them like a dark ribbon unwinding into the night. Inside, the atmosphere was a strange blend of calm and underlying tension. Grace, ever the wise observer, hadn't missed the tightening of Kris's shoulders during the brief roadside encounter, nor the way her eyes had widened at the sheer destructive power of the Behemoth.

"So," Grace said, turning back to Kris, her voice gentle. "Where were we? Ah, yes. Compassion and purpose. You see, Kris, it's not enough to simply want to be his. You have to understand why." Kris fidgeted, twisting her fingers in her lap. "He's…different." Kris's gaze flickering towards David, who was staring out the window, seemingly lost in thought. "He's… fair. He's not like the other guys I've met. They're always… opportunistic, you know? Trying to get something out of you. David… isn't."

Tiffany exchanged a knowing glance with Scott, who raised an eyebrow in amusement. She then turned back to Kris. "That's David. He has his… quirks. You could say." "Quirks?" Kris repeated, a skeptical tone coloring her voice. "That's putting it mildly. He's got more baggage than a 747!

But… I like him anyway." "It's more than quirks, Kris," Tiffany explained, her voice softening. "David has autism. He sees the world differently, processes information differently. He also has BPD, which means his emotions can be… intense at times. Add to that the trauma he carries from… well, before the regression, and you've got a pretty complex individual."

Kris absorbed this information, her smile replaced by a thoughtful frown. "So, he's… complicated?" "He's layered," Grace corrected gently. "Like an onion, but with more… well, less crying, hopefully." David, who had been staring out the window, quipped. "Ogres are like onions, darling." Tiffany chuckled. "See, Kris? Witty too."

"But," Grace continued, ignoring David's comment, "just because he has layers, doesn't mean it's complicated. It's important to understand the 'why' behind everything he does. His autism makes it impossible for him to be intentionally unfair, dishonest, or manipulative." "And the BPD?" Kris asked, her voice hesitant. "The BPD makes things… interesting," Tiffany admitted with a wry smile. "He feels things deeply. Joy, love, anger, sadness, it's all amplified. But it all gets filtered through his autism."

"Constant devotion and control," Grace echoed, nodding in agreement. "Not control of him, but a controlled environment for him. Predictability. Trust. Knowing that we are his and he is ours." "And the trauma?" Kris pressed. "It taught him," Grace answered, her voice firm. "It taught him the consequences of failure. That's why he's so decisive, so driven. He's not afraid to make the tough choices, because he knows what's at stake."

"So, he's not high-maintenance?" Kris asked, her voice laced with a hint of skepticism. "Because honestly, that sounds… intense." Tiffany and Grace exchanged another knowing look. "He's not high-maintenance, per se," Tiffany said. "He just needs… complete trust. Believe in him, support him, and he will literally give you the world. Doubt him, betray him, and… well, let's just say you wouldn't want to be on the receiving end of his displeasure."

Kris, perched beside Grace in the back, buzzed with a nervous energy that David found oddly endearing. Her eyes darted between the passing scenery and the enigmatic Grace, who sat perfectly still, her gaze fixed on the factory looming in the distance. "So," Kris began, her voice a breathless whisper, "like, is this a regular thing? Do you guys just…go around scouting factories all the time?"

Grace didn't break her stare, but Tiffany chuckled. "Let's just say this is our first run. But Grace and Kyle have been practicing for weeks. We needed Kyle's expertise." Kris's eyes widened further. "Expertise? Like, what kind of expertise?" "Kyle knows reloading, the different types of bullets, components, and how they are assembled to make the correct rounds." Tiffany explained.

David finally turned his attention from the road, a flicker of amusement dancing in his eyes. He found Kris's curiosity about the intricacies of his life with his wives and children endlessly entertaining. She asked so many questions. "He's our resident gunsmith, and he helped train Junior," David interjected, a playful smirk tugging at his lips.

As they pulled up to the factory gates, a tense silence settled over the vehicle. The factory was a hulking concrete behemoth that had been stripped bare by scavengers. The silence was broken only by the gentle hum of the engine. "Alright," David said, his voice calm and authoritative, "time to see what we're dealing with. Grace, you know the drill. Take Kyle in, assess the security, and report back. Quietly."

Grace nodded, "Yes Daddy." She slipped out of the van with the lithe grace of a predator, Kyle running to catch up. They moved with a practiced efficiency that spoke volumes about their training. David leaned back in his seat, watching the pair melt into the shadows. Kris, however, was practically vibrating with excitement. "Wow," she breathed, her eyes shining with admiration. "She's like a ninja! The way she moves…it's so cool!" David let out a low chuckle. "Why else did you think we named her Grace?" he quipped, earning a snort from Scott and a giggle from Kris.

The minutes stretched on. David didn't seem concerned, his gaze steady and unwavering, but Kris was a bundle of excited energy. She peppered Tiffany with questions about Grace's techniques, and her training. Finally, a small, almost imperceptible hand gesture from Grace signaled their return. She reappeared as silently as she had vanished, Kyle following close behind, a grim expression on his face. "Well?" David asked, his voice sharp but calm. "The warehouse has been picked over, severely," Kyle reported, his voice low and serious. "Not much left there. But…inside the factory, there's still a lot of loose ammo. Not organized, just scattered everywhere."

He continued. "There's also a lot of material; casings, bullets, primers and powder in the production area." David considered the information, his mind already formulating a plan. "Security?" "Minimal," Grace replied, her voice a quiet murmur. "A couple of stragglers, more interested in scavenging than guarding. Easily neutralized." David nodded. "Parker," he said into the radio, his voice calm and authoritative, "bring the Behemoth up. We're going in." There was a moment of static, then Parker's gruff voice crackled through the speaker. "Roger that, Boss." He turned to Tiffany. "Get ready to drive the van inside, once Parker makes an entry."

Tiffany simply nodded. Kris, however, was bouncing in her seat, practically bursting with excitement. "Oh my god, this is so cool!"

David sighed, considering her earnest plea. He knew Kris was eager to impress him, to prove her worth. And while he appreciated her enthusiasm, he couldn't afford any unnecessary risks. On the other hand, having an extra pair of eyes and hands could be useful, and even if things got bad, he was sure he could make sure that Kris would be safe. "Alright," he conceded, "but you listen to me, understood? Do exactly as I say, no questions asked. And if things get hairy, you stay close to me."

Kris squealed, throwing her arms around him in a tight hug. "Thank you, David! Thank you!" As she squeezed him, a surge of adrenaline and…something else, washed over her. Before she could think, she leaned in and pressed a quick, fervent kiss to the side of his neck. Her eyes widened in horror as she pulled back, her cheeks flushing deeply. Oh my god, what did I just do? He probably thinks I'm a total creep! She hoped he hadn't noticed, but the heat radiating from her face suggested otherwise. She quickly averted her gaze, focusing intently on the dashboard.

David, however, didn't react. His mind was already calculating angles, assessing threats, and formulating a plan. He knew Kris's intentions were a little impulsive, and he wasn't about to derail the mission with an awkward conversation about boundaries. "Parker," David said into the radio, "go ahead and breach."

A deafening roar ripped through the night as the Behemoth slammed into the fence. The chain-link buckled and splintered, creating a gaping hole in the perimeter. "Go, Tiffany!" David commanded. Tiffany expertly maneuvered the Ford Transit through the opening, following closely behind the behemoth.

Inside the factory, the scene was one of orchestrated chaos. Parker, Scott, Little David, and Kyle worked quickly, commandeering forklifts to move pallets of ammunition and reloading supplies. Grace, her small body dancing against the moonlight, watched the area from a high vantage point.

David, meanwhile, was directing the operation with calm precision. "Parker, load up on as much ammo and material as possible, prioritize what we need, but secure the rest within the factory's deep storage." He pointed to specific pallets. "Those crates of .223, get them on first. Then the 9mm. Scott, focus on the primers and powder. Junior, work with Kyle to secure the casings. We need to grab everything we can get our hands on." Anything that did not fit the current loadout was to be put into storage.

Kris, determined to prove her worth, scurried around, carrying boxes and relaying messages. She watched the forklifts with fascination. "David?" she asked tentatively, approaching him as he reviewed an inventory list. "How do those forklifts work, anyway?" David paused, a small smile forming. "They're counterbalance forklifts," he explained, his voice patient and informative. "Simple wiring, run on propane. Probably powered down and inside the factory when the EMP hit, which is why they still work. The key is the counterweight in the back, it balances the load in the front, allowing them to lift so much weight."

Kris listened intently, her brow furrowed in concentration. "So, the EMP didn't affect them because they were off and shielded inside the factory?" "Exactly," David confirmed, pleased with her quick grasp of the concept. He gave her head a gentle pat. "Smart girl." Kris beamed, her face lighting up. Emboldened by his praise, she impulsively grabbed his hand and playfully put his fingers in her mouth, a gesture both innocent and decidedly suggestive.

David, ever practical, simply stated, "Kris, my hands are dirty." He didn't pull away, didn't scold, just stated the obvious. It was enough. Kris's eyes widened as the realization of what she was doing crashed over her. Her cheeks flushed a deep crimson. She quickly released his hand, wiping her mouth with the back of her hand. "Oh! I... I didn't mean to," she stammered, mortified.

Chapter 20

Follow the Yellow Pages

David watched Kris's reaction with a detached amusement. He couldn't deny her spirit was… endearing. He rubbed her cheek gently, his thumb smoothing over her still-flushed skin. "No harm done, Kris. Just remember, we're working here. Let Tiffany know we should be done in a few hours." Kris, still mortified but buoyed by his lack of reprimand, nodded vigorously. "Okay, Master! I will!" She practically bounced away, her earlier awkwardness seemingly forgotten in her eagerness to please.

David chuckled softly as he watched Kris practically vibrate as she found Tiffany near the entrance, her earlier mortification replaced with an almost frantic energy. He turned back to the inventory list, his mind already calculating the amount of ammunition they could realistically transport back to the ranch. "Everything alright, David?" Scott asked, approaching him with a questioning look. "Fine, Scott. Just dealing with… Kris's enthusiasm," David replied, a hint of a smile playing on his lips. Scott raised an eyebrow. "Enthusiasm? Is that what we're calling it these days? Seems like the young lady has a bit of a crush." David nodded. "She certainly does, and apparently 'breeding' is right at the top of her list of kinks."

"Tiffany! Tiffany! I… I messed up!" Kris blurted out, her words tumbling over each other. Tiffany, ever vigilant, scanned the surroundings before focusing on Kris "Messed up how? Is everyone alright? Is someone hurt?" "No, no, nothing like that." Kris wrung her hands, her voice shaking. "I… I put David's fingers in my mouth." Tiffany blinked, a flicker of amusement dancing in her eyes. "You… what?" Kris's face flushed crimson again. "I know, I know, it was stupid! He was being so nice, praising me for understanding the EMP shielding, and I just… I don't know, I got carried away! He just said his hands were dirty, but I'm so worried he thinks I'm a total idiot now!"

Tiffany bit back a smile. She could only imagine David's reaction. "I doubt he thinks you're an idiot, Kris. David's not easily flustered. He's probably more concerned about the potential for lead poisoning." "But… but what if he thinks I'm too young? Lily's even older than me!" Kris wailed, the anxiety bubbling to the surface. "I don't want him to think I'm just some kid playing grown-up." Tiffany chuckled softly and laid a reassuring hand on Kris's shoulder. "Kris, don't worry so much. I highly doubt he thinks of you as a child." She paused, a mischievous glint in her eyes. "In fact, he probably appreciated your initiative."

Kris's eyes widened, hope warring with disbelief. "Really? You think so?" "Absolutely," Tiffany said with a wink. "Besides, David doesn't really do the whole sentimental 'you're too young' thing. He sees you as an adult, making adult decisions. As long as you understand the gravity of those decisions, he's not going to treat you like a child." Kris seemed to relax slightly, the frantic energy receding just a touch. "Okay… okay, that makes sense. But still, What about Lily, we're practically the same age? Won't he see me like a daughter?"

Tiffany laughed, shaking her head. "Honey, Lily is David's daughter, but that's a completely different dynamic. Try not to compare yourself. It's a recipe for madness, trust me." She leaned in conspiratorially. "Do you want to know a secret? When I first met David after… well, after everything, I was completely infatuated with him. Head over heels. I had just moved across the street. He was helping my mom and me with some work around the house, even teaching us how to cook. He just… radiated competence." Kris listened intently, completely captivated. "He could have… well, he could have had sex with me almost immediately. I was willing, eager even." Tiffany chuckled, a nostalgic smile on her face. "I was older than him by a couple of years, technically. But he made me wait. He said it wasn't about the age difference; it was about understanding. Understanding what he was, what he needed, what I wanted."

Kris frowned slightly. "Understanding? What do you mean?" "David wanted to make sure I understood that committing to him wasn't going to be a fleeting thing. People can get truly hurt if they rush things. David knew this, he experienced it." Tiffany cleared her throat. "You see, David knew where his life was going and he didn't want to burden me with that responsibility. If I wanted him, I had to go all in, no looking back. Only then, did he finally accept me."

She paused, a faraway look in her eyes. "And let me tell you, the wait was worth it." She chuckled again, a low, throaty sound that hinted at untold delights. "That man can fuck. If fucking was an Olympic sport, he'd be a gold medalist." Kris's eyes widened, a blush creeping up her neck. "Wow," she breathed, momentarily speechless. "So, it's not just about… you know… the bedroom stuff? It's about… everything else?"

Tiffany grinned, a wolfish glint in her eyes. "Oh, honey, the bedroom stuff is fantastic, don't get me wrong. But with David, it's about commitment, about responsibility, about being part of something bigger than yourself. It's about loyalty, trust, and knowing that no matter what happens, he'll always be there to protect you."

Then, Tiffany leaned forward, her voice dropping to a conspiratorial whisper. "Speaking of which… I have a confession to make myself." Kris's eyes widened with anticipation. "What is it?" Tiffany hesitated for a moment, then blurted out, "I have a kink. A… well, a somewhat extreme kink." Kris leaned closer, practically holding her breath. "Tell me!" Tiffany blushed slightly, looking around as if the walls had ears. "I… I kind of like being… unwilling."

Kris blinked, momentarily taken aback. "Unwilling? You mean…" "Yeah," Tiffany said, her voice almost inaudible. "I like the idea of… of being taken. Of being forced. It scares me sometimes, because it feels… wrong. But the orgasm? It's like nothing else. It's so much… stronger."

Kris's jaw dropped. "Wow," she breathed. "That's… intense." Then, a slow smile spread across her face. "But… I can see it. The contrast. The power dynamic. It's…" "Complicated," Tiffany finished for her. "It is. And it's something I struggle with sometimes. But David… he understands. He knows how to push my buttons, how to walk that line between pleasure and pain. He's… a master."

Kris turned to Tiffany, her voice a hushed plea, "Can… can I see? What that's like, I mean? With David?"

Tiffany paused. The request wasn't entirely unexpected. Kris had been peppering all of David's wives with questions for weeks, trying to understand the dynamics of their… arrangement. The idea of Kris watching… a small shiver ran down her spine. It was… kind of arousing. The thought of being observed, desired…

She considered the potential risks. Kris was… enthusiastic, to say the least. But she was also bright, resourceful, and fiercely loyal to those she cared about. And, let's be honest, a little exhibitionism never hurt anyone. "Alright," Tiffany finally said, her voice low. "But you have to be discreet. And you have to promise not to interfere, understand?"

Kris nodded vigorously, her eyes gleaming with excitement. "Yes! Of course! I promise!" "Good," Tiffany smiled, not entirely hiding her wolfish grin. "Watch David. Listen to what he says, and remember. Do not interfere." Then, Tiffany turned and walked towards David, who was overseeing the loading of the Behemoth with his usual calm efficiency. She leaned in close, whispering a few words in his ear.

David listened intently, his expression unchanging. He nodded once, a barely perceptible movement, and then returned to his task, seemingly unfazed. She returned to Kris, subtly licking her lips. "Alright, he's been informed. Now we wait." Tiffany, meanwhile, leaned against a stack of crates, watching Kris practically vibrate with anticipation. "Relax," she chuckled, nudging the younger woman with her elbow. "You're going to give yourself a hernia."

Kris jumped, startled. "I'm just… excited! I've never seen anything like this before. You and David… it's…" "A learning experience?" Tiffany offered, a playful glint in her eyes. "Just remember what I said. Observe, don't interfere. David doesn't like interruptions." Kris swallowed, nodding eagerly. "Yes, ma'am!"

Tiffany smiled. "Good girl." She glanced over at David, who was now conversing with Grace. The girl, perched atop the scaffolding, scanned the horizon with unnerving focus. Even from a distance, Tiffany could sense the intensity of his presence, the quiet authority that commanded respect and, let's be honest, sparked a certain level of primal fascination in everyone around him. "He's… amazing," Kris breathed, her voice barely audible. "He is," Tiffany agreed, her voice softening. "He's one of a kind."

After what felt like an eternity, Parker, his face smudged with grease, approached David. "All done, sir. Truck's loaded, ready to roll." David nodded, his gaze sweeping over the assembled group. "Good. Junior, take Scott, Kyle, and Parker. Take the truck and find some propane. Fill the tanks. We're burning through it faster than I'd like."

Little David nodded before they loaded back into the truck, in search of propane. "Tiffany," he said, his voice a low. "All preparations are complete?" "Yes, sir," she replied, pushing off the stack of crates. "The Behemoth is loaded, and Little David's team has departed to replenish our propane reserves." She paused, a hint of mischief dancing in her eyes.

He closed the distance between them in only a few steps, his movements fluid and deceptively quick. Before

Tiffany could fully register what was happening, David's hand shot out, clamping firmly around her neck. Not violently, not enough to cause real pain, but with a possessive grip that sent a shiver down her spine.

Kris gasped, her eyes widening in alarm. She'd been observing the scene, fascinated, from the doorway of a nearby office, but the sudden shift in David's demeanor sent a jolt of fear through her. The air crackled with a sudden, unexpected tension. What had started as playful observation had taken a sharp, unsettling turn. "Tiffany," David said, his voice still low, but now laced with an icy displeasure that was genuinely terrifying. "Do you think it is appropriate to address me so casually in front of others? Especially when they are not members of our family?"

Tiffany's smile faltered, replaced by a flicker of something akin to contrition. Heat flooded her face, and she stammered, "I...I just..." Before she could formulate a proper apology, David interjected, "Just because you are my first wife doesn't mean you can talk about me with impunity." "I apologize, David," she said, her voice barely a whisper. "It won't happen again."

The apology hung in the air, seemingly insufficient. David's grip tightened momentarily before releasing her neck. Then, with a swift, decisive movement that made Kris flinch, he struck Tiffany across the face. The sound echoed in the cavernous warehouse, a sharp, shocking slap that left a red mark blooming on her cheek.

Kris was too terrified to look away. She'd never seen David act like this. The stories she'd heard, the quiet dominance she'd witnessed with Jennifer, it was all different, controlled, almost playful. This was something else entirely. Without a word, David grasped Tiffany's arm and dragged her towards a heavy work table strewn with tools and blueprints. She stumbled slightly, following him with a mixture of shame and trepidation.

He stopped at the table, forcing her to face him, her eyes downcast. His voice was a low, controlled burn. "You are a petulant woman," he began, each word carefully enunciated. "You are the first, the foundation of our family, and you behave like a common barmaid. You are also a careless slut, parading your familiarity with me in front of someone who has yet to earn such privilege and finally, you are an ungrateful bitch, for failing to show me the respect that I deserve and that I have earned.

Tiffany remained silent, her shoulders slumped with shame. The red mark on her cheek stood out starkly against her pale skin. She nodded almost imperceptibly, a sign of understanding, but it didn't seem to appease David.

"If you want to behave like a common whore. showing off for her pimp, then I will use you as such. Do you understand?" David asked, not waiting for an answer before forcefully removing her clothes, leaving her vulnerable and exposed under the dim moonlight shining into the warehouse. The act was brutal, devoid of any tenderness, a stark display of dominance.

He then bent her over the table, his grip unyielding as he held her in place. Tiffany gasped, a small, choked sound that was swallowed by the vastness of the space. Kris's breath hitched in her throat. This was… beyond anything she had imagined. The stories, the glimpses she'd caught, hadn't prepared her for this raw, untamed power.

Without a word, David unsheathed his cock. The act was swift and decisive. He positioned himself behind her, and with a forceful thrust, he entered her. Tiffany cried out, a muffled sound of pain and perhaps, a strange kind of pleasure.

Kris felt a flush creep up her neck. The scene before her was shocking, undeniably harsh, yet she couldn't deny the burning curiosity that coursed through her veins. This wasn't the gentle, caring "Daddy" that Jessica spoke of, nor the attentive husband Summer described. This was a primal force, a man who demanded absolute obedience, and in that demand, Kris found a strange, unsettling allure. She had seen David's intelligence, his compassion, his wit. But she had never witnessed this raw dominance, this complete control. And a part of her, the part that yearned for structure, for security, was captivated.

Meanwhile, Parker, Little David, Scott and Kyle continued their work, seemingly oblivious to the drama unfolding nearby. Grace remained perched atop the warehouse scaffolding, an unmoving sentinel. The sounds of their activity, the clanking of metal, provided a strange counterpoint to the intense scene playing out near the work table.

Back at the table, David continued his brutal possession of Tiffany. Each thrust was a statement, a reaffirmation of his authority. Tiffany, despite the initial shock and pain, seemed to have surrendered to the moment, her body now moving in a rhythm dictated by his will.

The scene stretched on, an eternity of raw power and forced submission. Finally, after what felt like an hour, David stilled. He let out a guttural groan, his body shuddering with release. He remained inside Tiffany for a moment longer, before withdrawing and stepping away.

He didn't speak, didn't offer a word of comfort or apology. He simply turned and walked toward a stack of clean rags, wiping himself clean with methodical precision. Tiffany remained bent over the table, naked and vulnerable, her body trembling. The red mark on her cheek seemed to burn even brighter now. She slowly straightened, her eyes fixed on the floor.

Kris, finally able to move, retreated further into the shadows, her mind reeling. She had witnessed a side of David that she hadn't known existed, a side that was both terrifying and incredibly compelling. The experience had shaken her to her core, leaving her with a confusing mix of fear, fascination, and a burning desire to understand the man who held such absolute power. She knew one thing for certain: she wanted to be worthy of that power.

David turned to Tiffany. "Get dressed." His voice was devoid of emotion, a simple command. He then glanced in Kris's direction, his gaze piercing even from the distance. A ghost of a smile touched his lips. "Kris," he said, his voice now softer, almost inviting. "Come here."

Kris froze, her heart leaping into her throat. He knew she was there. He had known all along. Slowly, hesitantly, she stepped out of the shadows, drawn to him like a moth to a flame, a lamb to the slaughter. She had no idea what he wanted, but she knew she couldn't refuse him. Not now. Not after what she had just witnessed.

As she approached, David's gaze softened further. He saw the raw hunger in her eyes, the desperate yearning for acceptance, for belonging, for the power she'd just witnessed firsthand. He understood it. He'd cultivated it. It was a tool, like any other in his arsenal. "You were watching," he stated, his voice low and conversational. It wasn't an accusation, merely an observation.

Kris swallowed, her throat dry. "Yes, Sir." The word slipped out unbidden, a testament to the primal force he exerted. David nodded slightly. "And what did you think, Kris?" He waited, his eyes never leaving hers, probing the depths of her soul. She hesitated, fear warring with desire. "I… I want to understand." The truth hung in the air, raw and vulnerable. "I want to be worthy."

David took a step closer, closing the distance between them. He reached out, his hand gentle as he brushed a stray strand of hair from her face. "Worthy of what, Kris?" "Worthy of you, Sir. Worthy of… being like them." She gestured subtly towards where Tiffany was now buttoning up her shirt, her movements deliberate and controlled, as if nothing untoward had happened.

Tiffany, despite the lingering red mark blooming on her cheek, moved with a practiced grace, each button fastened with deliberate precision. The kiss she placed on David's lips was a stark contrast to the earlier violence, a display of unwavering devotion that both baffled and intrigued Kris. "I love you so fucking much, sir," Tiffany murmured against his mouth, the words laced with an intensity that resonated deep within Kris's soul.

He turned his attention back to Tiffany, recognizing the familiar warmth spreading through him as they connected. "I love you too, Tiffany," he said, his voice softer now, laced with genuine affection. He knew the toll these displays took on her, the strength it required to compartmentalize and endure. He appreciated her beyond measure.

The low rumble of the Behemoth's engine cut through the night, announcing its return. David nodded to Tiffany, a silent signal. Duty called. He turned back to Kris. "Think about what you said, Kris. Think about what you truly want. And be honest with yourself, more than anyone else." He paused, his gaze piercing. "Honesty is a valuable currency in these times. Don't waste it."

Then, he turned and strode towards the waiting vehicle, his movements purposeful and efficient. He spared no further glance at Kris, leaving her to grapple with his words and the whirlwind of emotions he had stirred within her. As David disappeared into the darkness, Tiffany turned to Kris, her expression shifting from the controlled composure she'd displayed for David to something altogether more knowing. The red mark on her cheek stood out starkly in the dim light, a silent testament to the raw encounter she'd witnessed.

"You were really captivated, weren't you?" Tiffany asked, her voice a low purr. Kris flushed, unable to meet Tiffany's gaze directly. "I... I don't know what to say." Tiffany chuckled, a sound that held both amusement and a hint of something else, something almost predatory. "To be honest, I came so hard, I can still feel it vibrating between my legs. It was rough," she said with a wicked glint in her eye, "but so, so good".

Kris's breath hitched. The image of Tiffany, moments ago submitting so completely to David's will, flashed through her mind. The contrast between the violence and the undeniable pleasure was intoxicating, terrifying, and utterly compelling. She felt a surge of heat pooling in her lower abdomen, a primal response that she couldn't control. The desire to experience that same intensity, that same surrender, overwhelmed her. It was all so intoxicating, and Tiffany was here, right in front of her. "Is it always… like that?" Kris blurted out, the question escaping before she could censor herself. Tiffany smiled. "Only if you want it to be," Tiffany answered.

Just then, David casually strolled back towards them, wiping his hands on a rag. "Alright ladies, ready to head home? Got almost everything we needed. This place is pretty much tapped out though, going to another factory now would be a waste of gas." He glanced from Tiffany to Kris. "Anything else you two wanted before we go home? Last call."

Tiffany, still riding the aftershocks of her earlier encounter, considered the question. "Well, we could use a good band saw and some other tools. We're gonna have to start slaughtering cattle soon, and I'd rather not use a dull axe." Before David could respond, Scott stepped forward. "I can build a small slaughterhouse. Got the skills, just need the materials."

David's lips quirked in a smile. "Now that's what I like to hear. Scott, you're a lifesaver. Okay, new mission. Let's find everything we need for Scott to build a slaughterhouse. Lumber, tools, roofing, the whole shebang. And Tiffany, we'll get your band saw." He clapped his hands together, a gesture that somehow managed to be both commanding and casual. "Little David, see if you can find out if there's any place around here that we can get those materials. Parker, start preppin' the Behemoth!"

Inside the dimly lit office of the munitions factory, little David worked with focused intensity. The power was still out, rendering the computer useless, but he wasn't deterred. He had found something better: a thick, dusty book filled with yellow pages. He illuminated the pages with his tactical flashlight, his brow furrowed in concentration as he scanned the listings.

Kris, drawn by the light and curiosity, walked into the office. She stopped short, her brow furrowing in confusion. "What are you doing, David?" she asked, peering at the open book. "Are you... reading a book? To find something? I thought we had the internet for that sort of thing?" Little David didn't look up, his fingers tracing down a column of text. "This is a directory of local businesses." He said matter-of-factly, as if it was the most obvious thing in the world. "Before the internet, people used these to find information."

Kris stared at the book, then at David, her expression a mixture of bewilderment and fascination. "A... pre-internet search engine? Seriously? That's wild!" The notion that people could find things without a screen and a keyboard seemed archaic and almost unbelievable. But then, she remembered where she was, when she was, and who she was with. Nothing was "normal" anymore.

He finally looked up, his youthful face serious despite the absurdity of the situation. "I'm trying to locate a slaughterhouse and a construction supply store. Scott needs materials to build a proper slaughterhouse back at the ranch, and Tiffany needs a bandsaw. So far it looks like, there's a slaughter house south of Dallas, they might have good equipment."

David, his face illuminated by the soft glow of his flashlight, meticulously studied the map. The munitions factory was proving to be a goldmine, but resources were finite, and they had to be strategic. Little David unfolded the large paper road map, checking the margin references before circling two locations on the lower portion. "Slaughterhouse south of Dallas," little David announced, his voice clear and precise, "and a construction supply store not too far from it. Good chance we can hit both in one run."

Kris, practically glued to David's side, leaned in, her eyes wide with genuine curiosity. "How did you even find those places?" she blurted out. "Tools from before the internet. I know how because my dad knows how." He tapped his temple, a silent acknowledgement of his gifted experience.

Little David made his way out of the office, clutching the marked maps, his footsteps echoing slightly in the cavernous factory. He found his father near the behemoth. Little David approached his father and held out the maps. "Slaughterhouse and construction supply store, south of

Dallas, like you asked. I marked the optimal route, factoring in potential road obstructions from the old maps."

David accepted the maps, his gaze sweeping over them with a practiced eye. "Good work, son. He clapped Little David on the shoulder, a display of affection that made the boy stand a little taller.

David watched as Parker expertly maneuvered the Behemoth out of the factory, the monstrous vehicle rumbling like a slumbering beast awakened. Inside the Ford Transit, Tiffany gripped the steering wheel, her focus absolute. Kris peppered David with questions about the maps, about the world before the internet, about everything that seemed so foreign and yet so appealing. "So, like, if you wanted to know something, you just… went to a library? And looked it up in a book? That's… insane!" she exclaimed, her tone a mix of disbelief and awe.

David answered patiently. "Libraries were repositories of knowledge, yes. And before them, scrolls and tablets. Humanity has always sought to record and preserve information." He paused, a thoughtful expression on his face. "The internet made access instant, but it also diluted the value of information. Anyone can post anything, regardless of its veracity."

"But… porn!" Kris interjected, her eyes widening. "What did people do before the internet had porn? That's… that's a world I don't even want to imagine!" Tiffany snorted from the driver's seat. "They used magazines, Kris. And imagination. Lots and lots of imagination." Kris's face scrunched up in a comical expression of disgust. "Ew, magazines? That sounds so… analog. And sticky."

David chuckled. "It had its merits, Kris. But I digress. We need to focus on the task at hand. We're looking for resources, not relics." As they drove, David observed Grace intently. He noticed her subtle shifts in posture, her keen observations of the environment. "Grace," he said softly, "do you notice anything unusual?" Grace paused, her brow furrowed in concentration. "The wind is shifting, Dad. And there's a… a metallic tang in the air. Like something burning." David's eyes narrowed. "Interesting. Keep a close watch."

The slaughterhouse loomed in the distance, a grim reminder of the world's current state. The stench of decay hung heavy in the air, a stark contrast to the crisp March night. The building was dilapidated, but potentially salvageable. "Scott, take point," David instructed. "Tiffany, cover the rear. Grace, stay close."

Chapter 21

The Slaughterhouse Salvage

As they approached, they could hear the faint sounds of movement inside. Scott cautiously pushed open the door, his gun at the ready. The interior was a scene of utter chaos. Bloodstained machinery lay scattered across the floor, and the air was thick with the smell of rot.

A chorus of gagging erupted, Kris leading the charge. "Oh, sweet baby Jesus, that is vile!" she wheezed, clutching her stomach dramatically. Tiffany, despite her years of dealing with… well, everything, also wrinkled her nose. "Even for this world, this is pushing it."

David, however, remained unfazed. He scanned the room with a calculating gaze, his mind already cataloging the salvageable equipment. "Focus, people. We're not here for a picnic. Kris, try to contain your theatrics. Scott, check for any… unwanted guests." Scott, ever the professional, moved quickly and efficiently, clearing the corners of the room. "All clear, David. Looks like we're the only ones brave (or stupid) enough to venture in here."

David nodded, his attention already on a massive bandsaw positioned near the back of the building. "That's what I'm after. See if you can find any extra blades." He turned to Tiffany. "Check the office for schematics or manuals. Anything that might help us reassemble and maintain this equipment."

Tiffany nodded and headed towards a door labeled "Office." Grace, true to form, stuck close to David, her eyes darting around. Kris, still struggling with the smell, fanned her face dramatically. "I swear, I'm going to need therapy after this. Or at least a really, really long shower. Maybe both, actually."

David, focused on the bandsaw, barely registered her comment. He ran a hand over the cold metal, his mind already working out the logistics of dismantling and transporting it. Meanwhile, Tiffany emerged from the office, her face a mixture of triumph and disgust. "Jackpot! I found a repair manual and a parts catalog. Also, a half-eaten sandwich that's probably older than Kris."

Kris gasped dramatically. "I'm not that old." Tiffany smirked. "Whatever you say, sweetie. Just try not to faint from the smell before we get out of here." She handed the manuals to David. "These look like they'll be invaluable. There's even a section on troubleshooting common problems."

David quickly scanned the manuals, his eyes darting across the schematics and diagrams. He looked at Scott. "Think you can handle dismantling the motor while I focus on the blade assembly?"

Scott cracked his knuckles. "Consider it done, David. I've wrestled with worse." He grabbed a wrench and began loosening bolts. Grace pointed to a pool of dark liquid on the floor. "Dad, what's that?" David knelt down, sniffing the air cautiously. "That's… rendering waste. Stay clear of it. It's highly contaminated."

Kris, who had finally managed to regain some semblance of composure, piped up. "Contaminated with what? The souls of the slaughtered?" David sighed. "Probably just bacteria and decaying organic matter. But let's not take any chances." He grabbed a bottle of bleach out of one of the nearby cabinets and handed it to Scott. "Pour that around the area before you start working."

As Scott splashed the bleach around, a voice crackled over the radio. It was Little David, his tone urgent. "Dad, we've got company. A small group, looks like scavengers. They're heading your way." David's head snapped up. "How far out?" "About a mile. They're on foot, but they're moving fast."

David's mind raced. He hadn't wanted a confrontation, but he wouldn't back down from one either. He needed the bandsaw, and he wouldn't leave it behind. "Tiffany, Kris, secure the perimeter. No unnecessary risks, but watch them."

Tiffany and Kris moved with practiced efficiency, melting into the shadows outside the loading bay doors. Tiffany took cover behind some stacked pallets. Kris, however, found a rusty barrel to crouch behind, her AR-15 held at the ready. "Showtime, ladies," she muttered, checking the magazine. "Let's hope these guys aren't fans of body art." David turned back to the others. "Scott, speed it up. We don't have much time." Scott grabbed a socket wrench and began attacking the bandsaw with renewed vigor.

Little David's voice came over the radio again, laced with concern. "Dad, they're getting closer. I can see them now. Looks like about five or six, armed with... what is that, a chainsaw?" David choked back a laugh. A chainsaw? At a slaughterhouse? The irony was almost too delicious. "Junior," he said into the radio, a smirk playing on his lips, "tell me, does this chainsaw-wielding gentleman happen to be wearing someone else's face as a mask?

Silence crackled over the comms for a moment. Then, Little David's voice, slightly bewildered, replied, "Uh, negative, Dad. No skin masks. Just… a guy with a chainsaw. And a really determined look on his face." "Damn," Kris said, disappointed. "And here I thought things were about to get interesting."

David shook his head, a genuine smile tugging at the corners of his mouth. "Alright, plan B. Tiffany, Kris, assess the situation. If they're just looking for supplies, try to negotiate. If they start any trouble, remind them why slaughterhouses are best left to, well, slaughtering." Tiffany's voice, calm and collected, responded from her position. "Understood, David. I'll try to appeal to their better natures. Though, considering the times, I'm not holding my breath that they have any."

Kris, on the other hand, was less optimistic. "Negotiate? Pfft. With a chainsaw? This is gonna be fun." Then, into her radio, "Grace, get ready to record. I wanna document this for posterity, I think everyone at home might enjoy this."

Grace, ever the stealth expert, had already positioned herself behind a stack of discarded meat trays, her phone held steady, recording the scene unfolding before her. She gave David a thumbs-up, a mischievous glint in her eye.

He strode towards the loading bay doors, holding his hands up in a gesture of peace. "Alright, folks! Let's talk!" he called out, his voice amplified by the acoustics of the slaughterhouse. "We're just looking for some equipment. We're happy to trade for it or even help you out with something."

The chainsaw sputtered to life, a high-pitched whine that echoed in the night air. The man wielding it, a burly figure in a stained jumpsuit, took a step forward. "Get off our property! This is our place now!" he roared, his voice raspy and uneven. David raised an eyebrow. "Your place? Last time I checked, this was Smithfield Processing. Did Smithfield Processing suddenly decide to embrace the post-apocalyptic raiding lifestyle? And if so, did they at least offer dental?"

The chainsaw man sputtered, momentarily thrown off by David's absurd question. "Dental? What the hell are you talking about? Get out! Before I… before I…" He trailed off, clearly lacking a threatening conclusion to his sentence. David pressed his advantage. "Before you what? Give me a complimentary haircut? Look, pal, I'm just trying to make an honest living. I need that bandsaw. I need the meat grinder. And I'm willing to trade. What do you need?"

From her flanking position, Tiffany subtly adjusted her grip on her AR-15, her eyes scanning the surrounding shadows. Kris leaned against the wall, looking utterly bored, but her hand never strayed far from the Glock on her hip. Grace, meanwhile, was zooming in on the chainsaw man's face, capturing every bead of sweat and nervous twitch. The chainsaw man hesitated, his grip on the roaring machine wavering slightly. "I… we… we need food."

David smiled, a genuine, warm smile that could disarm even the most hardened raider, or at least confuse them into inaction. "Food, huh? Well, you're in luck. My sister in law packed us enough sack lunches to feed a small army. Sandwiches, fruit, cookies, the works. Enough to last you guys a couple of days, easy. How's that sound for the bandsaw and the meat grinder?"

The chainsaw man glanced over his shoulder, seemingly consulting with someone unseen. After a brief, muffled conversation, punctuated by the occasional unintelligible grunt, he turned back to David, his expression slightly less menacing. "Alright. But we want all the lunches. Every last one." David smiled. "And I bet you'll make better use of them, than I would," he said with a wink. "Tiffany, bring out the feast!"

Tiffany grumbled something about spoiled brats getting perfectly good food, but dutifully retrieved the cooler from the Ford Transit. The chainsaw man and his unseen compatriots swarmed the lunches like locusts, tearing into the sandwiches with gusto. Within minutes, the air was filled with the sounds of chewing and satisfied groans.

Kris, who had been leaning against the wall with an air of utter indifference, now stepped fully into the flickering light. She stretched languidly, her movements drawing attention like moths to a flame. The raiders, mid-chew, paused to stare at her, their eyes widening with something akin to... well, Kris was no fool. It was lust. Pure, unadulterated, post-apocalyptic lust. "Damn," one of them breathed, a teenager with a patchy beard. "She's hot."

His comment seemed to embolden the others. Several of them exchanged glances, and a low murmur rippled through the group. The chainsaw man, his mouth full of ham and cheese, pointed a greasy finger at Kris. "We… we want her too."

David's smile vanished. The air around him seemed to thicken, and the temperature felt like it dropped a good ten degrees. David stepped forward, his voice dangerously low. "She belongs to me." He paused, letting the words hang in the air. "If any of you so much as lay a finger on her, I promise you, I will take your arm." He paused. "Do I make myself clear?"

The teenager, emboldened by embarrassment and a sudden rush of testosterone, reached for a handgun hidden in his waistband. Before anyone could react, Grace, a whisper of a girl with eyes that saw everything, moved with impossible speed. It was like watching a hummingbird in fast-forward. One moment, the kid was reaching; the next, his hand was pinned to the side of the rusty slaughterhouse wall by a throwing knife embedded precisely between his fingers.

The teenager screamed, a high-pitched, pathetic wail that echoed through the cavernous space. The chainsaw man, startled and clearly not used to such swift justice, dropped his half-eaten sandwich. The other raiders, a motley collection of scavengers and thugs, froze, their eyes wide with fear. "Grace," David said, his voice calm. "Retrieve your knife."

Grace, without a word, pulled the knife free, the teenager screaming again as the blade scraped along his knuckles. She wiped the blade clean on his greasy shirt with a look of utter disdain before returning to David's side. The chainsaw man swallowed hard, his Adam's apple bobbing nervously. "Okay, okay," he stammered, holding up his hands in a gesture of surrender. "Sheesh, no need to get all… stabby." David's gaze didn't waver. "You were saying?"

The chainsaw man's eyes darted from David to Grace, then to Tiffany, who stood vigilant off to the side. Kris, however, was a sight to behold. She was practically vibrating with suppressed laughter, her eyes sparkling with amusement. David's possessiveness, coupled with Grace's swift action, had clearly struck a chord.

"Look, man," the chainsaw man said, his voice now laced with genuine apprehension. "We just… we were just joking. You know? Post-apocalyptic humor. It's a thing." "Right," David said, his voice dripping with sarcasm. "Because threatening to take someone who clearly doesn't want to go with you is hilarious. I'll have to try that routine sometime." He turned to Kris, a slight smile playing on his lips. "Are you alright?"

Kris snorted, stifling a giggle. "Oh, I'm peachy. In fact, I haven't had this much fun in ages. Makes me wonder what it'll be like when you have to protect our kids." She raised an eyebrow. He cleared his throat, ignoring the snickers he heard from Tiffany. "Let's just focus on getting the equipment, shall we?"

Just then, Parker's voice crackled over the radio. "Dave? Found the blades. A whole freakin' box of 'em. Enough to keep us sawing through beef for the next decade." David sighed in relief. At least something was going right.

As if on cue, Little David rounded the corner, grunting with exertion. He was carrying a meat grinder that looked like it belonged in a small abattoir. It was easily 250 pounds of cast iron and steel. The raiders stared in stunned silence. "Found this bad boy in the back," Little David said. "Looks like it's in pretty good shape. Think it'll work?" David stared at his son, a mixture of pride swirling within him.

He clapped his hands together, the sound echoing in the cavernous slaughterhouse. "Alright, people. Let's get this show on the road. Kyle, help Scott disassemble that saw. Parker, bring the Behemoth closer. Tiffany, Kris, keep a close eye on our 'friends' here. Junior, set that… thing down gently. Grace, maybe practice your whittling on something less… sentient."

As Scott worked, he noticed the teenager clutching his hand, a thin trail of blood seeping between his fingers. With a sigh that suggested he'd seen far too much violence in his life, Scott pulled out a first-aid kit from his belt. "Here, let me take a look at that," he said gruffly.

The teenager hesitated, then hesitantly extended his hand. Scott gently unwrapped the fingers, revealing a nasty gash. "Looks like it missed the bone. Lucky it wasn't worse." Scott cleaned the wound with antiseptic, earning a yelp from the boy, and expertly applied a bandage. "There you go. Keep it clean." He patted the kid's shoulder, a gesture that looked strangely out of place in the grimy slaughterhouse.

With the saw disassembled, the grinder loaded, and the box of blades secured, David felt a wave of exhaustion wash over him. He wanted nothing more than to be back at the ranch, surrounded by his family, away from the stench of death and desperation. He turned to the apparent leader of the ragtag group, who was now watching him with a mixture of fear and grudging respect. David pulled the man aside, speaking in a low voice so the others wouldn't hear.

"Look," David began, his voice surprisingly gentle. "I get it. You're just trying to survive. And that chainsaw… well, it's a statement. But it's not a long-term solution." He paused, considering his words. "This EMP… it changed everything. The old rules don't apply anymore. Chainsaws are loud, they attract attention, and they run out of gas."

He pointed towards the highway. "Head east. Find an old property with a well. Stock up on non-perishable food. Learn to garden. And most importantly, learn to work together. You've got kids here. They deserve a chance." He reached into the back of the Ford Transit and pulled out an AR-15, offering it to the man with a case of ammo. The man stared at it, his eyes wide with disbelief. "Take it," David insisted. "It's better than a chainsaw. Learn to use it responsibly. Protect your family." The man hesitantly took the rifle, his fingers trembling. "Thank… thank you," he stammered. "I… I don't know what to say."

David clapped him on the shoulder. "Just survive. And maybe, someday, we'll see each other again." He gestured towards the Behemoth and the Ford Transit. "We're leaving now. Good luck."

The Behemoth roared to life, Parker's heavy foot pressing the accelerator. Little David, perched beside him, grinned, already fiddling with the radio. Kyle, in the back, checked the newly acquired supplies, a satisfied grunt escaping his lips. The Ford Transit followed, Tiffany expertly navigating the debris-strewn road. David watched the slaughterhouse recede in the rearview mirror, a knot of anxiety twisting in his gut. He knew the odds were stacked against those people. But he'd given them a chance, a fighting chance. And sometimes, that was all you could do. "Alright, team," David announced, turning to face the passengers. "Building supply store, next stop. Let's get this show on the road."

Kris, her eyes sparkling with mischief, leaned forward from the back. "David, you're so generous. Giving away that rifle. It's… inspiring." David raised an eyebrow, a slight smile playing on his lips. "They needed it more than we did." Scott chuckled from the passenger seat. "Besides, we've got enough firepower to start a small war."

Grace, sandwiched between them, piped up. "Daddy, can we get ice cream when we get back?" David's face softened. "Absolutely, sweetheart. Whatever flavor you want." Tiffany, overhearing the conversation, glanced back and grinned. "Don't spoil her, David. We need to keep her sharp. Stealth ninjas don't run on sugar." David smiled. "Darling, don't tell me how to love my daughter," he said, patting Tiffany's hand.

"Speaking of sharp," David said, changing the subject, "Scott, that was some impressive first aid back there. You handled that kid like a pro." Scott shrugged, a hint of a blush creeping up his neck. "Just basic stuff. Andrea taught me a few things." "And Grace," David continued, turning his attention to his daughter, "you were amazing. Staying calm, keeping an eye out. You've got the instincts of a seasoned scout." Grace beamed, puffing out her chest with pride. "It was like a scavenger hunt, Daddy! But… a smelly one."

David turned to look out the window. The lack of other travelers was both a blessing and a curse. Fewer threats, sure, but also a stark reminder of the devastation. He knew that the relative peace wouldn't last. Once summer hit, the heat would drive people out of their hiding places, desperate for resources, and night would become the new day. The thought spurred him to push harder, to prepare his ranch for the inevitable outbreak of violence.

Kris, never one to let a moment of silence linger, turned her attention to Grace. "So, sweetie," she purred, her voice laced with amusement, "how do you feel about having so many aunts?" Grace pondered the question, her brow furrowed in thought. "It's… fun! I like having lots of people to play with. And Aunt Tiffany makes the best cookies, and Aunt Jennifer tells the funniest jokes, and Aunt Elena teaches me cuss words… She trailed off, counting on her fingers. "Lily's my favorite though. We use to sneak popsicles at night."

Scott shifted in his seat. "David, I've been meaning to ask you something. You, uh, your kids… you all seem to bounce back from injuries pretty quickly. Do you heal faster than normal people?" David considered the question. It was a common assumption. "No, not really. Our healing rate is pretty standard. We just… endure better." Scott frowned. "But you're all so strong. I just figured that went hand in hand with accelerated healing."

David chuckled. "That's a misconception. We don't have superpowers, Scott. What we have is tighter muscular density. Think of it like tightly winding seventy pounds of muscle into a toddler's body. By the time they're full grown, with enough training, their maximal muscular force could end up being four or five times greater than an average person without taking up extra space."

"So, it's like they're… compressed?" Scott asked, still trying to wrap his head around it. "Essentially, yes," David confirmed. "And that compression, combined with their training, gives them a significant advantage in combat and survival situations." He paused, a touch of pride creeping into his voice. "It's not magic. It's just… efficient engineering."

Kris, who had been listening intently, leaned forward, her eyes sparkling with mischief. "Efficient engineering, huh? That sounds fascinating. I'm surprised you aren't filling up every woman within arm's reach with your engineering serum. You know, a little reproductive engineering for the sake of humanity."

David, who was already regretting opening this particular can of worms, subtly pinched the bridge of his nose. He could practically feel Tiffany's amusement radiating from the driver's seat. He enjoyed Kris's playful audacity, but her timing was, as usual, impeccable for maximum awkwardness.

Scott, oblivious to the undercurrents, looked genuinely intrigued. "So that's like... building a better baby? Like, stronger bones and stuff from the get-go?" Grace, ever the observant one, piped up. "Daddy, what's reproductive engineering?" David sighed inwardly. He needed to shut this down, and fast. "It's… complicated, Grace. We'll talk about it later.

Thankfully, salvation arrived in the form of their destination. "Alright, everyone," David announced, his voice regaining its authoritative tone. "Building supply store in sight. Let's get in, get what we need, and get out. Parker, Junior, Kyle, secure the perimeter. Tiffany, Kris, Scott, with me. Grace, you're on recon."

As the Ford Transit rumbled to a stop, dust devils danced in the headlights, painting grotesque shadows on the abandoned building supply store. David surveyed the scene, his eyes scanning for any immediate threats. "Remember the plan," he instructed, his voice calm and steady. "Efficiency and speed. We're not here to browse the paint samples." Grace smiled, adjusting her night vision goggles. "Yes Daddy!"

He watched as Parker expertly maneuvered the Behemoth into the loading dock, its massive frame a comforting reassurance. Little David and Kyle, already armed and alert, hopped out and began their perimeter sweep. Scott, still struggling with the concept of 'compressed muscular density,' stared wide-eyed at Grace. "But... she's just a kid," he stammered, gesturing at the petite blonde who barely reached his shoulders. "How can she be... I mean..." Before Scott could finish his bewildered sentence, Grace vanished. One moment she was there, a small figure amidst giants, the next she was gone, a whisper of movement swallowed by the darkness.

David smirked faintly. "Grace takes her stealth training seriously," he explained to the bewildered Scott. "Don't underestimate her, Scott. She's more than capable." He paused, his gaze hardening. "Remember, everyone, eyes open. This place is a potential death trap. Assume hostiles are present until proven otherwise."

David, Tiffany, and Kris entered the echoing warehouse, the air thick with the ghosts of forgotten projects and the dust of neglect. The flashlight beams danced across empty shelves, punctuated by the occasional towering rack laden with lumber – the dregs of what must have been a once-thriving business. "Well, this is… underwhelming," Tiffany declared, her voice bouncing off the corrugated metal walls. "Looks like everyone else had the same idea. Guess building materials are the new gold."

Kris skipped ahead, her Doc Martens crunching on scattered debris. "Don't worry, David," she chirped, her voice laced with playful confidence. "We'll make it work." She winked. David simply nodded. "Tiffany, focus on the smaller items, nails, screws, wiring. We'll need those for the finishing touches. Kris, help me assess the lumber. We need to prioritize what's usable and what's just taking up space." Scott, still reeling from Grace's vanishing act, trailed behind them, his eyes darting nervously around the cavernous space. He kept muttering, "Invisible ninja children… invisible ninja children…"

The warehouse was eerily empty, save for the towering racks of lumber. It was clear that the prime cuts had long been scavenged, leaving only the less desirable pieces strewn about. David surveyed the situation with a critical eye, his mind already calculating the angles and loads required for his new slaughterhouse.

"David," Tiffany called out, her voice echoing slightly. "I've found a decent stash of nails and screws, but the wiring's mostly gone. "Not surprising," David replied, his voice calm. "We anticipated that. We'll make do with what we have and supplement it with what we have back home."

Kris, meanwhile, was attempting to scale one of the lumber racks, her short stature proving a hindrance. "David, these top shelves are loaded! But I can't reach! What do you want me to do?" she called down, her voice a mix of frustration and eagerness.

David sighed again. "Just take it easy, Kris. We'll figure something out. I don't want you getting hurt or breaking your neck." He weighed his options. Then he remembered Grace. "Grace," he said, his voice low but clear. Immediately, and with a startling pop of displaced air, Grace materialized directly behind Scott.

Scott screamed. It wasn't a manly yell, not even a grunt of surprise. It was a high-pitched, ear-splitting screech that echoed through the warehouse, causing a flock of pigeons roosting in the rafters to take flight in a flurry of wings and panicked cooing. He stumbled forward, tripping over his own feet and landing in a heap on the dusty floor.

Scott lay sprawled, a whimpering mess of limbs and suppressed sobs. His eyes darted around, searching for the source of his terror. "Invisible ninja children… they're real… they're really real…" he mumbled, his voice barely audible above the rustling of pigeons overhead.

Tiffany simply stepped over him. "Honestly, Scott, pull yourself together. You're embarrassing yourself." Kris, still perched precariously on the lower rungs of the lumber rack, watched Scott with a mixture of amusement and impatience. "David, are we just going to leave him there? I still need help getting this wood down!"

David, however, was already focused on the task at hand. He knelt beside Scott, placing a reassuring hand on his shoulder. "Scott, are you alright? Take a deep breath." Scott looked up at David, his eyes wide with disbelief. "Stealth? She teleported! She just appeared! That's not stealth, that's... demonic!"

David sighed inwardly. "Grace," David said, his voice calm and even. "I need you to do something for me. Can you find out where the forklifts are?" Grace nodded once, and with another almost imperceptible pop, she vanished. Scott flinched violently and dove behind Tiffany, using her thin frame as a shield. "Seriously, Scott?" Tiffany grumbled, pushing him away. "I'm trying to be supportive here, but you're cramping my style."

A few minutes later, Grace reappeared, her expression unreadable. "They're in the back, near the loading docks," she reported. "But the keys are gone."

David frowned. That was a setback. The lumber at the top of the racks was the only decent stuff left, and without forklifts, getting it down would be a major challenge. Plus, they needed to get moving. Sunrise was approaching fast, and he wanted to be out of here before others came out.

He pulled out his radio and keyed the transmit button. "Junior, this is Dad. Do you read me?" A crackle of static filled the air, followed by Little David's crisp, professional voice. "Reading you loud and clear, sir. What's the situation?" "We need to get some lumber down from the top racks," David explained. "The forklifts are back by the loading docks, but the keys are missing. Think you can hotwire them?" There was a brief pause. "Affirmative. Give me a few minutes."

"Alright, everyone, let's get moving," David announced, clapping his hands together. Kris, who had finally managed to clamber down from the lumber rack with a few choice planks, strutted over to David. "Can I assist you in any way? "Thank you, Kris, but I think we have it covered. Why don't you make sure the Ford Transit is ready to go? We'll need it for the smaller stuff."

Kris deflated only slightly, shooting a glare at Tiffany, who winked in response. "Of course, David. Anything for you." She sauntered off towards the Transit, muttering something about "unappreciated talent."

David turned his attention back to his radio. "Junior, any progress?" "Almost there, Dad," Little David's voice crackled back. "Just bypassed the ignition switch. Stand by." A moment later, a roar echoed from the back of the building, followed by the unmistakable sound of a forklift engine sputtering to life. "We're in business, sir. Two forklifts operational."

David let out a relieved sigh. "Excellent work, son. Parker, Kyle, you're up. Follow Junior's lead and start loading the Behemoth. Tiffany, Scott, you can help load the smaller items in the Transit. Grace, keep an eye out for any… unwanted attention."

Little David, with the confident swagger of someone who'd mastered forklift operation in under five minutes, expertly maneuvered the heavy machinery. Parker barked out orders with calm precision, guiding Little David's movements. Kyle secured each load with military-grade straps, ensuring nothing would shift during the bumpy ride back to the ranch. The Behemoth, parked at the loading dock, seemed to groan with satisfaction as it devoured stack after stack of lumber, plywood, and roofing shingles.

Inside, Tiffany and Scott loaded smaller items like nails, screws, tools, and wiring into the Ford Transit, organizing everything with Tetris-like precision. Tiffany, despite her athletic build, occasionally grunted under the weight of particularly heavy boxes, while Scott, a mountain of a man, barely seemed to notice the strain. Grace, meanwhile, remained a silent sentinel, her keen eyes scanning the perimeter for any signs of trouble.

"Alright, that's the last of it," Parker announced, wiping sweat from his brow. "Behemoth's packed tighter than a drum. Good work, Junior." Little David hopped down from the forklift, his eyes sparkling with pride. "Thanks, Parker. Just doing my job, sir." Tiffany slammed the back doors of the Transit shut. "All loaded up here too, David. Ready to roll." "Excellent," David said, clapping his hands together. "Let's move out. Parker, you take the lead. Tiffany, you're on point. Grace, ride shotgun with Tiffany, and keep your eyes peeled."

Chapter 22

The Hard Road Home

David watched as Grace approached Tiffany with a straightforward request. "Tiffany, can I switch places with David?" she asked, her voice surprisingly steady. "I'd rather ride in the Behemoth with Parker and Kyle." Tiffany raised an eyebrow, a hint of amusement playing on her lips. "And why is that, Grace? Don't you like riding with us?"

Grace hesitated for a moment, her cheeks flushing slightly. "It's not that. It's just… I think I can be more useful in the Behemoth. More visibility, better vantage point." It wasn't a complete lie. The Behemoth's elevated position offered a wider field of view, ideal for spotting potential threats. But David, and likely Tiffany, suspected there was more to it than that.

David suppressed a chuckle. He knew about Grace's not-so-secret crush on Kyle. The girl was as subtle as a sledgehammer when it came to the young gunsmith. While she was a master of stealth, her affections were broadcasted in neon lights. "Well, now, that's a very mature and responsible request, Grace," David said, stepping forward. "I think it's a good idea. Junior is good to have around me, to keep me on my toes. Tiffany, what do you think?"

Tiffany glanced at David, a knowing smile gracing her lips. "Suit yourself, boss. Grace, you're welcome to ride with the big boys. But don't let Kyle distract you from your duties. We need those eyes sharp." She winked, causing

Grace's blush to deepen. "I won't, Tiffany. Thank you," Grace mumbled, already halfway to the Behemoth.

David watched her go, a fond smile on his face. He turned to Tiffany, his smile softening. "She's sweet on him, isn't she?" "Sweet on him? David, she's practically wearing a 'Kyle is my future husband' t-shirt," Tiffany said, chuckling. "I swear, the girl follows him around like a shadow. And Kyle, bless his heart, is completely oblivious."

David laughed, shaking his head. "He's a good man, Kyle. Focused. Doesn't let much distract him. And Grace, well, she's…persistent." He paused, considering. "They actually make a good team. They work well together in training, push each other. He doesn't treat her like a kid, but he still looks out for her, which is important."

Tiffany nodded. "True. Kyle respects her skills, and Grace…well, she probably appreciates being taken seriously. He made a mental note to talk to Grace and Kyle, see if they needed anything. Maybe a little extra training, or just someone to talk to. "Alright, let's get a move on," David said, clapping his hands together. "We're not getting any closer to home standing around here."

As the Ford Transit idled, waiting for Parker to fire up the behemoth, Kris sidled up to David, her eyes wide with concern. "Aren't you worried about Grace?" David raised an eyebrow, the corner of his mouth twitching. "Worried? About what, Kris?" "Well," she started, "she's, like, fourteen. And Kyle…he's, like, thirty-two. Isn't that, like, a little… weird?" Kris watched David carefully, trying to gauge his reaction. David chuckled. "Kris, you're sweet to be concerned. I appreciate that. But I know both of them quite well, and they are both fairly well-rounded, mature even. There's nothing inappropriate going on.

Kyle is a good man, and a responsible one. He would never do anything to hurt Grace. And Grace, she respects him, admires his skills, and treats him like a peer in many ways. He paused, considering how best to explain. "Look, this isn't like some ordinary teen crush. Grace is... observant, and she knows a lot. She sees Kyle for who he is: a skilled, dependable person, someone she can trust. And Kyle sees her potential, her dedication, her intelligence. They have a connection, based on mutual respect and shared skills. It's a valuable thing, especially in these times."

Kris still looked a little unconvinced. "But... marriage? Shouldn't she be, like, playing with dolls or something?" David smiled gently. "Aren't you like… twenty-eight years younger than me? And yes, she does play with dolls, sometimes. But she also knows everything I knew when I regressed. Besides," he added with a wink, "it's not like they're getting married tomorrow. They have plenty of time to figure things out."

He leaned in closer, lowering his voice. "And honestly, Kris, between you and me? I trust Grace's judgment implicitly. She's a smart cookie. If she thinks they have that potential, then I'm inclined to believe her." Kris seemed to relax a little, though a flicker of something else, perhaps envy, crossed her face. "Okay, I trust you," she said, her voice softer. David patted her hand. "Good."

As the van rumbled down the ravaged Texas highway, Scott, crammed in the back beside Kris, couldn't help but observe the interaction between her and David. The subtle tremor that ran through Kris's body after David's casual "Good girl" hadn't escaped his notice. And what he saw was… intriguing, to say the least. He leaned closer to Kris, lowering his voice. "You okay, Kris? You seem a little… flushed." Kris jumped, startled. "Oh! Uh, yeah, Scott. Fine. Just… thinking."

Scott raised a skeptical eyebrow, but didn't press. He had his suspicions. He'd seen David in action before, witnessed the almost hypnotic effect he had on people. Kris was young, impressionable, and clearly, deeply smitten. His gaze shifted to David, who was now engrossed in a conversation with Tiffany in the passenger seat, seemingly oblivious to the undercurrents in the back. Scott furrowed his brow. Was David aware of the effect he had? Or was he truly as oblivious as he appeared?

A sudden thought struck Scott, one so outlandish it almost made him laugh. Could it be possible? Were David's… "gifts," for lack of a better word, amplified by his regressive experience? Maybe his pheromones were concentrated, supercharged somehow, making him irresistible, especially to certain… predisposed individuals.

Meanwhile, Little David, oblivious to the simmering tension in the back, continued to provide a running commentary on the passing scenery. "That's a dead armadillo, Kris! See? And over there… more rubble! I bet there used to be a Wal-Mart there. I liked Wal-Mart." Kris, still attempting to regain her composure, managed a weak smile. "Yeah, Wal-Mart was… something."

David, his conversation with Tiffany winding down, turned his attention to the younger occupants of the van.

"You doing alright back there, you two?" he asked, his voice laced with genuine concern. "Yep! Just sightseeing," Little David chirped. Kris, however, chose that exact moment to completely lose her mind. "No," she blurted out, the word hanging in the air like a pungent fart. "I'm not alright. I… I want you to get me pregnant!"

Little David, oblivious to the tension, continued to gaze out the window, pointing excitedly at a flock of buzzards circling overhead. Tiffany, ever the maternal one, shot David a knowing glance, a mixture of amusement and concern in her eyes. David, however, remained unfazed. He simply smiled gently at Kris, his eyes filled with an unreadable depth. "We'll discuss it later, Kris," he said calmly, his voice laced with a subtle authority that somehow managed to be both reassuring and absolute. "Right now, we need to focus on getting home safe."

Scott, however, was floored. He stifled a cough, trying to mask his shock, and met David's eyes in the rearview mirror. David's gaze was steady, knowing, and for the briefest of moments, Scott swore he saw a flicker of amusement dance in the depths of David's pupils. That was it. Scott was convinced. It wasn't just intelligence, tactical skill, or even the inherent leadership qualities that drew people to David. It was something… else. Something almost supernatural, a potent cocktail of charisma, pheromones, and the unquantifiable weight of a life lived, lost, and relived. And David, this motherfucker, he knew it. He was playing a game with levels Scott couldn't even comprehend.

The tension in the back of the Ford Transit was now so thick you could cut it with a knife – a knife, Scott noted wryly, that Seth would probably be able to identify by its make and model just by glancing at the handle. Just then, Kris leaned closer to David, her voice trembling. "David?" she asked, her eyes wide and pleading. "Could I… could I maybe… give you a blowjob? If I promise to be really discreet?"

Scott nearly choked on his own spit. He fumbled for the door handle, contemplating jumping out of the moving vehicle. This was beyond awkward; this was bordering on the absurd. He glanced at Tiffany, expecting outrage or at least a raised eyebrow. But Tiffany merely sighed, a weary expression on her face. It was the look of a mother who had seen it all before, a veteran of countless teenage dramas. "Kris," she said firmly, "not in the car. Have some respect." Kris was not disappointed, because David didn't say 'No'.

David, having endured Kris's brazen seduction for the entirety of the mission, decided to teach Kris a lesson. Tiffany was driving when David had her pull over to the side of the desolate highway. "Kris," David said, his voice devoid of its usual warmth. It was the tone he used when issuing orders to his paramilitary team, a tone that brooked no argument. "Get out of the van."

Kris, her eyes sparkling with a mixture of anticipation and trepidation, obeyed instantly. She scrambled out of the van, her heart pounding against her ribs. She glanced at David, trying to decipher his expression. Was this it? Was her dream about to come true? "Bend over," David commanded, his voice still flat and emotionless.

The sparkle in Kris's eyes dimmed slightly, replaced by a flicker of confusion. "Bend over?" she repeated, her voice barely a whisper. "But… I thought…" "No arguments, Kris," David said, his tone leaving no room for discussion. "Bend over my knee." Scott, who had been watching the unfolding drama with a mixture of horror and fascination, nearly lost it. His knee? He was going to spank her? This was getting weirder by the second. He surreptitiously pulled out his phone and started recording. This was too good to miss.

Tiffany, however, simply turned off the engine and leaned back in her seat, a small smile playing on her lips. With a sigh, and a look that bordered on resignation, Kris bent over David's knee, presenting her posterior to the world. She wore jeans, but David methodically lowered them. David, without a word, raised his hand and delivered the first swat. It landed with a sharp crack against Kris's bare bottom, eliciting a gasp of surprise from her. "One," David said, his voice still measured.

He continued, each swat delivered with the same precise force and rhythm. "Two… three… four…" Kris, now red-faced and whimpering, tried to stifle her moans. This wasn't exactly the erotic encounter she had envisioned. It hurt. It was humiliating. And yet… there was a strange thrill mixed in with the pain and the shame.

Scott, recording from inside the van, was struggling to contain his laughter. The absurdity of the situation was almost too much to bear. He glanced at Tiffany, who was now calmly filing her nails, seemingly oblivious to the spectacle unfolding outside. David continued the spanking, counting each stroke with unwavering precision. "Fifteen… sixteen… seventeen…"

By the time he reached twenty-five, Kris was a sobbing mess, her bottom stinging and throbbing. "Alright, Kris," David said, straightening up. "Dry your tears and pull up your pants." Kris, sniffling and wiping her eyes, obeyed without a word. She was still trying to process what had just happened. Was she being punished? Or was this some kind of... weird initiation?

David, watching her with a detached expression, seemed to read her thoughts. "This was a lesson, Kris," he said. "To learn respect, discipline and boundaries. You need to practice self control and tact. Do you understand?" Kris nodded meekly, still too stunned to speak. "Good," David said. "Now get back in the van. We have a long drive ahead of us."

As Kris limped back to the Ford Transit, Scott cut off the recording on his cellphone. He knew that this would be a story he would be telling, and retelling, for years to come. Once everyone was back inside, and Tiffany had resumed driving, an uneasy silence settled over the vehicle. Little David had fallen asleep, his head resting against the window.

Finally, Scott couldn't contain himself any longer. "So," he said, addressing the group. "That was... interesting." Tiffany chuckled, shaking her head. "You get used to it," she said. "David has his methods." Kris, still sniffling in the back seat, glared at Scott. David, however, simply smiled, a hint of amusement in his eyes. "Sometimes," he said, "a little bit of discipline is necessary." He looked at Kris, his gaze softening slightly. "Do you understand, Kris?"

Kris, her pride wounded but her admiration for him undeterred, met his gaze. "Yes, Sir," she whispered, a faint blush creeping up her cheeks.

The Ford Transit rumbled along, the earlier spectacle fading into a surreal memory. Scott, however, was still buzzing, replaying the scene in his head. He glanced at the rearview mirror, catching Kris's eye. She quickly looked away, but not before he saw the mix of humiliation and… something else flicker across her face. He stifled another chuckle. This was going to be a long ride.

Suddenly, Tiffany slammed on the brakes. "What is it?" David asked, his senses immediately on high alert. "Another roadblock," Tiffany said grimly, pointing ahead. "And this one looks… bigger."

David peered through the windshield. This wasn't just a few abandoned cars and debris like before. This was a wall of vehicles, trucks, vans, even a school bus, reinforced with tires, scrap metal, and what looked suspiciously like stolen barricades. He could see figures moving amongst the vehicles, armed and looking decidedly unfriendly. "Definitely more ambitious than our last meet-and-greet," David observed dryly.

He reached for the radio. "Parker, you copy?" A gruff voice crackled back. "Loud and clear, David. What's the situation?" "Roadblock. Looks significant," David replied. "Prepare for a… forceful entry. Stand by for my signal." He paused, then added, "And Parker? Try not to kill anyone. Maiming is generally more persuasive." A low chuckle rumbled over the radio. "Understood, David. Maiming it is."

David turned his attention back to the roadblock. These weren't desperate survivors scrabbling for scraps. This was organized. The barricade was too well-constructed, the figures too purposeful. This was a gang, likely preying on those fleeing the cities. He sighed inwardly. He was getting too old for this. "Tiffany," he said, "back us up a hundred yards. Give Parker a clear run." Tiffany nodded grimly and shifted the van into reverse. Scott braced himself, while Kris, momentarily forgetting her earlier humiliation, peered nervously out the back window. Little David remained blissfully asleep.

He watched as the Behemoth, a monstrous behemoth of metal and muscle, lumbered into view. The morning sun glinted off its armored plating, making it look like a mechanical rhino ready to charge. The sound of its modified engine, a deep, guttural growl, filled the air, sending vibrations through the ground. "Now," David said into the radio, "Parker, you have the green light. Unleash the beast."

The Behemoth roared. With a terrifying surge of power, it accelerated towards the roadblock. There was no finesse, no attempt to navigate around the obstacles. It simply smashed through them, a metal tidal wave obliterating everything in its path. Cars were sent flying, tires exploded, and the screams of the would-be bandits were swallowed by the engine's thunderous roar.

The Ford Transit shuddered as debris rained down around it. Scott, his eyes wide, gripped the radio tightly, ready to relay any important information. Kris, despite her fear, found herself strangely captivated by the sheer spectacle of destruction. Gunfire erupted from the roadblock, but the bullets pinged harmlessly off the Behemoth's armor. It was like throwing pebbles at a tank. The behemoth never slowed, never faltered. It plowed through the barricade, leaving a trail of twisted metal and broken bodies in its wake.

Within seconds, the roadblock was nothing more than a smoking ruin. The Behemoth, its mission accomplished, slowed to a stop on the other side of the wreckage, its engine idling menacingly. David surveyed the scene. A few of the bandits were still standing, dazed and bleeding. Most were either unconscious or fleeing in terror. He shook his head. "Amateurs," he muttered.

Tiffany expertly steered the Ford Transit around the wreckage, careful to avoid the larger debris. As they passed the Behemoth, David saw Parker leaning against it, casually smoking a cigarette. The scene was surreal, a bizarre tableau of post-apocalyptic normalcy. They didn't linger, Tiffany simply kept driving. Parker, of course, would trail behind.

The Ford Transit bounced along the potholed road, leaving the wreckage of the Dallas roadblock behind. David leaned back in his seat, a quiet satisfaction settling over him. Beside him, Tiffany kept a steady hand on the wheel, her gaze fixed on the road ahead. In the back, little David was back asleep, his head resting against the glass. Scott, still gripping the radio, occasionally glanced out the window, a mixture of pride and grim satisfaction on his face. And then there was Kris.

David glanced at her. She was staring out the window, her expression unreadable. The Texas landscape blurred past, a monotonous mix of scrub brush and withered trees. He knew she was likely still processing the spanking he'd administered earlier, coupled with the raw display of power she'd just witnessed. The combination was probably a bit overwhelming. "Everything alright, Kris?" he asked, his voice calm and even.

She turned, a flicker of something, perhaps awe or something else entirely, in her eyes. "David," she began, "that was… incredible." David raised an eyebrow, a smile playing on his lips. "Effective, certainly. But hardly what I'd call 'incredible'. Just practical." "No," she insisted, her voice gaining strength. "The way it just… crushed everything. It was like watching a titan at work. And knowing… knowing you orchestrated it all…"

David chuckled. "I assure you, Kris, there's nothing particularly divine about reinforcing an Oshkosh with steel plating and a really big engine. Though," he added, a mischievous glint entering his eye, "I suppose it does inspire a certain… intimidation." Scott, who had been trying his best to fade into the background, coughed awkwardly. "So, uh, David," he stammered, "what's the plan for the rest of the day? Think we'll be able to get back to the ranch before breakfast?"

David appreciated Scott's attempt to steer the conversation away from the increasingly… charged atmosphere. "That's the intention, Scott. Barring any unexpected roadblocks manned by equally ill-prepared thugs, we should be back by 8:00 am." He paused, considering. "Once we're back, I want a full inventory of the supplies we picked up today. Have Mark, Eric and Elena help with that. I want you guys to get some rest."

The Ford Transit pulled into the ranch, kicking up a cloud of dust that momentarily obscured the house. As the vehicle rolled to a stop, a welcoming committee materialized – Andrea, Janet, Jessica, Jill, Jennifer, and Nicole, all eager to greet the returning crew. David didn't need to issue a single command; his household sprang into action.

Eric immediately took the keys to the Behemoth from parker at they disembarked. With a nod of understanding, he lumbered towards the monstrous vehicle, ready to unload the supplies retrieved from Dallas. Meanwhile, Aidan hopped into the Ford Transit, grabbing the keys from his mother. His destination was the garage, where the van would be meticulously unloaded, refueled, and cleaned, ensuring it was ready for the next run.

As David stepped out of the van, a chorus of greetings washed over him. The women, bless their hearts, had already anticipated their arrival. The aroma of freshly brewed coffee mingled with the savory scent of breakfast burritos, wafted around them.

But before David could say a word, Jessica launched herself into his arms. "Daddy!" she squealed, her petite frame practically vibrating with excitement. David chuckled, catching her easily. "Easy there, Baby," he said, tightening his hold. "Don't want you squishing the little one." He glanced down at her burgeoning belly, a soft smile gracing his lips. "How are you feeling?" "Perfect, now that you're back!" she declared, peppering his face with kisses. "I missed you, Daddy. I was worried sick!"

Scott, not used to this type of reception, hugged his wife, grabbing some breakfast and coffee before returning to his apartment with his wife. Mark approached, his expression a mix of gratitude and eagerness. "Welcome back, David. Ready to get started on the unloading and inventory." He gave David a respectful nod before glancing over at Kris, who seemed reluctant to look him in the eye.

Kayla followed close behind. She paused briefly, pulling David to her for a longing kiss. "Welcome home. I'll get the inventory sheets ready." With a brisk wave, she strode towards the work shed where Eric was already wrestling with the Behemoth's massive cargo straps. David watched them go, a sense of quiet satisfaction settling over him.

Nicole had been watching the interactions with a knowing smile. She nudged David gently, her eyes twinkling. "Grace seems awfully interested in Kyle." David followed her gaze. "Well, she could do worse. Kyle's a good man, and a damn fine gunsmith." He chuckled softly. Across the yard, Jennifer's sharp eyes hadn't missed anything either. She sauntered over, a playful smirk dancing on her lips. "Someone had a rough trip," she purred, her gaze flicking from the faint handprint still visible on Tiffany's cheek to Kris, who was discreetly rubbing her backside. She winked suggestively. "I'll bet you had a busy night, Master."

David sighed inwardly. Of course, nothing escaped Jennifer's notice. He wrapped an arm around her waist, pulling her close. "Let's just say that protocol was… enforced." He lowered his voice, "Tiffany wanted special attention, and Kris needed to be punished. As for you.. You need to be patient." He whispered in her ear, earning a shiver of pleasure. "I have plans for you later, my dear." Jennifer leaned into him, a throaty chuckle escaping her lips.

"Promises, promises," she murmured, but her eyes sparkled with anticipation. "I'll look forward to it, Master."

David shook his head, a fond smile playing on his lips. It was never a dull moment with these women. He turned his attention back to the group. "Alright, everyone, listen up!" he called out, his voice carrying across the yard. He pointed to Parker, little David, Grace, Kyle, Kris, and Tiffany. "You six, get some sleep. You all worked hard on this run, and I need you rested and ready for whatever comes next." He emphasized the word 'rested', shooting a pointed look at Tiffany and Kris. "No arguments. Go. Sleep."

Parker, who was already halfway to his apartment, muttering something about needing a shower and a very long nap. Little David simply nodded and disappeared into the main house. Grace, with a reluctant glance at Kyle, pouted but obeyed, trailing after her older brother. Kyle, looking slightly dazed by Grace's attention, mumbled a good night and headed towards his own apartment. Kris, with a final, lingering look at David, a look that clearly conveyed both longing and a hint of masochistic pleasure, turned and sauntered toward the work shed. Tiffany, after giving David one last look, followed Grace into the house.

David, feeling the grime of Dallas clinging to him, decided a shower was in order before he attempted any form of rest. The idea of a nap, however, was quite appealing. He lumbered towards the main house, the weight of responsibility, both present and future, settled heavily on his shoulders.

He stripped in the bathroom, the sound of the water drumming against the tile momentarily drowning out the ever-present anxieties that gnawed at the edges of his mind. As he stepped under the hot spray, he let the tension seep from his muscles. He scrubbed away the dirt and the day's weariness, letting the simple act of cleansing ground him.

He emerged from the bathroom, refreshed and slightly less burdened, only to be met with a sight that made him pause. Jessica was sprawled across the bed, completely naked. Her petite frame seemed almost swallowed by the king-sized mattress, but her confidence was undeniable. Her long hair cascaded across the pillow, and her eyes, wide and expectant, sparkled with mischief. She patted the space next to her.

"Daddy," she purred, her voice a deliberate whisper that sent a jolt of unexpected heat through him. "I need you inside of me." David stared at her, momentarily speechless. The logical part of his brain was screaming that he needed rest. But the primal part of him, the part that responded to beauty and desire, was already halfway across the room.

He was not an emotionless robot, although he sometimes wished he was. "Jessica," he said, his voice rough. "You know I've had a long night." She giggled, a sound that was both innocent and utterly seductive. "And I know exactly how to help you fall asleep." She reached out, her fingers tracing a path across his chest. "Besides," she added, her voice dropping to a conspiratorial whisper, "pregnancy makes me horny."

Chapter 23

A Woman's Desperation

As David stepped out of the shower, he didn't bother drying off or getting dressed. Jessica, his young wife, was waiting for him in their bed, naked and eager. Jessica would seldom allow David to enter or exit his bed without first filling herself with him, both literally and figuratively.

David approached the bed with a predatory grace, his eyes locked on Jessica's. "Come here," he growled, his voice low and rough. Jessica obeyed, moving to the edge of the bed. David grabbed her around the neck, pulling her face close as her body went partially limp. He kissed her fiercely, his tongue plunging into her mouth as his hands roamed her body. Jessica moaned, her hands clutching at his shoulders as she returned the kiss. David loved Jessica more than anything, and his grip on her reflected his desire.

David pulled back, his breath ragged. He gazed down at Jessica, her face flushed and her lips swollen from his kisses. Her eyes, usually bright with youthful energy, were now glazed with desire, reflecting the raw passion he ignited within her. Even pregnant, she was a vibrant, intoxicating creature. He ran a hand through her hair, the damp strands clinging to his fingers.

"You're mine, Jessica," he murmured, his voice a possessive rasp. "Completely and utterly mine." Jessica shivered, her body responding to the primal claim in his tone.

"Yes, Daddy," she whispered, the word a soft offering. "I am."

He leaned down, kissing her again, a slow, deliberate exploration that rekindled the fire that had briefly subsided. His hands traced the curves of her body, lingering on the gentle swell of her belly, a constant reminder of the precious life they were creating together. Even with the life growing within her, he felt no need to be gentle. She wasn't a porcelain doll to be handled with care, but a wild and untamed beauty that thrived under his dominance.

He moved lower, his lips trailing down her neck, her chest, until he reached her breasts, swollen and sensitive. He suckled gently, drawing a moan from her lips. He continued his descent, his tongue tracing a path down her stomach, around her navel, until he reached her lips.

Jessica gasped as his tongue flicked against her, igniting a wildfire of pleasure. She arched her back, her fingers digging into his shoulders as she surrendered to the sensations washing over her. He knew exactly how to drive her wild, how to push her to the edge of ecstasy and then pull her back, prolonging her pleasure.

He took his time, dragging the tip of his tongue along the seam of her labia, occasionally wrapping his tongue around her clit, until she was begging him for more. "Please, Daddy," she cried, her voice thick with need. "I need you inside me." David chuckled. "Patience, Baby girl," he murmured, his voice laced with playful cruelty. "You'll get what you want. But first, you'll earn it."

He rose above her, his eyes burning with a fierce intensity. He straddled her, his weight pressing down on her, a tangible expression of his dominance. Jessica welcomed the pressure, her body instinctively seeking his control. He leaned down, whispering in her ear, his words a litany of lust and degradation. "You're a good girl, Jessica," he murmured, "but you're also a dirty little slut. Admit that you crave my touch, my control. Admit that you want me to use you, to break you, to make you mine in every way possible."

Jessica whimpered, her body trembling with anticipation. "Yes, Daddy," she gasped. "Please, fuck me, fill me up." Satisfied with her response, David finally entered her, his movements slow and deliberate, each thrust designed to maximize her pleasure and his own. Jessica cried out, her body contracting around him as she met his thrusts with a fervor that mirrored his own. The rhythm was primal, a dance of dominance and submission, of need and fulfillment.

He pushed her harder, faster, his control absolute. He watched her face, enjoying the expressions that flickered across her features, the pleasure, the pain, the surrender. He loved the way she responded to him, the way she gave herself to him completely, without reservation.

The morning sun climbed higher, painting the room in warmer hues as their joined bodies moved in a frantic ballet. He felt her building towards her peak, her muscles tightening, her breath coming in ragged gasps. A wave of possessiveness washed over him. He slowed his movements, drawing back, denying her the release she so desperately craved.

Jessica moaned, her eyes fluttering open. "Daddy, please," she begged, her voice laced with desperation. "Let me come." He brushed a stray strand of hair from her forehead, his expression unreadable. "Not yet, Baby girl," he whispered. "You're not quite there yet. You need to suffer a little longer. Enjoy the anticipation, savor the pleasure."

He continued to move inside her, but with a teasing slowness that bordered on torture. He could feel her frustration mounting, her body coiling tighter and tighter. Her nails dug into his back, leaving shallow red marks. "Daddy, I can't," she cried, tears welling in her eyes. "Please, I need it. I need you."

David watched her, his heart softening. He knew he was pushing her to the edge, but he also knew that the release would be all the more intense for the wait. He saw the genuine desperation in her eyes, the complete trust she placed in him. "Almost there, Jessica," he murmured, his voice softening. "Just a little bit longer. Think of me, think of how good it feels to be filled with me. Let the pleasure build, let it consume you."

He increased the pace, his movements becoming more urgent, more demanding. He could feel her teetering on the precipice, her body vibrating with barely suppressed energy. "Daddy," she screamed, her voice cracking with emotion. "I'm going to come! I'm going to come!" He finally relented, giving her what she craved. He thrust into her with all his force, his own body shuddering with the intensity of the moment. He felt her muscles clench around him as she finally surrendered to the overwhelming pleasure.

Jessica cried out, her body arching off the bed as wave after wave of ecstasy washed over her. He held her tight, her sweat-slicked body trembling against his. He felt her nails digging into his back, her teeth nipping at his shoulder.

Jessica cried out as David, still slick with their shared passion, rolled her to her side. The abruptness of the movement caught her off guard, pulling a gasp from her lips. Before she could fully register what was happening, he expertly positioned her, straddling one leg while holding the other aloft. A thrill, sharp and electric, shot through her as she anticipated his next move.

He didn't disappoint. With a deliberate, almost predatory grace, he plunged back into her. The sensation was immediate and intense, amplified by the lingering echoes of her recent orgasm. A fresh wave of pleasure threatened to overwhelm her, even as a knot of delicious anticipation tightened in her belly.

Then came the grip. Not a harsh or painful one, but firm and possessive. He took hold of the front of her neck, his fingers wrapping around with surprising gentleness. Simultaneously, his other hand clenched a fistful of her hair, not yanking, but using it as leverage, anchoring her to him.

The world tilted slightly, her perspective shifting as he used her body as his anchor. Every thrust was deep, deliberate, and utterly consuming. The pressure on her neck and the tug on her hair heightened the feeling of submission, of being completely and utterly at his mercy, a feeling that she craved more than air itself. Her body responded with unrestrained fervor, her hips meeting his with eager abandon. "Daddy," she gasped, the word a ragged prayer on her lips. "Oh, Daddy…"

He didn't reply verbally, but his actions spoke volumes. Each movement was a testament to his control, his dominance, and his understanding of her deepest desires. He knew exactly how to push her, how to tease her, how to bring her to the brink of madness with pleasure.

The combination of the intense physical sensations, the possessive grip on her neck, and the anchoring pull of her hair sent her spiraling into a vortex of pure sensation. Her mind emptied, her thoughts dissolving into nothing but the present moment, the feel of his body against hers, the sound of their mingled breaths, the overwhelming pleasure that threatened to shatter her completely.

He continued to move, relentless in his pursuit of her pleasure, until she felt herself teetering on the edge once more. This time, there was no holding back. The dam broke, and she surrendered to the tide, her body convulsing with the force of her release. "Daddy! Daddy! Daddy!" she cried out, the words echoing through the room, a testament to his mastery, her complete and utter surrender.

Jessica's body was flush, slick with sweat, a testament to the raw energy that had just consumed them. The mattress beneath them was damp, the air thick with the scent of sex. David, his breathing still ragged, shifted slightly, a predatory gleam in his eyes. He ran a hand down her spine, a slow, deliberate caress that sent shivers down her skin.

Without a word, he flipped her onto her knees, her back arching in anticipation. Her eyes, glazed with desire, met his as she looked back at him. She knew what was coming, and the knowledge ignited a fresh wave of heat within her. He lifted her thighs, his grip sending a jolt of electricity through her. Her breath hitched in her throat as she felt the moist heat of his mouth against her.

Then, his tongue. It was a deliberate invasion, a probing exploration that left no part of her untouched. He tasted her, explored her, savored her, each stroke of his tongue sending waves of pleasure radiating through her body. She gripped the sheets, her knuckles white, her body trembling with the intensity of the sensation.

"Daddy…" she moaned, the word a plea, a demand, a surrender. Her hips pulsed rhythmically, instinctively seeking more, craving the depths of his touch. He responded with a low growl, a primal sound that resonated deep within her soul. His grip tightened on her thighs, holding her firmly in place as he continued to devour her.

Time seemed to dissolve, the world narrowing to the feel of his tongue, the movement of his mouth, the overwhelming pleasure that threatened to consume her entirely. She was lost, adrift in a sea of sensation, with David as her only anchor. His name became a mantra, a litany of desire that spilled from her lips with each ragged breath.

He continued until she was shaking, until every nerve ending in her body was screaming for release. And then, with a final act of cruelty, he stopped, leaving her teetering on the edge. The feeling of his mouth on her skin faded, leaving behind a void that ached to be filled. She whimpered, a small, desperate sound that tugged at something deep within him. He watched her, his expression unreadable, a complex mix of desire and control warring within his eyes.

Then, with a swift, decisive action, he slapped her ass. The sharp crack echoed in the room, a shocking burst of sensation that made her gasp. Her body jolted, momentarily stunned by the unexpected sting. But before the surprise could fully register, he gripped her hips, his hands strong and sure, and thrust his cock deep inside her.

The sudden, forceful entry sent a jolt of pure pleasure through Jessica, obliterating the lingering shock of the slap. She cried out, a mixture of pain and ecstasy, her body arching to meet his. He filled her completely, stretching her, possessing her, claiming her as his own.

He began to move, a slow, deliberate rhythm that built with each stroke. He held her firmly, his grip unyielding, his body a powerful force driving her towards the brink. Jessica surrendered to the sensation, her head falling forward, her hair cascading over her face. She moaned, her voice raw with need, her nails digging into the sheets beneath her. "Daddy..." she gasped, the word a prayer, a plea, a command.

Again, he didn't answer with words, but with action. His thrusts grew deeper, harder, faster. He was relentless, his focus laser-locked on her pleasure. The air in the room grew thick with the sounds of their labored breathing, the slap of skin against skin, the soft whimpers and moans that escaped Jessica's lips.

He was going to continue until he was completely exhausted, no matter how much she begged him to stop. This was his intent, his will, a force as immutable as the laws of physics. He was driven by a deep-seated need to give her pleasure, to push her to the edge of her limits, to claim her body and soul as his own. It was an expression of dominance, yes, but also an act of profound intimacy, a merging of two bodies and two souls into one.

Jessica's body was screaming, every nerve ending alight with pure, raw sensation. She was on the verge, teetering on the precipice of oblivion, her mind dissolving into a kaleidoscope of pleasure. Her legs became weak as her body began to sink into the bed. "Daddy, please…" she begged, her voice a broken whisper. "Please…"

He ignored her plea, his pace unwavering, his focus absolute. He wanted her to break, to shatter, to surrender completely to the power of his touch. He wanted to hear her scream his name, to feel her body convulse beneath his, to know that he had driven her to the very edge of ecstasy.

He continued to pound into her, his body a relentless machine, his will unyielding. Jessica's cries grew louder, more desperate, her body trembling uncontrollably. She was lost, adrift in a sea of sensation, with David as her only anchor.

And then, finally, it happened. A wave of pure, unadulterated pleasure washed over her, consuming her completely. Her body convulsed, her muscles clenched, and she cried out his name, a long, drawn-out moan that echoed through the room. She shattered, broke, surrendered, her body completely consumed by the force of her orgasm.

Yet, he didn't stop. He continued to thrust, his movements becoming more frantic, more desperate, driven by his own mounting desire. He felt her contractions gripping him tightly, pulling him deeper, drawing him closer to his own release. He closed his eyes, his jaw clenched, his body straining with the effort. He pushed harder, faster, his breathing ragged, his heart pounding in his chest. He felt himself teetering on the edge, the world around him dissolving into a blur of sensation.

And then, with a final, earth-shattering thrust, he exploded, filling her with his cum. His body shuddered, his muscles spasmed, and he let out a guttural groan that was a mixture of pain and pure, unadulterated pleasure. He collapsed on top of her, his body heavy, his breathing labored. He stayed there for a long moment, savoring the afterglow of their lovemaking, feeling the warmth of her body beneath his, the softness of her skin against his.

Finally, he stirred, lifting himself slightly and looking down at her. Her face was flushed, her hair tangled, her eyes glazed with contentment. A small smile played on her lips. "Daddy…" she whispered, reaching up to touch his face. "That was… incredible." He smiled back at her, a genuine smile that lit up his face. He leaned down and kissed her gently on the forehead. "You're incredible," he said softly, his voice filled with affection.

He rolled off her and lay beside her, pulling her close. He held her tightly, feeling the gentle rise and fall of her chest, the soft warmth of her body against his. He closed his eyes, feeling a deep sense of peace and contentment wash over him.

David stretched, the lingering ache of spent muscles a pleasant reminder of his earlier exertion. He glanced at the digital clock on the nightstand – 3:17 PM. He truly had slept deeply. He carefully swung his legs over the side of the bed, making sure not to disturb Jessica, who was still sound asleep, her petite frame curled into a comfortable ball amongst the plush sheets.

He walked silently to the bathroom, relieved himself, and splashed some cool water on his face. He avoided looking in the mirror; he wasn't particularly concerned with his appearance. After grabbing a fresh cup of coffee from the kitchen, he decided to head down to the recreational bunker. The thought of the cool, chlorine-tinged air and the sight of his wives enjoying themselves was appealing.

As he descended the stairs, the scent of chlorine and the faint, tinge of coconut filled his nostrils. The vast, brightly lit space stretched before him, the pool shimmering under the lights. Tiffany, Jennifer, Kris, Elena, and Tanya were already there, their laughter echoing off the concrete walls.

He settled into one of the lounge chairs near the edge of the pool, his pajama pants feeling incongruous in the slightly humid environment. He took a sip of coffee, the rich aroma filling his nostrils, and leaned back, watching his wives with a quiet sense of pride.

Jennifer, ever attuned to David's presence, noticed him almost immediately. She gracefully swam towards the edge of the pool, her blonde hair plastered to her face, her eyes sparkling with playful mischief. She pulled herself out of the water, a slight shiver running down her spine as the cool air hit her damp skin. Wrapping a towel around herself, she padded over to David, leaving a trail of wet footprints on the concrete.

"Master," she purred, her voice laced with a teasing tone. She leaned down, placing a soft kiss on his cheek. "Sleeping well?" David took another sip of his coffee, his expression unreadable. "Absolutely." Jennifer chuckled, running a hand through her wet hair. "I heard you and Jessica having a... vigorous morning. Sounds like someone was making up for lost time." She playfully nudged him with her elbow. "You still owe me one, you know."

David remained unperturbed, his gaze fixed on the shimmering surface of the pool. Tiffany was now doing laps, her athletic frame slicing through the water with effortless power. Tanya was meticulously applying sunscreen, as Kris and Elena were eavesdropping, trying their best at being unsuspecting.

He finally turned his attention back to Jennifer, his blue eyes meeting hers with a steady gaze. He took another slow sip of his coffee, the silence stretching between them. "Then take it," he said simply, his voice calm and even.

Jennifer, not one to waste an opportunity and gloriously shameless, grinned. Her eyes danced with a mixture of arousal and amusement. Without a word, she straddled David in the lounge chair, her movements fluid and practiced. She easily pulled his pajama pants down, her fingers nimble and efficient, and then adjusted the lower portion of her swimsuit, exposing enough skin to make contact.

A soft gasp escaped her lips as she settled onto him, the girth of his cock opening her up as her body naturally conformed to him. She leaned forward, her breasts pressing against his chest, and whispered in his ear, "You know, Master, I love how easy you make this." Her breath was warm against his skin, a stark contrast to her swimsuit. Which was leaving wet imprints on his dry clothes.

David merely hummed in response, his hands resting lightly on Jennifer's hips as she began to move. He closed his eyes, focusing on the sensation, the warmth of her body against his, the gentle rocking motion that threatened to lull him back to sleep. The faint scent of chlorine and Jennifer's vanilla perfume filled his senses.

Tiffany, mid-lap, paused at the edge of the pool, lifting her goggles onto her head. A small smile played on her lips as she watched the scene unfold. She shook her head, a low chuckle escaping her throat. "Show off," she muttered good-naturedly, before pushing off again, resuming her laps with renewed vigor. The rhythmic splashing of the water was a counterpoint to the soft sounds emanating from the lounge chair.

Elena, feigning disinterest, turned a page in her book, but her eyes kept darting towards David and Jennifer. A smirk tugged at the corner of her mouth. She found Jennifer's brazenness both amusing and, admittedly, a little arousing. She wondered how long Jennifer could last against David.

Tanya, ever the picture of composure, dabbed more sunscreen onto her nose, but her movements were slightly hurried, her gaze fixed on the couple. A flush crept up her neck, and she subtly adjusted her own swimsuit, a sudden awareness of her own body washing over her.

Kris was practically vibrating with anticipation. She leaned forward, her chin resting on the side of the pool, her eyes glued to the performance. "Damn, Jennifer," she whispered under her breath, loud enough for Elena and Tanya to hear, "You are a lucky woman." She sighed dramatically, fanning herself with her hand. "I swear, just looking at them makes me wet."

Jennifer moaned softly, her pace quickening. "Oh, Master," she breathed, her voice laced with pleasure, "You feel so good." She punctuated each word with a deliberate thrust, her hips rocking against his. David remained still, a small smile playing on his lips.

Tiffany, after completing her fifth lap, hauled herself out of the pool, droplets of water clinging to her body. She grabbed a towel, casually drying herself as she strolled over to the lounge chairs. "Need a hand, Jen?" she asked, her voice dripping with mock concern. Jennifer gasped, momentarily losing her rhythm. "Tiffany!" she exclaimed, half-laughing, half-exasperated. "You're going to distract me!"

David, now shirtless and radiating primal energy, simply chuckled. "Distraction is part of the fun, isn't it?" He continued his ministrations, his touch precise and knowing, pushing Jennifer closer to the edge. Elena, observing the scene, couldn't help but be impressed. She closed her book, the words blurring before her eyes as a sudden wave of heat washed over her.

Tiffany, unfazed by the spectacle, shrugged, a playful glint in her eyes. "He has a way of bringing out the best, and the horniest, in all of us." She casually stretched. "Speaking of which," she added, turning to Elena with a mischievous grin, "Are you going to let Jennifer have all the fun?" Elena scoffed, but her eyes betrayed her. "I'm thinking about it," she admitted.

Tanya, unable to contain herself any longer, abruptly stood up, tossing her towel aside. "I need a cold shower," she announced, her voice slightly strained. "Or maybe two." She hurried towards the house, her hips swaying with each step.

Jennifer, fueled by the attention and David's skillful touch, reached her peak with a cry of pure pleasure. She collapsed against him, breathing heavily, her body trembling as David held her close, stroking her hair soothingly. "Good girl," he murmured, his voice low and affectionate. He kissed her forehead, then looked up at Tiffany and Elena, a knowing smile on his face. "Next?"

Elena didn't hesitate. She rose gracefully from her lounge chair, her dark eyes blazing with desire. "My turn," she declared, striding towards David with a confidence that bordered on theatrical. She didn't simply sit; she ascended, gracefully straddling him on the lounge chair. But, in a move that was pure Elena, she faced the pool, her back to David, effectively presenting a panoramic view of her assets to Kris, Tiffany, and the rest of the afternoon sunbathers. "Show off," Tiffany muttered good-naturedly, grabbing a glass of iced tea from a nearby table.

Elena winked over her shoulder, a flash of white teeth against her sun-kissed skin. "Darling, if you've got it, flaunt it. Especially when it's driving my magnificent Master wild." She lowered her voice, just enough for David to hear. "Isn't that right, my love?" David chuckled, his hands finding their way to Elena's hips. "You know exactly what you're doing."

"Of course I do," she purred. "Intelligence is wasted if it's not used for maximum… impact." And with that, she began to move, her movements fluid and deliberate, a silent symphony of seduction performed for an audience of appreciative women.

Kris, clinging to the edge of the pool, was indeed having a moment. The water around her rippled as she discreetly explored her own body, a silent offering to the spectacle unfolding before her. The chlorine stung slightly, but the discomfort was a welcome distraction, a counterpoint to the rising tide of desire threatening to overwhelm her. She wanted that. She wanted him. The fact that he was already claimed by so many only amplified the allure. He was a force of nature, a sun around which they all orbited, and she desperately wanted to be closer, even if it meant getting burned.

Tanya, meanwhile, was not having a cold shower. She had made it as far as the hallway before collapsing against the wall, her breath coming in ragged gasps. The image of David was seared into her mind. She knew she couldn't go back out there, not yet. She needed a moment to compose herself, to regain some semblance of composure. "Damn you, David," she whispered, a mixture of frustration and adoration in her voice. "You make it so hard to be good."

Back by the pool, Elena was reaching her crescendo. Her breath came in short, sharp gasps, her body trembling with each thrust. "Master…" she moaned, the word a heavy plea. Elena's climax echoed in the high-ceilinged recreational bunker, a throaty cry of pleasure that reverberated through the humid air. As her body shuddered, the tension slowly bled away, leaving her flushed and breathless against David.

Kris, however, was not watching Elena. Her eyes were locked, laser-focused, on something far more… immediate. She saw the glistening trail of pearly fluid sliding down the seam between Elena's labia and David's cock, a testament to David's potent masculinity. It was a sight that sent a jolt of pure, unadulterated desire through her. A desire so sharp, so primal, that it shattered the last vestiges of her carefully constructed composure.

Without a word, without a second thought, she surged from the pool. David, ever adaptable, simply adjusted his grip on Elena, supporting her as Kris, with surprising strength, lifted her off with a grunt of effort. Elena, dazed and giggling a little from the post-coital bliss, mumbled a protest that was mostly air. "Kris! What are you…"

Before Elena could finish, Kris was a whirlwind of motion. Her hands, now moved with a determined, almost ruthless efficiency. The discarded bikini bottom lay forgotten on the edge of the pool, a testament to her current priorities. With a swift, practiced movement, she scooped the sticky mess from Elena's yielding flesh. Then, with a satisfied sigh that bordered on a growl, she plunged her fingers into herself, ensuring that every last drop of David's essence found its mark. The act was primal, possessive, a blatant declaration of ownership that resonated deep within David's core.

Elena, now fully aware of what was happening, watched with wide-eyed astonishment. A slow grin spread across her face, a mixture of amusement and arousal dancing in her dark eyes. "Well," she drawled, now leaning back against a concrete pillar, "that's one way to cut to the chase."

Kris, not pausing for breath, immediately straddled David, her wet body sliding against his with a delightful friction. Her eyes, usually sparkling with mischief, were now dark with a raw, urgent need. "David," she gasped, her voice thick with longing, "I'm so sorry, I couldn't wait. I need your baby."

Chapter 24

The Probationary Concubine

The chlorine-tinged air of the recreational bunker hung thick with confusion and longing. David, momentarily stunned, lay back against the lounge chair, his expression uncertain. Tiffany, perched on the edge of a lounge chair, let out a low whistle. "Well, that's one way to claim a baby daddy," she quipped, a mischievous glint in her eye.

Jennifer's shock quickly morphed into something akin to understanding. She knew that desperate ache, that primal need to be connected to David in the most fundamental way possible. Getting off the lounge chair, she knelt beside David, placing a reassuring hand on his arm. "Easy, love," she murmured, her voice soft. "Go easy on her, she didn't mean any harm. You don't realize how… consuming it can be, wanting you."

Kris, riding David with a frantic energy, was a whirlwind of contradictions. Tears streamed down her face, mixing with the pool water clinging to her skin. "Please forgive me!" she sobbed, her voice ragged. "I didn't mean to… I just… I want your baby so badly. Please don't kick me out! Please, David, please!"

Elena watched the scene unfold with a detached amusement. She crossed her arms, a sardonic smile playing on her lips. "It's really comical that you think Master will throw you away after all that," Elena said, a playful smile on her face. "I thought you were smarter than this. You are literally begging him not to send you away, but you haven't stopped riding him, the entire time."

With a sigh, David reached up, cupping Kris's face between his hands. His touch was gentle, firm, and instantly effective. Kris paused, her frantic movements momentarily ceasing. Her tear-filled eyes met his, searching for any sign of rejection. "Kris," David began, his voice calm and measured, "Breathe. I understand."

His words seemed to have a calming effect. Kris's breathing slowed, though the tears continued to stream. But, the effect was short lived. Driven by her desire for motherhood and the intoxicating pleasure, she disregarded rational thinking. She leaned forward, kissing David deeply, and with a soft whimper, she resumed her rhythmic riding, the tears unrelenting.

David, internally, was starting to find the whole situation... well, actually quite funny. The sheer, unadulterated desperation was almost cartoonish. He could feel the others watching, probably placing bets on how long this performance would last. He decided to watch and see, at least for a little while. "David, please," Kris gasped between moans, her voice thick with tears and raw need. "Please, let me have your baby. I'll be a good mother, I promise. I'll do anything. Please, David, please give me your cum!"

Just then, Tanya walked back into the recreational bunker, a towel wrapped around her. She had hoped to escape the sensory overload in the main house, but it seemed chaos had waited for her downstairs. Her eyes widened, her jaw dropping slightly as she took in the spectacle before her. Kris, tears streaming, straddling David with wild abandon.

Jennifer kneeling with an understanding expression. Tiffany, wearing a bemused smirk. And Elena, still bottomless, looking like she was watching a particularly interesting documentary.

"What... what is going on here?" Tanya stammered, completely dumbfounded. Elena shrugged, not bothering to turn her head. "Kris is... expressing her needs," she said dryly. "Expressing? She looks like she's trying to break David!" Tanya exclaimed, her voice rising in pitch. "Shouldn't someone stop her? Is David even conscious?" "Oh, he's conscious," Jennifer assured her, patting David's leg. "Just... slightly overwhelmed, I think." "Overwhelmed? He looks like he's trying not to laugh!" Tanya said, squinting at David. She could see the corners of his mouth twitching. "I'm afraid to stop her in the middle," Elena said, her tone surprisingly serious. "She might actually explode. And I really don't want to clean that up."

Kris, oblivious to the conversation happening around her, continued her fervent pleas. "Please, Sir, please, I need this. I need you. Please, please, please!" Tanya, still trying to process the tableau, asked, "Okay, I'll bite. What exactly is she after?" Jennifer, with a wry smile, answered, "She wants David's... seed. She wants a baby."

Tanya's eyebrows shot up. "She... okay. That's... direct." She looked from Kris, grinding away with the force of a small jackhammer, to David, whose stoic expression was cracking under the pressure of suppressed laughter, then back to Elena. "But why the tears? Is it that difficult?"

Elena shrugged, a mischievous glint in her eyes. "Let's just say Kris took a, uh, proactive approach." Tanya tilted her head, puzzled. "Proactive? What does that mean?" Elena sighed dramatically. "Okay, fine. She scooped David's baby load from me after we were done and... self-administered."

Tanya's jaw dropped. "She... she scooped? From you? And then...?" She gestured vaguely towards Kris's lower half. Elena nodded, a smug expression on her face. "Yep. And now she's trying to... top it off, shall we say?" Tanya glanced back at Elena, and then down at her bare legs. Her eyes widened in horror. "Wait a minute! You're... still bottomless! Were you planning on going back upstairs like that?" Elena blinked, a slow blush creeping up her neck. "Oh. Crap. I forgot."

Tanya's eyes flicked from Kris, still enthusiastically pleading her case while still riding a very bewildered David, to Elena, suddenly self-conscious about her lack of apparel, and back to David. The absurdity of the situation finally cracked her composure. She burst out laughing, a sound that echoed in the vast recreational bunker.

"This... this is insane!" she gasped, clutching her stomach. "You know what, David? Just... just finish. Just give her what she wants! It's not like we're exactly lacking in resources, or willing hands to help raise a kid." She waved her hand dismissively. David finally spoke. "Tanya, are you sure? I mean, I appreciate the... encouragement, but..." He trailed off, glancing at Kris, who had momentarily paused her... ministrations... to listen. Her eyes were wide with hope.

Jennifer, ever the pragmatist, gently squeezed David's arm. "Honey, Tanya's right in principle, but maybe let's think this through. You were with Jessica all morning, then me, then Elena. I'm not sure your… boys… are exactly brimming with viable swimmers right now. Kris might be riding a dry well, so to speak."

Jennifer's delicately phrased assessment hung in the air. Kris's hopeful expression wavered, replaced by a dawning horror. "Dry… well?" she croaked, her voice stricken with worry. She looked down at David, then back at Jennifer, then back down at David again. The color drained from her face. Elena snorted with laughter. "Oh, honey, you didn't think he'd be fully loaded after that marathon, did you? This isn't a video game, there's a recharge time!"

Tanya, recovered from her initial fit of laughter, chimed in. "Yeah, David, maybe a strategic withdrawal is in order. We don't want Kris expending all that… effort… for nothing. We can schedule a more… optimal… session later."

David, finally free from Kris's enthusiastic but potentially fruitless endeavor, retreated upstairs feeling a strange mix of amusement, exhaustion, and a faint sense of guilt. He showered quickly, then pulled on a pair of pants, a simple grey t-shirt, and his trusty work boots. Stepping out onto the front porch, the late afternoon sun warmed his face. David immediately set off toward the opposite side of the barn.

The scene before him was a testament to the industrious spirit that had taken root on his little slice of Texas. Scott was already hard at work. The rhythmic clang of his hammer echoed in the air as Scott drove in wooden stakes into the ground on the opposite side of the work shed. Using brightly colored spray paint, he was meticulously marking out the perimeter of the future slaughterhouse, its footprint snaking around the back of the existing workshop.

David watched him for a moment, appreciating his efficiency. He was a man who simply got things done, a quality David valued above almost all others, especially in their current circumstances. He walked down the steps and approached Scott, a slight smile playing on his lips. "Looking good, Scott. You're not wasting any time." Scott paused his hammering, wiped his brow with the back of his hand, and nodded. "Need to get it done. Meat won't butcher itself."

David chuckled. "True enough. Anything I can do to help?" Scott grinned. "Actually, yeah. A concrete mixer would be a godsend. Mixing by hand is going to be a killer. And another set of hands wouldn't hurt either, prepping the ground."

David nodded thoughtfully. "Concrete mixer, got it. Mark has some experience in road construction. I'll get him out here too." He paused, considering. "Don't try to do this yourself, I'll bring my boys out here to help dig. They've got the strength and energy, might as well take advantage of it."

Scott leaned on his hammer, a grateful look on his face. "That would be fantastic, David. Really appreciate it." "No problem," David said, already turning back towards the main house. "Teamwork makes the dream work, right?" He called out as he walked away, "I'll wrangle Mark and the boys. Be back in a bit."

David strode into the cool interior of the main house, the transition from the Texas sun a welcome relief. He found Aidan in his room in the garage bunker, the air filled with the soft strumming of his guitar. Alissa sat beside him, surrounded by pictures from books and magazines, her brow furrowed in concentration. The domestic scene warmed David; their desire to start a family, even now, was a testament to their hope and resilience.

Aidan paused his playing, a question in his eyes. "Hey, Dad. Everything alright?" "Everything's fine," David assured him, his gaze softening as he took in Alissa's focused expression. "Just checking in. And I need a favor." Alissa looked up, a smile gracing her lips. "What's up, David?" "Scott is starting on the slaughterhouse," David explained. "He could use some extra hands. I was hoping you and the boys could lend him a hand."

Aidan nodded immediately. "Of course. Just say when." "Scott mentioned prepping the ground mostly. Said a concrete mixer would be nice too. Mark has road construction experience, so I'll wrangle him too." David clarified. "He wants to get it done quickly, which I agree with. The sooner we have a dedicated butchering space, the better." Aidan considered this for a moment. "Is there any way we can start after dinner?" David nodded. "After dinner works. Gives everyone a chance to relax and recharge. I just wanted to get everyone spun up anyway."

Aidan smirked, a hint of mischief dancing in his eyes. "So, Dad," he began, his tone laced with playful sarcasm, "did Kris finally manage to trap you? Any little mini-Davids on the way?" Alissa playfully slapped Aidan's arm, a blush creeping up her neck, her eyes asking David for forgiveness.

David chuckled, choosing to sidestep the loaded question. "Just making sure you two are behaving yourselves. And that Alissa isn't working herself into a stupor over all those baby books." He reached out, flicking off the light switch, plunging the room into a playful darkness before quietly shutting the door.

David appreciated Aidan's candor, especially nowadays. David stopped by the classroom, but, of course, it was empty, as he expected. Janet was diligent about keeping to the schedule she'd painstakingly created. Next door, Andrea was indeed scrubbing away, her brow furrowed in concentration. "Having fun, Andrea?" David asked, his voice deliberately quieter than usual.

Andrea jumped, a startled yelp escaping her lips. "God, David! You scared the shit out of me!" She clutched at her chest, her heart visibly pounding against her ribcage. David chuckled, a flash of genuine remorse crossing his face. "Sorry about that. Didn't mean to startle you. Expecting company?"

Andrea nodded, taking a deep breath to steady herself. "Mm hmm, Jessica's stopping by for a checkup in a few hours. This baby is really important to her." She ran a gentle hand over the exam table, her expression softening. "To all of us, really." David smiled warmly. "Of course, Andrea. We all want what's best for Jessica and the little one." He paused, a thoughtful expression on his face. "Do you need any help getting ready? I'm sure the girls would love to lend a hand. Tiffany is particularly good at calming nerves, and Summer has a knack for organization."

Andrea smiled back, relaxing slightly. "That's really nice of you, David, but I think I'm good for now. He left Andrea to her preparations and headed towards the work shed. Scott was no longer outside and the sound of Kyle's music reached his ears even before he reached the entrance. Inside, Kyle and Little David were a whirlwind of organized chaos, sorting through the mountain of reloading supplies hauled back from Dallas this morning.

"Morning, gentlemen," David greeted, leaning against the doorframe. "How's everything coming along?" Kyle turned down his music before answering. "So far so good. We have plenty of supplies, but I'm going to prioritize the best loads first." Junior, who was consolidating the powders added. "We want to max out our operational rounds first. Training ammo doesn't require fancy ballistics, so if we can burn-up out excess powder there, might as well." David agreed wholeheartedly. It didn't make sense to invest time and the best materials in high quality ammo if it was only was used for general training.

David left Kyle and Little David to their tasks. He descended the concrete stairs that led to the apartment bunker below. He found Mark's apartment door ajar, sounds of muted laughter and the tantalizing aroma of something baking wafting into the hallway. He rapped lightly on the doorframe. "Mark? You got a minute?"

Mark appeared in the doorway, a dishtowel slung over his shoulder, a slightly harried but happy expression on his face. "David! Come on in. Just trying to keep the wolves at bay." He gestured towards the interior of the apartment, where Janet was wrangling Lori and Beth, who were attempting to decorate cupcakes with more enthusiasm than skill.

David stepped inside, a small smile playing on his lips. "Looks like you have your hands full," he observed, his gaze lingering on Janet, who offered him a weary but grateful smile. "Tell me about it," Mark chuckled, running a hand through his hair. "But it's good to have some normalcy, you know? Lori and Beth love getting their hands dirty. It's like they forgot about what happened."

"I'm really happy to hear that, Mark. Getting back to normal," David replied, his voice firm. "That's what we're building here." He paused, his expression turning serious. "Speaking of building, I need to ask you a favor." Mark straightened up, sensing a change in tone. "What's up?" "Scott's started on the foundation for the slaughterhouse today. He could use an extra set of hands. I was hoping you could lend him yours."

"The slaughterhouse, huh? Figured we'd get to that eventually," Mark said, resignation blending with a hint of grim determination. "Yeah, okay, I can do that. Anything to keep busy. Keeps the… thoughts away." He looked towards his daughters again, his expression softening. "Besides, someone's gotta provide for these little monsters."

David clapped him on the shoulder. "I appreciate it, Mark. It'll be a big help. Scott's marking the area now, and the boys are gonna dig it up after dinner, so you enjoy your night." David looked at Janet. "Besides, you've already done your fair share for the day. Plus, your family needs you. You can worry about work in the morning, when the girls go off to school."

Mark and Janet exchanged a glance, relief washing over their faces. "Thanks, David," Janet said, her voice laced with genuine gratitude. "It means a lot." Mark nodded in agreement. David simply smiled, a flash of genuine warmth in his eyes. "Don't mention it. We're all in this together, right?"

As David spoke, a figure flitted past in the hallway, headed towards the next apartment. It was Kris, her usual vivacious energy seemingly dimmed, her head down. "Stop," David commanded, his voice carrying through the open doorway. To Mark's surprise, Kris froze instantly, mid-stride. She didn't turn around, didn't even twitch. It was as if she'd been turned to stone, a statue of youthful shame. Mark knew Kris was usually the most boisterous and unapologetically forward person in any setting. However, this sudden stillness was unsettling, almost unnatural.

"Kris," he said, his voice gentle but firm, carrying just enough authority to command her attention without attracting unwanted ears. "Wait for me in your apartment. We'll talk." Kris didn't respond verbally, but the subtle dip of her head was acknowledgement enough. She resumed her movement, but this time, it was with a subdued, almost hesitant gait. She disappeared into the doorway of her apartment, leaving a lingering silence in her wake.

David turned back to Mark, his expression carefully neutral. "You two have a good night," he said, offering a reassuring smile. "Get some rest. We'll hit the ground running tomorrow." Mark nodded, a hint of concern still etched on his face as he glanced towards Kris's apartment. He clearly sensed that something was amiss, but he wisely refrained from prying. "We will," he said. "Thanks again, David. For everything."

David watched Mark and Janet head back to their apartment, a thoughtful frown creasing his forehead. He could practically feel the conflicting emotions radiating from Kris's apartment; shame, desire, and a potent confusion that only a young woman grappling with intense feelings could generate. He sighed inwardly. Navigating the complexities of human emotions, especially when compounded by the pressures of their current reality, was a challenge, even for him.

He turned towards Kris's apartment, a simple, space that she had somehow managed to infuse with her own unique brand of quirky personality. He knocked softly, and the door opened almost immediately. Kris stood there, her eyes downcast, her shoulders slumped. She looked smaller than usual, her usual fiery spirit momentarily extinguished. And then, she knelt.

It wasn't a graceful, practiced movement. It was abrupt, almost clumsy, born of panic. She lowered her head, her long hair falling forward to obscure her face. "Master," she whispered, the word barely audible. David's eyebrows shot up. He hadn't expected that. He preferred Kris's usual boldness to this display of... well, what was it exactly? Guilt? Adoration? A potent cocktail of both, perhaps? "Kris," he said, his voice gentle but firm. "Stand up."

She hesitated for a moment, then slowly, rose to her feet. She didn't meet his eyes. "Look at me," David instructed, and after a moment, she complied. Her eyes were red-rimmed, her expression a mix of shame and a desperate plea for understanding.

"I'm sorry," she blurted out, the words tumbling over each other in her haste. "I didn't mean to... I just... I got carried away. I know it was wrong. I know you were in the middle of… and your wives… I just…" She trailed off, unable to articulate the jumble of thoughts and emotions that had propelled her into her earlier impulsive act.

David stepped closer, his gaze unwavering. "Kris," he said softly, "I'm not angry." Her eyes widened in disbelief. "But… you should be! I practically… it was… inappropriate." He smiled, a small, reassuring smile that reached his eyes. "Inappropriate, perhaps. But not malicious. I understand that you have… strong motivations." A blush crept up her neck, staining her cheeks a vibrant red. "Strong is an understatement," she mumbled, then winced as soon as the words left her mouth.

David chuckled. At least the sass was still there, lurking beneath the surface. "Indeed. Look, Kris, I appreciate your… excitement. And I'm not going to pretend that I don't find you attractive. You're a beautiful young woman, and I do value you. But…" He paused, searching for the right words. "There's a time and a place for everything. And jumping someone by the pool, especially when his wives are nearby, is generally not considered good etiquette, even in these circumstances."

He saw a flicker of a smile play on her lips. "So, what you're saying is, next time, I should check for wives first?" Kris quipped, a mischievous look returning to her eyes. David laughed, the sound echoing in the room. "That's the spirit, Kris! I much prefer this version of you. But, in all seriousness, while I appreciate the sentiment, perhaps a little more… finesse is required." He sobered slightly. "And it's not just about proper procedure. My wives aren't mad, at least, not the ones who were around to witness your… moment. But there are others, like Jessica, who might have a slightly different perspective. Jessica is very protective of me, and she is pregnant, after all."

Kris's face fell. "Oh. Right. Jessica. I… I didn't think." A hint of irritation washed over her, eclipsing the earlier embarrassment and desire. She hadn't considered the ramifications of her actions, how they might cause trouble. "Exactly," David said, his voice gentle. He placed a hand on her shoulder, a light, comforting gesture. "You need to think, Kris. Not just about what you want, but about the impact of your actions on everyone else. We're a family here, even if it's not a conventional one. And families look out for each other."

He paused, then continued, "Look, I'm not going to lie. Your desire is flattering. But this constant pressure, this… manic energy… it's not sustainable, Kris. Not for you, and certainly not for me. I need you to be… you. The smart, funny, insightful Kris I know you can be. The one who can hold a conversation without immediately trying to jump my bones." He winked, hoping to lighten the mood. Kris managed a weak smile. "Okay, okay, I get it. I'm too much. Like a horny puppy that won't stop humping your leg."

David chuckled. "A… vivid analogy, but not entirely inaccurate." He removed his hand from her shoulder and stepped back slightly. "So, here's the deal, Kris. I'll meet you halfway. But only if you promise to dial it back. Way back." He held up a hand, ticking off points on his fingers. "One, no more sexual ambushes. Two, no more theatrical declarations of baby making and the responsibility of mankind. Three, and this is important, you must respect my wives. Friends or not, there is a lot more there than you can imagine."

Kris's eyes widened, a spark of hope igniting within them. "So… you're saying there's a chance?" The question hung in the air, thick with anticipation. She knew this was a precarious position, walking a tightrope between her overwhelming desire and the established order of David's unique family.

David met her gaze, his expression softening slightly. He understood her desperation, her longing for connection and belonging. He also recognized a genuine intelligence beneath the surface of her sometimes-abrasive pursuit. "Yes, Kris," he said, a hint of a smile playing on his lips. "There's a chance. But it's not a free pass. It's a probationary period."

Kris tilted her head, a flicker of confusion crossing her face. "Probationary?" "Exactly. You noticed I said 'halfway,' right? That means there's something in it for you, if you can meet me there." David paused for dramatic effect. "Effective immediately, you will be considered a… probationary concubine."

The word hung in the small apartment, heavy with implications. Kris blinked, processing the information. A concubine? It wasn't exactly the same as being a wife, but it was certainly a step in the right direction. A chance to prove herself, to earn a place within David's inner circle. A wave of giddy excitement washed over her, tempered by a healthy dose of apprehension.

Before Kris could fully formulate a response, David pulled out his phone. "Time to get some input." He started typing. "Tiffany? Summer? Could you come to apartment seven for a quick pow-wow? Thanks." "On our way, David," Tiffany's response was instantaneous. David pocketed his phone and turned back to Kris. "They'll want to know what's going on. Transparency is key, remember?"

Kris nodded, her stomach doing acrobatic flips. The thought of facing Tiffany and Summer, two of David's most established and respected wives, in this situation, filled her with a mixture of apprehension and dread. Within moments, there was a soft knock on the door. David opened it to reveal Tiffany and Summer, her empathetic eyes scanning the room. "What's up, David?" Tiffany asked, stepping inside. Summer followed, her gaze immediately settling on Kris, assessing her with quiet curiosity.

David gestured for them to sit on the small sofa. "Kris and I have been discussing… some things. And we've reached an agreement. One that I wanted to run by you both." He looked at Kris, offering her a reassuring nod. "Kris has agreed to try and curb her… enthusiasm. In return, I've offered her an opportunity to earn a more preferential position with me here."

He turned back to Tiffany and Summer, explaining his decision in concise, logical terms. He carefully worded his explanation, emphasizing that this was a probationary arrangement and that Kris would be subject to their approval. Tiffany listened intently, her expression thoughtful. Summer, ever perceptive, picked up on Kris's anxiety. "So, what does this 'probationary concubine' thing entail, exactly?" Tiffany asked, cutting to the chase.

David leaned forward, his hands clasped between his knees. "Kris will be able to reap the benefits of being… my woman. However," he held up a finger, "she'll remain in her apartment. She won't be sleeping in my bed, at least not yet. And she won't be involved in my decision-making processes." He paused, letting the information sink in. "Think of it as a trial run. Full access to the perks, but none of the responsibilities or the privileges that come with being a full member of the family."

Summer raised an eyebrow. "And the condition?" David's gaze met Summer's, a hint of a smile playing on his lips. "The condition is simple, yet potentially challenging. She must be completely accepted by each of you. All of you. Every single one of my wives." Kris paled slightly. That sounded significantly harder than she initially thought. Winning over David was one thing, but convincing all of his wives that she wasn't just some crazed groupie? That felt like climbing Everest in flip-flops. "Okay," Tiffany said slowly, "and how is she supposed to achieve this... universal acceptance?"

David turned to Kris. "She'll integrate herself willingly into all of your duties. Tiffany runs the ranch's day-to-day operations, making sure everything is running smoothly. Jennifer manages the hydroponics, ensuring a steady supply of fresh produce. Elena organizes the training regimens, keeping everyone sharp and combat-ready. Summer plans the meals, and she's also our on-call pharmacist. Kayla tracks our supplies, meticulously cataloging everything we have. Taylor is the nanny, caring for the younger children. Nicole oversees the cleaning, and Jessica helps her, ensuring the house remains sanitary. Tanya is the esthetician, and she also helps make soap, lotion, and other skincare products. She'll learn from each of you, assist you, and prove her worth through action, not just words."

He paused, his eyes locking with Kris's. "And she'll do it willingly. No complaining, no half-assing. Complete and utter dedication." Kris swallowed hard, the sheer scale of the undertaking beginning to dawn on her. "Right. Got it. All in." she said, trying for a confidence she didn't quite feel.

David nodded, his expression softening. "Each of my wives contributes, not because they have to, or because I demand it. It's not about obligation, Kris. It's about ownership. This isn't just a house; it's our home. Our legacy. We're building something together, something that will hopefully last. And everyone here wants to contribute to that, not because they feel they need to, but because they want to."

Summer leaned forward, her usual calm demeanor taking on a sharper edge. "None of us get a free ride, Kris. Some of us, like Tiffany, have committed years of our lives to build this from the ground up. Others commit their lives to making it better, refining it, expanding it. But everyone, without exception, works to keep it going. David has given us everything, and we give back in our own ways."

Tiffany added, her voice firm but kind, "And remember, David is the one who taught us how to do nearly everything we do. He's incredibly patient and supportive. He doesn't just delegate; he empowers. He'll show you the ropes, guide you, and help you find your place within the family."

Kris absorbed all of this, realization dawning on her face. It wasn't just about winning David over; it was about earning her place within a complex, well-oiled machine. A machine fueled by love, loyalty, and a shared vision. "So, where do I start?" she asked, her voice a little less shaky.

David smiled, a genuine, warm expression that crinkled the corners of his eyes. "You start right now." "Tiffany and Summer will inform the rest of the wives," he added. As Tiffany and Summer headed to the door, David leaned closer to Kris, lowering his voice. "After they leave," he whispered, a glint in his eye, "Protocol training begins." Kris's eyes widened.

Chapter 25

The Cattle Drive and Canvas

The air in the living room was a symphony of domesticity, a fragrant blend of beeswax polish and the rich aroma of freshly brewed coffee. Sunlight, a cheerful golden intruder, sliced through the bullet-resistant glass, illuminating a chaotic ballet of dust motes. In the eye of this domestic hurricane sat David, presiding over the morning meeting like a benevolent, albeit slightly exasperated, king.

Jessica, radiating the subtle glow of impending motherhood, occupied a privileged position on David's lap, her feet swinging precariously like a toddler on an oversized chair. Jennifer leaned against the armrest, radiating artistic angst. Kris disguised in tattoos and a newly found penchant for servitude, stood stoically to David's left.

Tiffany, Summer, and Kayla, the resident record-keepers, perched attentively on one couch, notepads and tablets at the ready. Tanya, Nicole, and Taylor circulated with coffee and juice, ensuring everyone was adequately caffeinated and hydrated for the day's deliberations. Elena, lost in the labyrinth of her book, remained blissfully oblivious, sprawled languidly on another couch. And the rest? They milled about, a diverse collection of survivors united by a shared dependence on David and a healthy dose of apocalypse-induced Stockholm Syndrome.

"Alright," David began, his voice a soothing balm amidst the morning's bustle, a voice that could calm a feral goat and still be heard over a shotgun blast, "let's get started. What triumphs and tribulations do we have to discuss today?"

Scott, the newly appointed butcher-in-chief, spoke first, his voice booming with pride. "The slaughterhouse is finished, David. Fully operational. Ventilation, drainage, everything's up to snuff." A beat of silence hung in the air, thick with the unspoken question: "Can we start turning those adorable miniature cows into burgers now?"

David stroked his chin, a picture of thoughtful deliberation. "Excellent work, Scott. However, I still want to prioritize finding wild cattle before we start culling from our miniature herd. I'm not heartless, you know." He glanced at Tiffany. "Tiffany, have you scouted any likely areas recently?"

Tiffany nodded, her expression all business. "I've seen some tracks near the creek bed, about five miles west. Could be a small herd. Aidan and Alissa are eager to check it out, see if anyone else already claimed it." The unspoken implication hung heavy: finding wild cattle was a race against other, potentially less friendly, survivor groups.

David nodded. "Aidan, Alissa, prepare to leave within the hour. Brian, can you ensure Behemoth is ready to go? Check the propane levels, and the tires. I want it ready, just in case." Behemoth, the group's armored, propane-powered behemoth of a vehicle, was their answer to pretty much any problem. Bad weather? Behemoth. Hostile neighbors? Behemoth. Need to pick up a particularly large pizza order? You guessed it, Behemoth. Brian simply nodded.

Little David, the group's resident weapons expert, cleared his throat. "I have something to report as well." He looked at Lynn, a woman who still seemed slightly overwhelmed by her new life. "Lynn has officially earned her open carry privileges. She consistently demonstrated safe handling and tactical awareness on the firing range. She's ready."

Lynn, Josh's mother, shifted nervously under the collective gaze, her eyes wide with a mixture of pride and trepidation. All eyes turned to her, and David offered a warm, encouraging smile. "Congratulations, Lynn. You've earned it." A hesitant smile bloomed on Lynn's face. "Thank you, David. It... it means a lot." She paused, then took a deep breath, gathering her courage. "Actually... now that I'm... proficient... would it be alright if I tried to find my parents? I haven't heard from them since the day I left."

David studied her, his expression softening with empathy. He saw a flicker of fear, but also a spark of hope. He nodded slowly. "Of course, Lynn. Josh, Lily, you'll accompany Lynn. Take the van, but don't take unnecessary risks. And Lynn, be prepared for anything, we don't even know if they're still alive." Lynn nodded, understanding the gravity of the situation. The apocalypse wasn't exactly known for its happy reunions.

David turned to Jessica, his voice softening further, becoming almost a purr. "How are you feeling, baby girl?" Jessica's face lit up, her mood as sunny as the morning light streaming through the windows. "Great, Daddy. Kris has been spoiling me rotten." She playfully nudged Kris, who, subtly rolled her eyes. "Although," she added, a mischievous glint in her eyes, "I think I need a foot massage. This little one is getting heavy."

The room erupted in a chorus of amused groans and knowing sighs. Jessica's pregnancy, while a joyous occasion, was also a masterclass in manipulation. Jennifer snorted, "Of course you do, Jess. You always need a foot massage," though her tone was more affectionate than annoyed. Kayla rolled her eyes, but a smile played on her lips. Jessica's 'needs' were a running joke, but everyone catered to them, knowing that a happy Jessica meant a happy ranch.

Kris, already kneeling, gently took Jessica's foot in her hands. "Yes, Mistress Jessica," she murmured, her voice a low whisper. The subservient address, usually reserved for David, caused another wave of chuckles. Jessica simply batted her eyelashes and wriggled her toes, clearly enjoying the attention.

While Jessica basked in the glow of David's doting gaze, Summer, the resident meteorologist, brought them crashing back to reality. She tapped on her tablet, her brow furrowed with concern. "David, the weather is becoming increasingly concerning. The average temperatures are rising faster than predicted, and the models are showing an increased risk of tornadoes in the coming weeks."

David sighed, rubbing his temples. "I knew it. This climate is getting more and more unpredictable. I wasn't in the area last time, but I imagine hurricane season will start early as well." He paused, considering their options. "We'll be safe on the ranch," he said, his voice reassuring, "but we still need to take precautions, especially if we're out and about."

The collective shrug that rippled through the room was almost palpable. Tornadoes? Hurricanes? They lived in a fortress that could probably survive a bombing run and a nuclear winter. A little bad weather wasn't exactly raising their pulses.

"So," David continued, clapping his hands together, "that's settled. Lynn, get your things, and Josh and Lily, gear up. Everyone else, carry on as usual. And..." he paused, a twinkle in his eye, "don't forget, tonight is arts and crafts night. Painting. Everyone's welcome. Even you, Jennifer, even if your 'abstract expressionism' looks suspiciously like a toddler threw up on a canvas."

Jennifer gasped dramatically, clutching her chest. "My art is a reflection of the soul, David! You just don't understand the layers of emotion!" "The only layer I see is a thick coat of… well, never mind," David chuckled. "Just try to keep the paint off the furniture this time."

The meeting adjourned with a flurry of activity. Lynn, looking slightly overwhelmed but grateful, started packing a small bag. Josh and Lily, always eager for a mission, headed towards the armory, their youthful faces alight with anticipation. Jennifer, still feigning offense at David's art critique, sashayed towards the kitchen, muttering about the philistine nature of men.

Eric approached David with a hesitant gait. "David," he began, his voice rough around the edges, "I was thinking… maybe I could take Lynn, Josh, and Lily in the Behemoth tonight? Try to find Lynn's parents?" David regarded him with a thoughtful expression. He appreciated Eric's initiative, plus, it wasn't a bad idea. "That's a good idea, Eric. But, it's dangerous out there. Are you sure you're up for it?" "I can handle it," Eric replied, his eyes holding a steely glint. "And with Josh and Lily, we'll be alright."

David nodded slowly. "Alright. Let Lynn and the others know there's been a change of plans." He paused, placing a hand on Eric's shoulder. "Don't get too sidetracked while you're out there. And we'll just have Bonnie stay with Grace tonight." Eric offered a rare, small smile. "Thanks, David."

David watched Eric walk away, a strange mix of emotions tumbling within him. He was simultaneously impressed by Eric's resolve, concerned for his safety, and slightly amused by the ripple effect of his seemingly simple decisions. The apocalypse, it seemed, was a catalyst for both profound loss and unexpected growth. He then turned to find Aidan and Alissa, who were already tinkering with the Beast in preparation for their cattle scouting mission, ready to face whatever the post-apocalyptic world threw their way, be it feral cows, hostile neighbors, or Jennifer's questionable art. After all, running a ranch in the apocalypse was never a dull affair.

"Alright, cowpokes!" David hollered, swaggering into the garage like a gunslinger entering a dusty saloon. Only instead of a six-shooter, he was armed with... well, the general authority of being in charge. "Remember, we're looking for cows, not trouble. But if trouble finds you, give it hell."

His words were met with varying levels of enthusiasm. Aidan, ever the stoic, simply nodded. Alissa, on the other hand, flashed a grin that could curdle milk. They hopped into the "Beast" and roared off, leaving David to survey his chaotic domain. Clearly, the apocalypse wasn't slowing anyone down.

As the Beast's engine faded, David witnessed a scene that could only be described as… multilingual courtship. Brian, usually a man of few words, was mumbling surprisingly decent Korean to a giggling Seo-Yeon. David chuckled to himself. Junior was clearly a phenomenal teacher, but the irony of Seo-Yeon ending up with the one who didn't speak Korean or Thai still amused him.

Before he could even contemplate the complexities of post-apocalyptic romance, David nearly collided with a human stampede led by Taylor, Andrea, and Janet. Their charges? A gaggle of excitable children being herded toward the recreational bunker for a day of aquatic mayhem. Mike, Seth, Lori, Beth, Bonnie, and Jessica were a bubbling cauldron of energy, practically vibrating with anticipation. "Pool time, huh?" David asked, watching them pass. "Yes," Taylor replied, her voice a calming balm amidst the youthful shrieks. "No classroom work today. Plus, Jessica needs to stay in shape for the baby."

Jessica, looking slightly less thrilled than the others, grumbled, "It's hard to swim with a watermelon attached to your stomach." She did manage a smile, though. Apparently, even impending motherhood couldn't dampen the spirit of a good swim. David, eyebrows raised, then asked, "Are you swimming?" Jessica shook her head. "Nah, Tanya's coming down for water Yoga in a bit." David, ever the playful leader, playfully smacked Jessica on the rear as she passed, already imaging the chaos that would ensue when the kids hit the water.

So there you have it. One minute, you're sending out a posse to wrangle rogue cattle. The next, you're refereeing international flirting and managing a swimming pool full of potentially radioactive children.

In the work shed, the rhythmic thunk-click of the reloading press provided the soundtrack to another productive afternoon in the ranch's workshop. Little David expertly fed spent casings into the machine while Kyle, with the precision of a Swiss watchmaker, measured powder charges. 9mm, .308, and .223, the ranch's staples, were accumulating faster than doomsday preppers hoarded toilet paper. After all, the end of the world hadn't stopped target practice, and David, ever the pragmatist, insisted on economical reloads.

Downstairs, in the generator room but now also served as the community armory, Grace, a whirlwind of meticulous organization, was boxing the finished ammunition. Each box was labeled with the caliber, grain, and date, a testament to David's preparedness and Grace's borderline obsessive orderliness. Shelves groaned under the weight of enough ammunition to equip a small army, along with spare parts and cleaning supplies that would make a gun enthusiast weep with joy.

David paused, wiping carbon residue from his hands. "So, Kyle," he began, a mischievous glint in his eye, "I hear congratulations are in order. Engagement, is it?" Kyle, normally unflappable, nearly choked on a sunflower seed. "Engagement? What the hell are you talking about?"

Before Kyle could launch into a full-blown denial, Grace's voice floated up from the stairwell, as clear and unwavering as a sniper's aim. "He's talking about you and me, Kyle. And yes, we are engaged. We're going to get married as soon as I'm old enough." She popped her head over the edge of the floor, like a prairie dog emerging from its burrow. "After all, Daddy needs his family united."

Kyle's jaw dropped so far he risked dislocating it. Little David burst into laughter, slapping his knee. "I knew it! I knew something was brewing between you two lovebirds!" Kyle rounded on Grace, his face a mask of bewildered exasperation. "Grace, we've talked about this! You're… you're only fourteen! I'm almost thirty-two! This is… this is insane!"

Grace, utterly unfazed, calmly placed a tray of completed boxes on the workbench. "Age is just a number, Kyle. Besides, I've already got everything planned out." Kyle buried his face in his hands, murmuring something about needing a drink – a strong drink. David, still chortling, added fuel to the fire. "Don't fight it, Kyle. You two already work well together. Besides, Grace has a plan. Always does. You're just a pawn in her grand scheme."

"Exactly," Grace said, a self-satisfied smirk playing on her lips. She patted Kyle's arm condescendingly, like he was a particularly slow toddler. "Don't worry, Kyle. I'll take good care of you."

Kyle understood. He really did. Grace, despite her age, possessed the strategic mind of a five-star general and the ruthlessness of a Fortune 500 CEO. She probably saw him as a loyal, if slightly dim-witted, asset. And, he had to admit, he was quite fond of her. Though also understandably unnerved.

Little David clapped Kyle on the shoulder. "Cheer up, old man! You're marrying into the family. That makes you invincible. And hey," he added with a wink, "when she turns eighteen, you'll have a smoking hot, lethal bride. What's there to worry about?"

Several miles west of the ranch, Aidan gripped the steering wheel like he was trying to strangle it. He navigated the beast down a precarious dirt road leading to the parched riverbed of what was optimistically labeled on the map as Orion Creek. His brow was furrowed in a concentration usually reserved for defusing ticking time bombs, but in this case, it involved avoiding snapping an axle on a rogue mesquite root.

Beside him, Alissa, his partner in crime, held her cell phone to her ear, a radiant smile illuminating her face. "Yeah, Tiffany, we found three! Near Orion Creek, looking a little thirsty but otherwise okay. Aidan thinks he can coax them back." She paused, absorbing Tiffany's squeals of excitement. "Okay, great! We'll start heading back as soon as we get there. Love you too."

With a dramatic flourish, she disconnected the call and beamed at Aidan. "Tiffany's thrilled! She's already preparing what I'm sure will be a champion's welcome."

Aidan chuckled, a sound as rare and precious as a genuine antique at a flea market. "Champion's welcome? It's going to be an adjustment nonetheless with full-sized cattle. Not miniature ones like the rest." He glanced at Alissa, a mischievous glint in his eye. "Think you can handle driving this beast for a bit? My hands are starting to cramp. Probably from the death grip I've had on this wheel."

Alissa, a woman who considered "backing down" a foreign phrase, grinned like a Cheshire cat. "You know it!

Hand it over, Daddy-O." Aidan's eyebrows shot up so high they threatened to disappear into his hairline. "Daddy-O? Where'd you pick that one up? It sounds like it escaped from a 1950s beatnik convention."

"Kris happened to be doing tattoos for Lily last night, and I was flipping through her tattoo books. I saw the phrase 'Daddy-O' and I liked it, so I asked her what it meant. Figured I'd give it a try. What's life without a little experimentation?" Alissa replied, already reaching for the door handle.

Aidan hopped out, and walked around to the passenger side. Alissa slid over to the driver's seat with an eagerness that bordered on reckless, and Aidan, bracing himself for the inevitable swerving, hopped in the passenger seat. "Alright, but if we end up listening to big band music and wearing zoot suits, I'm drawing the line. My Stetson is as far as I'm willing to go."

Alissa cackled, the sound bouncing off the interior of the cab. "No promises! But seriously, thanks for bringing me out here. I know we both needed a break after being cooped up at the ranch with everyone watching our every move."

He cracked a window, letting in the hot, dry air that smelled of dust and freedom. "You know," he said, leaning back in his seat, "for someone who grew up in Tucson, you handle this whole 'country life' thing pretty well." Alissa grinned, her hands surprisingly steady on the steering wheel. "Learned from the best. Besides," she added with a playful wink, "my husband makes a pretty convincing cowboy. Even if he does complain about getting dirt under his fingernails."

Aidan rolled his eyes, but a smile betrayed his amusement. "So," Aidan began, addressing the issue at hand, "any brilliant ideas on how we're going to convince three stubborn cows to walk four miles in the right direction? Because last time I checked, cattle weren't exactly known for their enthusiasm for brisk walks in the desert."

Alissa downshifted as they approached the small herd, who were now peacefully munching on some scrub grass near Orion Creek, blissfully unaware of the drama they were about to unleash. "Well," she said, thoughtfully, "I was thinking we could try the 'gentle persuasion' method. You know, talk nicely, offer them some water, maybe a little back scratch behind the ears. Channel our inner Dr. Doolittle."

She slowed the Beast to a halt a safe distance from the cattle. "Alright, gentle persuasion it is. But if that doesn't work, I'm not ruling out the lasso. Although I'm not sure I remember exactly how to use it…"

As they climbed out of the vehicle, Aidan grabbing two large buckets of water while Alissa rummaged in the back for some rope. As they approached the cows, Aidan spoke in a calm, soothing voice, the kind one might use to pacify a grumpy toddler. "Hey there, ladies. Just wanted to offer you a little refreshment. It's a hot one out here, isn't it?"

The cows, predictably, stared back at him with blank, bovine expressions. One of them let out a loud moo, which Aidan interpreted as either a greeting from an alien or a threat to his life. He wasn't entirely sure which.

Alissa, meanwhile, was attempting to loop the rope around the neck of the largest cow, a mottled brown and white behemoth that looked like it could bench press the Behemoth. The cow, however, was having none of it. It snorted, took a step back, and glared at Alissa. "Easy girl, easy," Alissa cooed, inching closer. "I just want to be friends—and maybe guide you home."

The cow responded by kicking out its back legs, narrowly missing Alissa's shins. Alissa yelped and jumped back, dropping the rope in the process. "Okay," she said, dusting herself off, "gentle persuasion is officially off the table. Time for Plan B, and I'm open to suggestions at this point."

Aidan grinned, a flash of devilment in his eyes. "I told you so." He held out a bucket of water to the cows, who finally seemed interested. They cautiously approached, lapping up the water with gusto, momentarily forgetting their distrust of humans. "Alright," Alissa said, picking up the rope again, "plan B. We're going to have to herd them. Aidan, you take the left flank, I'll take the right. Let's try to keep them moving in the direction of the ranch. I'll call dad about the car to help block them."

And so began the great Texas cow drive of 2027. Aidan and Alissa, armed with nothing but their wits, a couple of lengths of rope, and a rapidly dwindling supply of patience, attempted to coax, cajole, and occasionally yell at the three stubbornly independent cows to move in the general direction of home.

The cows, of course, had other ideas. They wandered off the trail, stopped to eat every patch of grass they could find (even the ones that looked suspiciously like weeds), and generally made life as difficult as possible. At one point, the largest cow, affectionately named 'This son of a bitch' in Aidan's increasingly colorful inner monologue, decided to take a nap in the middle of the road, forcing Aidan and Alissa to resort to desperate measures, including throwing small rocks and making ridiculous noises.

Despite the challenges, there was a certain satisfaction in the task. It was a simple, honest kind of work, a connection to the land that they rarely experienced back at the ranch. And, more importantly, it was a chance to spend some quality time together, away from the ever-present responsibilities and the watchful eyes of their extended family. Even if that quality time involved dodging cow pies and arguing about the best way to motivate a bovine nap enthusiast.

After what felt like an eternity, they finally reached the outskirts of the ranch. The cows, sensing that they were close to food, water, and the promise of a good, long nap, perked up and started moving with a surprising amount of enthusiasm. As they approached the gate, they were greeted by a chorus of cheers from the ranch residents, who had gathered to witness their triumphant return. Though if someone had asked Aidan at that moment, he probably would have preferred a medal and a long, silent nap.

Tiffany, the ever-vigilant mother hen of the group, practically vibrated with pride as Aidan and Alissa walked towards her. "You did it!" she squealed, enveloping them in a hug. "I knew you could! Now, let's get these ladies settled in." The "ladies" in question were three full-sized, and frankly, rather weary-looking cows being gently nudged toward the barn. It was an odd sight, but this group had a knack for the unusual.

What followed was a scene straight out of a rural sitcom. Tiffany, bless her heart, acted as a bovine entertainer, likely whispering sweet nothings about the benefits of organic fertilizer. Meanwhile, Andrea, Mark, Janet, Summer, Parker, Jill, and Eric swarmed the cows, combing them with the fervor of archaeologists on a dig, searching for ticks and other unwanted hitchhikers. Once de-bugged, the cows were subjected to an impromptu spa day, courtesy of Lily and Nicole, whose calming presence seemed to reassure the bewildered beasts that this was, in fact, not some elaborate cow-napping scheme.

Finally, freshly scrubbed and inoculated, Tiffany led the trio into the promised land: a high-tech barn that looked like something out of a sci-fi dairy farm. Inside, a bizarre welcoming committee awaited. Twenty miniature cows, resembling fluffy, disproportionate calves, stared with wide-eyed curiosity. Goats bleated greetings, their calls sounding suspiciously like laughter, while a chaotic flock of chickens scurried underfoot, seemingly unfazed by the momentous arrival.

For the new cows, however, this was no laughing matter. After weeks of fending for themselves in a Texas landscape that looked like it had lost a fight with a particularly angry dust storm, the climate-controlled barn was nothing short of paradise. An automatic watering system offered sweet relief from the muddy creek beds that had been their only source of hydration. The soft bedding was a luxurious upgrade from the hard, unforgiving ground they'd been forced to sleep on. As they munched contentedly on the provided feed, the stress of survival slowly began to melt away, replaced by the bovine equivalent of a sigh of contentment.

As the cows settled into their new digs, David, the ranch's stoic leader, surveyed the scene with a critical eye. Alissa, still buzzing from the successful cow-wrangling adventure, was regaling Summer and Elena with tales of daring and bovine bravery. Summer, ever the pragmatist, peppered her with questions about milk yield and potential beef quality. Elena, never one to miss a golden opportunity for teasing, winked at Aidan. "So, did you sweet-talk them into following you, or did you have to use your… persuasive techniques? Did The Beast have to flex its muscles?"

Just then, the man himself, David, pulled into the driveway, expertly parking Aidan's red "Beast" in the garage. Hot on his heels was Brian in David's unassuming sedan, the very picture of responsible driving – despite the fact that he probably could hotwire either vehicle in under thirty seconds.

Tiffany, having finished her initial health check, joined the group, her brow furrowed with concern. "They're malnourished," she announced. "It'll take at least a month to get them back to peak condition before…" She trailed off, delicately avoiding the dreaded "S" word. The group knew what she meant; they weren't squeamish, but they approached the realities of ranching with a certain respect.

Suddenly, Mike and Bonnie, the ranch's resident animal enthusiasts, practically vibrated with excitement. "Can we name them?" Mike burst out, his eyes shining with pleading desperation. Bonnie, not to be outdone, echoed, "Yeah! Please, can we?" Parker, scenting an opportunity for comedic gold, seized it with both hands. "I've got some great names! How about T-Bone, Brisket, and… Meatloaf?"

Jill, his long-suffering wife, promptly elbowed him in the ribs. "Parker! Be serious." Parker's wince was Oscar-worthy. "Okay, okay! But seriously, think about it! T-Bone has a certain ring to it, doesn't it?" Mike and Bonnie, however, were completely sold on Parker's culinary-inspired suggestions. "T-Bone is awesome!" Mike declared, bouncing on the balls of his feet. Bonnie nodded enthusiastically. "And Meatloaf is so much better than Bessie!" Apparently, she had already started brainstorming names.

Tiffany chuckled, shaking her head. "Alright, alright, let's not get ahead of ourselves. We need to get them settled first. Then we can have a naming contest." She glanced at David, a silent question in her eyes, and received a nearly imperceptible nod. The bovine naming ceremony was officially on hold, but the ranch was officially open for business, one rescued cow at a time.

Summer swept through the main house, arms laden with art supplies. "Alright, everyone!" she announced, her voice carrying a cheerful authority. "Tonight is all about unleashing your inner Picasso! Or, you know, just painting something vaguely resembling a tree. No pressure!" She winked, dumping the supplies onto the living room's sprawling coffee table. Canvases of all sizes leaned precariously against each other, tubes of paint threatened to roll onto the floor, and easels stood like expectant soldiers, ready for battle.

"I call dibs on the 3D paints!" Jennifer shouted from her usual spot on the couch. David, observing the scene with a fond smile, felt a familiar warmth spread through him. He appreciated Summer's efforts to maintain normalcy, to create pockets of joy amidst the post-apocalyptic gloom. The artistic inclinations of the family varied wildly, from Summer's near professional skill, to Jennifer's abstract splatter art and Jessica's stick figures.

Meanwhile, a different kind of preparation was underway. Josh, Lily, and Lynn were a trio forged in apprehension and determination. Josh meticulously checked his weapons, a Sig P226 and AR-15 rifle. Lily, a miniature version of her father in terms of discipline and tactical prowess, adjusted her plate carrier to fit her smaller frame. Lynn, still a bundle of nerves, quadruple checked her Glock and ammo.

"Are you sure about this, Lynn?" David asked gently, approaching her. He could sense her fear, her uncertainty. "We can send someone else, you know." Lynn shook her head, her jaw set with a newfound resolve. "No. I need to do this, David. They're my parents. I have to try." David nodded, placing a reassuring hand on her shoulder. "Then we'll make sure you're safe. Josh and Lily will look after you." He gave Josh a nod of approval. "And Eric is preparing the Behemoth. You'll be traveling in style, and relative safety."

Speaking of the Behemoth, it rumbled to life with an earth-shaking roar. The monstrous vehicle, a testament to Aidan's custom modifications, loomed large in the courtyard, its armored plating gleaming in the setting sun. Eric gave Lynn a thumbs-up. "She's ready to roll! Just try not to scratch the paint job, alright?" David sighed inwardly. Eric couldn't help but add a touch of levity, even in the face of a potentially dangerous mission. Lynn managed a weak smile. "I'll try my best."

As Lynn, Josh, and Lily climbed into the Behemoth, ready to embark on their rescue mission, the air crackled with a strange mixture of tension and excitement. David watched them go, a knot of worry tightening in his stomach. He trusted in their abilities, in their training, but the world outside the ranch was becoming increasingly unpredictable, unforgiving.

He turned back towards the house, where the sounds of laughter were already starting to emanate from the living room. Summer's art therapy was in full swing, a chaotic symphony of color, creativity, and the faint scent of glitter glue. Perhaps, he thought, a little bit of normalcy was exactly what they all needed right now. And maybe, just maybe, he'd contribute by painting something himself.

Chapter 26

The Mailbox Invitation

The air in the main house crackled with creative energy. Summer, ever the organizer, had transformed the living room into an impromptu art studio. Canvases leaned against the furniture, tubes of paint littered the coffee table, and the scent of linseed oil hung heavy in the air. Kris, perched on the edge of a plush armchair, surveyed the scene with a smug grin. She'd envisioned herself as the resident artiste, ready to unleash a torrent of post-apocalyptic angst onto the unsuspecting canvases.

She'd even mentally composed a dramatic artist statement: "Through charcoal and shadow, I expose the raw nerve of our shattered reality! Observe the gnarled trees, scarred by the EMP, whispering tales of a world consumed by darkness!"

But her self-aggrandizing thoughts screeched to a halt as she took in the others. Kayla, with her brow furrowed in concentration, was meticulously layering oil paints onto a canvas, a vibrant Texas landscape slowly emerging. Elena, hunched over a large sheet of paper, was sketching with rapid, precise strokes, a dizzying perspective drawing of the ranch taking shape, stylized like a warped theme park map. And Nicole, humming softly to herself, was creating a chaotic yet charming scene of muscular superheroes riding dachshunds into battle, wielding oversized spatulas and rolling pins instead of swords.

Kris's smugness deflated like a punctured tire. These weren't just dabblers; they were artists. Real artists. Then there was David. He sat behind his own easel, a mischievous glint in his eyes. He faced a large canvas, brush in hand, and was outlining what appeared to be a… well, a rather explicit, pop art, BDSM scene featuring Jessica. He paused, tilted his head, and added a delicate lace detail to the… restraint. He looked up, caught Kris's eye, and winked.

"Alright, everyone," Kris announced, forcing a bravado she didn't quite feel. "Let's have an artistic showdown! May the best angst win!" Summer chuckled. "It's not a competition, Kris. Just… let it flow." And so, they did. Kayla's landscape bloomed with wildflowers and rolling hills, a testament to the enduring beauty of nature even in the face of chaos. Elena's perspective piece morphed into a whimsical representation of their safe haven, complete with tiny stick-figure residents happily tending their farm. Nicole's superhero squad charged onward, their wiener dog steeds sporting tiny capes and determined expressions.

David's piece continued to evolve. The initial outline filled with detail – the play of light on Jessica's skin, the texture of the leather, the subtle expressions of both dominance and submission. It was… surprisingly tasteful, despite the subject matter.

Kris, initially thrown off by the unexpectedly high level of artistic talent, found herself drawn into the therapeutic chaos. She abandoned her overly-dramatic intentions and simply let her feelings guide her hand. Just then, the door swung open, revealing Lynn, her face etched with a mixture of anxiety and determination. She was dressed in practical clothing, accessorized with body armor and a gun belt, her eyes searching for David. "David, we're ready to go. Lily and Josh are prepping the jeep now and Eric is getting his stuff together."

The festive atmosphere of the art session seemed to blow out like a candle in a window. The women exchanged concerned glances. David rose to his feet, his expression hardening with resolve. He crossed the room to Lynn. "Alright," he said, his voice low and steady. "You ready for this?" Lynn swallowed hard, her lip trembling slightly. "As I'll ever be."

David nodded once, a brief, reassuring gesture. "Alright. Lily and Josh will keep you safe. And Eric's got your back." He paused, his gaze softening slightly. "We'll be here waiting for you." As Lynn instinctively reached for a hug, David stopped her, a flicker of aversion crossing his face. "Here, hug her for me, I can't do it," he said, gently pushing Lynn towards Tiffany. Tiffany enveloped Lynn in a warm embrace, whispering words of comfort and encouragement.

Turning back to the others, David clapped his hands together. "Alright, ladies, let's not let Lynn's mission ruin our fun. Art is a powerful tool, even in the face of adversity." He walked over to Kris and ran his hand through her hair. "How's it coming, my little raven?" He peered at her untouched paper, a flicker of amusement dancing in his eyes. "Is that a polar bear in a blizzard?"

Kris flinched, the playful jab landing with unexpected force. The truth was, she hadn't even started. The blank page mocked her bravado, a stark representation of the artistic paralysis that had gripped her since Summer announced the art session. Surrounded by the genuinely talented women in David's life, her carefully constructed aura of dark artistry crumbled. Kayla was swirling vibrant landscapes in oil, Elena meticulously drafting intricate ink drawings, and even Nicole, usually doodling superheroes, was capturing a vibrant scene of heroic wiener cavalry.

She had envisioned herself creating something edgy, something profound, something dark. But faced with the reality of their talent and the rawness of the post-apocalyptic world, her attempts felt childish and pretentious. "Uh... I'm still thinking," she mumbled, avoiding his gaze. "Just... brainstorming themes, Master."

David grabbed her hips from behind, his breath tickling her neck as he leaned close, the warmth of his body pressing against her back. His lips brushed against Kris's ear, his voice a low rumble that sent shivers down her spine, a potent mix of anticipation and something she couldn't quite name. "Your theme is submission," he murmured, his fingers tightening slightly on her hips, "the exquisite purpose of slavery." The words hung in the air, heavy with implication, and Kris found herself both intrigued and a little breathless.

The words were a jolt, a spark igniting a fire within her. It wasn't the literal act of servitude he spoke of, but the surrender of ego, the relinquishing of control to something greater. In that moment, Kris understood. Her artistic paralysis wasn't about a lack of talent, but a fear of vulnerability. She had hidden behind darkness, using it as a shield against revealing her true self.

The charcoal pencil felt different in her hand now, no longer a tool for crafting an edgy persona but a conduit for expressing something real. She closed her eyes, picturing a woman, strong and defiant, yet bound by chains. But these weren't chains of oppression; they were links to an overshadowing figure, a source of immense power. The figure wasn't subduing her, but empowering her, grounding her, giving her a purpose.

Kris began to sketch, the charcoal dancing across the paper with newfound confidence. The woman's face was fierce, her eyes blazing with determination. The chains, rendered in intricate detail, weren't shackles but vibrant strands of energy connecting her to the towering figure behind her. The figure itself was shrouded in shadow, its form suggestive yet undefined, representing the complex dynamic of submission and power.

As she worked, she could feel David's presence beside her, not judging or directing, but simply observing, his energy a comforting weight. The therapeutic effect of the art session washed over her, melting away the anxiety and self-doubt. She wasn't trying to be someone else; she was simply expressing what was within her, the complex interplay of darkness and light, strength and surrender.

Meanwhile, the Behemoth, a monument to overkill and David's particular brand of pragmatic paranoia, lumbered down the abandoned highway. Inside, Eric gripped the steering wheel, navigating the obstacle course of derelict vehicles with surprising grace for a man whose pre-apocalypse life revolved delivering food in buckets. Beside him, Lynn fidgeted, her hands clasped tightly in her lap. The passing scenery was a blur of contorted metal and darkness, a grim reminder of the world's sudden, violent collapse.

In the back, Lily and Josh sat shoulder-to-shoulder, a silent, coordinated force. Lily, watching out the side window, seemed captivated by the scenery. On the other side, Josh watched his mother with concern and determination. "It's... it's been a while," Lynn said, her voice barely noticeable over the Behemoth's mechanical symphony. "Almost two months. I hope they're okay."

Eric glanced at her, his expression softening. "They're tough, Lynn. And you said they had supplies. They're probably just waiting it out." Lynn offered a weak smile, but her anxiety was palpable. She hadn't seen her parents since before she abandoned them to find Josh. The guilt gnawed at her, a constant, unwelcome companion. "Mee-maw and Pee-paw probably wouldn't recognize you now, Mom," Josh said from the back, a hint of amusement in his voice. "All that tactical gear, knowing which end of a gun goes bang... you've gone all hardcore."

Lynn chuckled, a genuine, if fleeting, moment of levity. "Hardcore is relative, honey. Compared to David and his wives, I'm still a damsel in distress." Suddenly, Lynn's breath hitched. "Stop! Stop the truck!" she exclaimed, her voice rising in panic. Eric, startled by her sudden outburst, slammed on the brakes. The Behemoth shuddered, its reinforced frame protesting the abrupt stop. Lily and Josh were instantly alert, their eyes scanning the surroundings for any sign of threat. "What is it?" Eric asked, his hand instinctively reaching for the pistol holstered on his thigh.

Lynn pointed a trembling finger towards the side of the road. "That... that's my car. My SUV. The one I abandoned." The Behemoth idled, its propane-fueled engine chugging steadily as they all stared at the pathetic remains of Lynn's pre-apocalypse life. It was a faded blue Ford Explorer, now covered in dust and grime, its tires flat and windows smeared with what looked suspiciously like blood.

The scene triggered a cascade of memories for Lynn: the desperation, the fear, the utter hopelessness she felt as she left it behind, praying for a miracle. "That's where... that's where David found me," she whispered, her voice thick with emotion. Lily, sensing her rising anxiety, grabbed her shoulder. "Are you going to be okay?"

Lynn took a deep breath, trying to regain her composure. "I'm fine. Just… it's a lot to process. It feels like a lifetime ago." Josh, ever practical, chimed in. "Do you want to take a look? Maybe there's something useful left inside?"

Lynn hesitated. A part of her wanted to stay as far away from that metal tomb as possible, to bury the memory and never look back. But another part of her, the part that was slowly learning to survive in this brutal new world, knew that every resource was precious. "Yeah," she said finally, her voice firmer now. "Yeah, let's take a look."

Eric pulled the Behemoth over, the massive vehicle sighing as its engine settled into a lower rumble. Lynn, Lily, and Josh climbed out, surveying the scene. The abandoned SUV sat like a forgotten monument to a life that no longer existed. "Looks like someone's already been through it," Josh observed, pointing to a shattered window. "Probably scavengers."

As they approached the vehicle, Lily's keen eyes scanned the surrounding area. "The bodies are gone," she stated matter-of-factly. "The men dad killed that night." She glanced at Lynn, a hint of concern in her expression. Lynn nodded, a shiver running down her spine despite the warm evening air. "Yeah. The men David… dealt with." She still had nightmares about that night. The speed, the precision, the absolute lack of hesitation in David's movements. It had been horrifying, yet… strangely reassuring.

"Someone probably dragged them off the road," Eric suggested, joining them near the SUV. "Animals, maybe. Or someone looking for supplies." He grimaced. "This whole area is probably picked clean by now, but it's worth a look."

Josh tried the door handle, but it was locked. With a shrug, he pulled a crowbar from his pack and expertly pried the door open. The hinges groaned in protest, and the interior of the SUV was revealed. Dust, debris, and the lingering scent of stale air filled their nostrils. "Wow, what a mess," Josh said, wrinkling his nose. "Looks like you left in a hurry." Lynn sighed, stepping closer. "I did. I didn't have time to pack. I just grabbed what I could and ran." She began sifting through the junk on the passenger seat: crumpled maps, empty water bottles, a half-eaten bag of chips.

Lily, meanwhile, was carefully examining the exterior of the SUV. She ran her fingers along the bullet holes in the door, her brow furrowed in concentration. "These shots… they were close range," she said, her voice barely a whisper. "Were these here before?" Lily's words hung heavy in the air, the implications thick with unspoken dread.

Josh, ever vigilant, had already circled the vehicle, his eyes darting over every inch of its battered frame. He stopped abruptly at the rear tire, squatting down for a closer look. "Mom," he said, his voice low and serious. "Your flat… it's not just a flat. See these?" He pointed to a series of small, neat holes clustered around the valve stem. "Bullet holes. Someone shot out your tire."

Lynn gasped, her hand flying to her mouth. "Shot it out? But… why?" Lily stepped closer, examining the damage. "They weren't trying to kill you, Lynn. These shots were deliberately placed to disable the vehicle. Make you a sitting duck." She glanced at Josh, a silent understanding passing between them. "Someone used you as bait." The realization hit Lynn like a physical blow. She stumbled back, her face paling. "Bait? For what? Who would do that?" Eric, who had been rummaging through the back of the SUV, paused, a look of concern etching itself onto his face. "This is bad," he muttered. "Real bad. We need to get out of here."

The engine of the truck roared to life, shattering the oppressive silence that had descended upon the scene. Lynn scrambled into the passenger seat, her mind reeling from Lily's chilling assessment. Josh hopped in beside her, his hand instinctively reaching for the small pistol holstered at his hip. Lily slid into the back, her eyes scanning the road side.

As Eric wrestled the truck back onto the road, Lily turned to Lynn, her voice calm and steady despite the gravity of the situation. "Think about it, Lynn," she said, "You were alone, vulnerable, and clearly heading somewhere. You didn't have anything of value they could take, so what else could you offer?"

Lynn wracked her brain, trying to make sense of the madness. "I… I don't know! I had some food, some water… but it wasn't much. Why would anyone want to use me as bait? What were they trying to catch?" "That's what we need to figure out," Josh interjected, his brow furrowed. "It could be anything. Other survivors, a vehicle… maybe they were just trying to lure someone in for a robbery."

Lily shook her head. "Too risky. Shooting out the tire like that, waiting for someone to come along… that's a planned ambush. They had a specific target in mind, and they were willing to use Lynn as a lure." Eric, his knuckles white on the steering wheel, glanced at Lynn in the rearview mirror. "We're getting you to Margaret and Clarence, Lynn. No more detours, no more stopping for anything. Straight there and straight back."

Josh was quiet, lost in thought. He remembered a similar situation, when they'd gone to rescue Summer, Andrea, Scott and the others. Summer's group had been stranded, their vehicle disabled, and waiting for rescue. Just like Lynn. "Lily, remember when we went to get Summer and the others?" he asked, his voice low. "Summer's car and Scott's ruck were both immobilized."

Lily's eyes widened, a spark of recognition igniting within them. "You're right, Josh. And Summer did have supplies, some medical stuff…" She sucked in a breath. "Dad said they used Summer as bait. Then too."

Eric gripped the steering wheel, the massive truck struggling to squeeze through the small streets. Lily, ever vigilant, scanned the passing scenery. "This town looks like a tornado magnet," she muttered, her voice barely audible above the rumble of the engine. Beside her, Josh nodded in agreement, his gaze equally sharp, picking apart the details of the landscape.

They turned off the main road onto a narrow country lane, the truck bouncing precariously over the potholes. The houses here were few and far between, each one a testament to the isolation of rural living. As they rounded a bend, Lynn gasped. "It's there, it's in there!"

Eric slammed on the brakes, the Behemoth groaning in protest as it lurched to a halt. "Lights?" he questioned, brow furrowed. "Lynn, are you sure this is the right place?" Lynn, her face a mixture of hope and apprehension, nodded vigorously. "Yes, I'm sure! That's their house. I know it is. But... they never had a generator." Lily thought a moment. "That's suspicious. This far out, a generator running at this time of night is a beacon." She glanced at Josh, who nodded in agreement.

Eric shifted in his seat, his gaze sweeping the surroundings. "Lynn, I hate to say it, but Lily's right. This feels off. What's this place usually like?" "Overgrown, cluttered, full of half-finished projects..." Lynn offered. "Dad was always tinkering with something. Mom would complain, but she secretly loved it. They... They were stubborn. They thought the government would fix everything." Her voice cracked.

The scene hung heavy with unanswered questions. The house, bathed in the unnatural glow of electric lights, was jarringly out of place against the backdrop of the star-dusted sky and silent, powerless world.

Lily leaned forward, her eyes narrowed, the youthful innocence of her face replaced with the hard-won pragmatism of a survivor. "Josh, perimeter sweep. Now. I want to know what we're walking into before we even think about knocking on that door."

Josh, ever attuned to her, was already moving, the rifle in his hands an extension of his own body. He slipped out of the Behemoth with a silent grace that belied his age, disappearing into the shadows surrounding the house. Eric watched them, a flicker of unease in his eyes. "You think… you think they're in danger?"

Lily didn't answer immediately, her gaze fixed on the house. "Someone wanted Lynn out here. Someone shot up her SUV to make sure she was stranded. That wasn't random. And now we find her parents' place lit up like a Christmas tree when they should be living like everyone else, scraping by in the dark? No, Eric. This isn't right."

Lynn, her face pale, finally spoke, her voice barely a whisper. "But… what if they're just… happy to see me? What if they found a generator?" Lily turned to her, her expression softening slightly. "I hope that's it, Lynn. I truly do. But we have to be prepared for the worst. This whole thing stinks of a setup."

She paused, chewing on her lip, her mind racing. Then, her eyes widened slightly as a horrifyingly logical thought dawned. "Wait a minute… Dad." Eric frowned. "David? What does he have to do with this?" "Think about it," Lily said, her voice rising in urgency. "The SUV, Summer's group, now this… someone is using Dad's family as bait. They're trying to draw him out." "But why?" Lynn asked, bewildered. "Why would anyone want to hurt David? He's… he's amazing. He helps everyone."

"Exactly," Lily said, frustration lacing her tone. "He's a threat. A powerful, organized, good threat in a world where power comes from exploiting others. They can't take him on at the ranch, not with everything he's built. So they try to lure him out, catch him off guard." She looked at Lynn, her eyes filled with a dawning horror. "Lynn, your SUV… it wasn't just to get to you. It was to get to him. You were bait, and so am I if we go walking in there."

Lynn gasped, her hand flying to her mouth. "Oh my God… I didn't even think…" Lily chewed on her lip, her mind racing. The air hung thick with the implications of her realization. Her mom, Summer, had been targeted. Lynn had been targeted. The common denominator wasn't just David, it was his family. And right now, she and Lynn were standing on the precipice of walking right into a carefully laid trap.

"Okay, okay, don't panic," Josh said, his voice calm and steady. He placed a reassuring hand on Lily's shoulder. "We assess. We adapt. That's what we do." Lily took a deep breath, trying to emulate Josh's composure. Panic wouldn't help anyone. "Right. Options." Lynn looked lost, her eyes darting between Lily and Josh. "So, what do we do? Just… leave my parents?"

"We don't leave them," Lily corrected, her voice firm. "We just don't walk into a kill zone. Option one: we go in, guns blazing, try to extract them. High risk, potentially high reward. Option two: we fall back, regroup, tell Dad what's going on, and come back with reinforcements. Lower risk, but buys the enemy time." Josh nodded. "Option three: something in between. We scout the place out, see what we're up against. Maybe we can find a way to get your parents out without a full-blown assault.”

Lily considered it. Scouting was always a good idea, but time was of the essence. Her gut screamed at her to get back to David, to warn him, but she couldn’t abandon Lynn’s parents. “Scouting is good, but we can’t take too long,” Lily said, her gaze fixed on the seemingly innocuous house. “This feels… deliberate. Too neat. Someone wants us here, and they’re probably expecting us to do exactly what we’re thinking of doing.”

Josh frowned. “True. It’s too easy. Almost like they’re daring us to come in.” Lily glanced at Lynn, her face etched with worry. “Lynn, what are your parents like? What are their habits? Any quirks that might help us?” Lynn wrung her hands. “My dad... he’s kind of a hoarder. The garage is always a mess, full of junk. My mom likes to sit on the porch and read in the evenings. They usually have the TV on in the living room.”

Suddenly, Lynn gasped, grabbing Lily’s arm. “Wait… look!” They followed her gaze to the front of the house. In the dim glow of the moon, a figure emerged from the front door. It was an older man, stocky and hunched – Clarence, Lynn’s father. He shuffled towards the mailbox at the end of the driveway. In the dark. Lily’s eyes narrowed. “What’s he doing?” Lynn’s voice trembled. “My dad… he never walks out here at night. Never. He hates the dark.” Adding to the strangeness, Clarence carefully placed something in the mailbox. “The mail hasn’t been running either,” Lily muttered, her mind racing. “So what’s he putting in there?”

Josh rubbed his chin, his expression hardening. "That's not right. That's definitely not right." The pieces were starting to click into place, forming a disturbing picture. The sabotaged SUV. The eerily undisturbed house. And now, Clarence, engaging in decidedly un-Clarence-like behavior. "Okay," Lily said, her voice low and decisive. "Something's definitely wrong. This isn't just a random encounter. Someone knows we're here."

Josh let out a frustrated sigh. "Damn it. They're watching us. They know we're out here analyzing the situation." Lynn covered her mouth with her hands, tears welling in her eyes. "What do we do? What if… what if they've hurt my parents?"

Josh pointed at the mailbox, a wicked glint in his eye. "Why don't we just check the mail? See what Grandpa Clarence is so eager to deposit at this ungodly hour? Might give us a clue as to what kind of welcome party they've planned inside." Lynn stared at him, aghast. "Are you crazy? We can't just walk up to the mailbox! They'll see us!"

Josh stated plainly, cutting through Lynn's rising panic. "We have to assume we're being watched, and obviously, sending pee-paw out here was a message, a proof of life, maybe even an invitation. The only thing missing is the red carpet." Josh ignored Lynn's rising panic. "We're already compromised, Lynn. Hiding in the bushes isn't going to magically make us invisible. We need information, and that mailbox is the closest thing we have to a clue right now." He glanced at Lily, a silent question in his eyes. Lily, ever the partner, simply nodded.

He took a deep breath and walked towards the mailbox, moving with a casual swagger that belied the tension coiled tight within him. He whistled a jaunty tune, scanning the surroundings, his senses on high alert. The air hung heavy with the scent of pine and something else… a faint metallic tang that made the hairs on the back of his neck prickle.

After grabbing the letter. Josh sauntered back to the Behemoth, the jaunty whistle replaced with a low hum of barely contained fury. He climbed into the passenger seat, tossing the letter onto the dashboard like it was a week-old trout. "Well?" Lily asked, her voice sharp with anticipation. Eric fidgeted in the back, his face a mask of worry. Lynn just stared, her eyes wide and pleading.

Josh leaned back, his face grim. "It's… an invitation. Of the less-than-hospitable variety. 'Welcome home, Lynn. Your parents are safe…for now.' Pleasant, right? The kicker is for you, Lily. 'Tell Lily to bring her father over for a visit if you want them to stay that way.'"

The silence in the cab of the Behemoth was thick enough to choke on. Eric's face went from worried to ashen. Lynn began to sob quietly, burying her face in her hands. Josh, however, remained infuriatingly calm. "Well, shit," Lily said, her voice flat. "They want to play games. Fine. Daddy always said I was good at games." "Lily, no," Lynn wailed, her head snapping up. "They have my parents! You can't just… just bring David into this! He'll get hurt! We'll all get hurt!"

Lily turned to Lynn, her expression softening slightly. "Lynn, sweetheart, they've already brought Dad into this. You being used as bait? Mom almost getting killed? That wasn't a coincidence. They want him. They're just too chicken to come get him themselves." She turned her attention to Josh, her eyes blazing with a cold fire. "They want a visit from my father? Fine. They're going to get one."

Josh nodded, a predatory grin spreading across his face. "That's my girl. Always thinking strategically." He turned to Lynn, his voice gentle but firm. "Mom, mee-maw and pee-paw are in danger, yes. But the best chance they have is if we hit these bastards hard and fast, and nobody hits harder or faster than David."

How strong is David and his family?

Strength usage is dependent on several factors, for the sake of simplicity, we'll say that there are 7 levels of strength. Untrained, Average, Beginner, Trained, Highly Trained, Peak and Elite. Each level has a percentage of their own body weight they can handle.

Additionally, Men and women, on average, have different strength levels for their upper body and lower body.

Group	UNTR	AVG	BEG	TNG	HIGH	PEAK	ELITE
Upper Body (Men)	55%	66%	91%	111%	152%	166%	191%
Lower Body (Men)	110%	125%	165%	200%	225%	250%	275%
Upper Body (Women)	29%	34%	47%	58%	79%	86%	99%
Lower Body (Women)	77%	88%	116%	140%	158%	175%	193%

If you consider David's strength at the time of his regression, then plug that into the body of a 13 year old, at 1/3 the weight, or even a toddler. Well, then you have a multiplier to add to the equation. Then consider everyone's strength training, their body weight and their age.

At birth, Aidan, at 6.5 lbs, with the temporal strength of his father, would be able to bench press 27 lbs. With regular training, Lily, during the shot-put incident in Chapter 32 of the first book, at 36 lbs, would be able to bench 49 lbs. Mainly because girls have a much lower upper body strength percentage.

David, immediately after his regression, at 13 years old, could bench 184 lbs. Now, the strongest people will never exceed 3 times greater than average, unless serious drugs are used. Consider Brian Shaw; at 454 lbs. can lift 202%, which is reasonably close to an Elite trainer. With that out of the way, here are the stats.

	Height (in)	Weight (lbs)	Upper (lbs)	Lower (lbs)	Upper %	Lower %	Diff of Average
David	72	180	604	909	335%	505%	4.6
Tiffany	69	150	119	237	79%	158%	2.1
Jennifer	63	134	78	188	58%	140%	1.6
Summer	66	130	75	182	58%	140%	1.6
Elena	68	126	73	176	58%	140%	1.6
Taylor	65	115	59	147	52%	128%	1.5
Nicole	61	140	79	195	56%	139%	1.6
Jessica	62	110	96	231	87%	210%	2.5
Kayla	63	135	82	204	61%	151%	1.8
Tanya	64	142	73	181	52%	128%	1.5
Aidan	72	171	524	944	306%	552%	4.5
Brian	75	200	613	1104	306%	552%	4.5
David Jr.	69	175	734	1087	420%	621%	5.7
Lily	65	125	297	604	237%	483%	6.2
Seth	60	121	377	680	312%	562%	4.6
Grace	59	110	179	433	163%	393%	4.6

This means Lily could carry a full-sized man around, as easily as most of us would carry a crate of ammunition. Junior, however, could easily throw that man about 50 feet with a bit of effort.

When did everything happen?

After Blackout/EMP (ABO). Before Blackout/EMP (BBO). Regression happened 33 years and 6 months BBO. After Regression (AR).

7yrs ABO – SR: Ch 1

34 yrs BBO – SR: Ch 2, David's Regression.

11 mos AR – SR: Ch 3, David meets Tiffany

3 yrs, 4 mos AR – SR: Ch 7, David meets Jennifer

4 yrs, 3 mos AR – SR: Ch 9, Summer confronts David

4 yrs, 10 mos AR – SR: Ch 11-12, Prom night

5 yrs, 11 mos AR – David marries Tiffany

8 yrs AR – SR: Ch 17, Jennifer moves in

8 yrs, 11 mos AR – Aidan is born

10 yrs, 10 mos AR – SR: Ch 19, Brian is born

11 yrs, 2 mos AR – David moves to California

11 yrs, 4 mos AR – SR: Ch 20, Summer moves in

11 yrs, 8 mos AR   SR: Ch 22, David marries Jennifer

12 yrs, 1 mos AR – SR: Ch 23, David Jr. is born

13 yrs, 8 mos AR – SR: Ch 24, Lily is born

14 yrs, 10 mos AR – SR: Ch 26, David meets Parker, Scott and Eric for the first time

15 yrs, 1 mos AR – SR: Ch 26, David marries Summer

16 yrs, 5 mos AR – SR: Ch 28, Bunker construction begins

17 yrs, 8 mos AR – SR: Ch 30, Taylor joins David's group

17 yrs, 11 mos AR – SR: Ch 33, Jessica meets David

18 yrs, 10 mos AR – SR: Ch 24, Nicole sleeps with David

19 yrs, 7 mos AR – SR: Ch 36, Seth and Grace are born

20 yrs AR – SR: Ch 37, David marries Nicole

21 yrs, 6 mos AR – David retires from the Army

21 yrs, 7 mos AR – SR: Ch 39, David meets Kayla

22 yrs, 4 mos AR – Jessica moves in with David

23 yrs AR – Jessica gives herself to David

23 yrs, 3 mos AR – Kayla joins David, David marries Jessica

24 yrs, 1 mos AR – Aidan meets Alissa

24 yrs, 7 mos AR – SR: Ch 46, David and Jessica's world tour

26 yrs, 4 mos AR – SR: Ch 48, Move to Texas, Alissa joints David's family

27 yrs, 8 mos AR – SR: Ch 50, Aidan and Alissa finally consummate

28 yrs, 3 mos AR – SR: Ch 51, Windows installed, Lily meets Josh

30 yrs AR – SR: Ch 52, David meets Lynn

30 yrs, 6 mos AR – Ch 54, David meets Tanya

31 yrs, 8 mos AR – Ch 55, Tanya gives herself to David

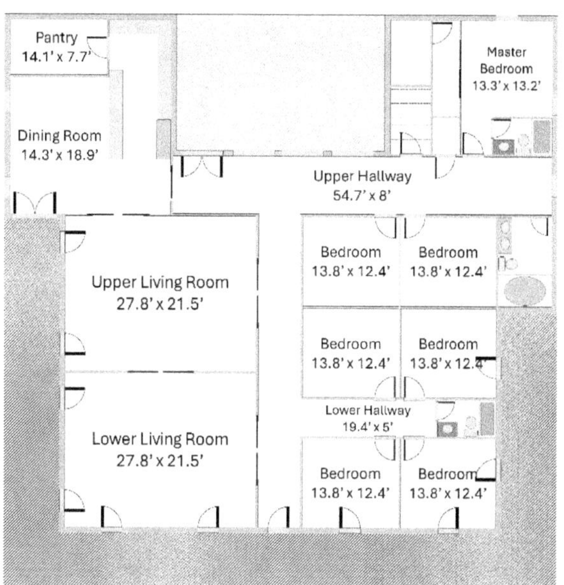

First (Main) floor of the main house

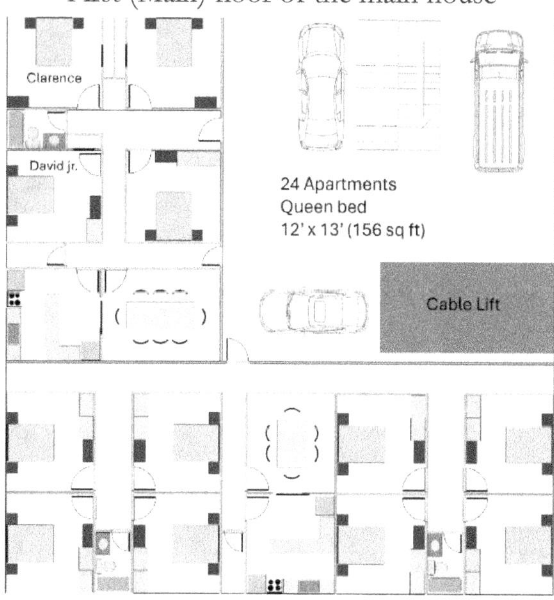

Garage (Top Bunker) of the main house

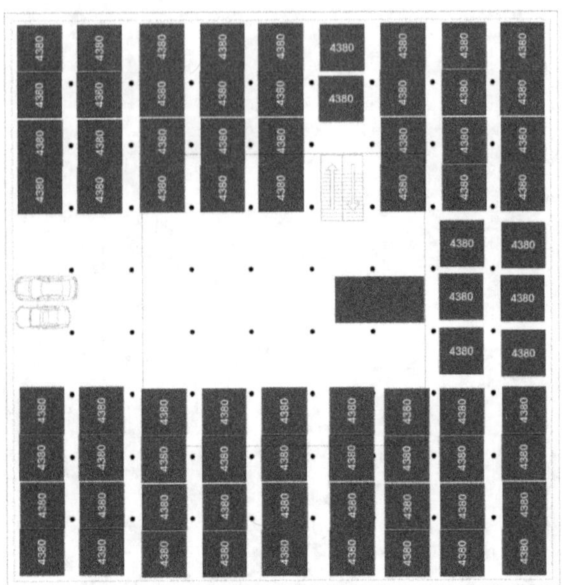

Storage Bunker

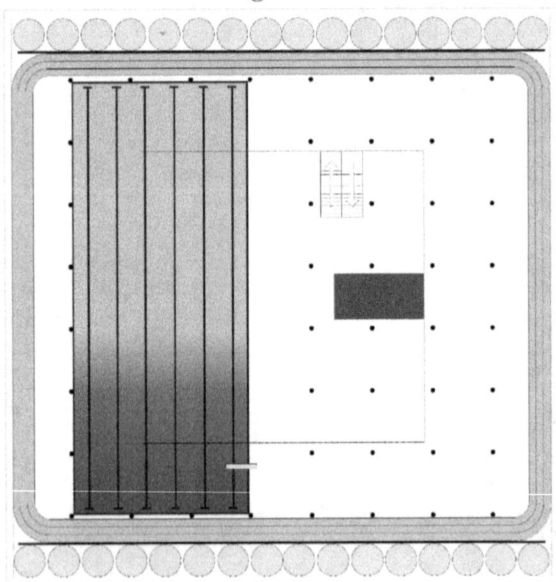

Recreational Bunker

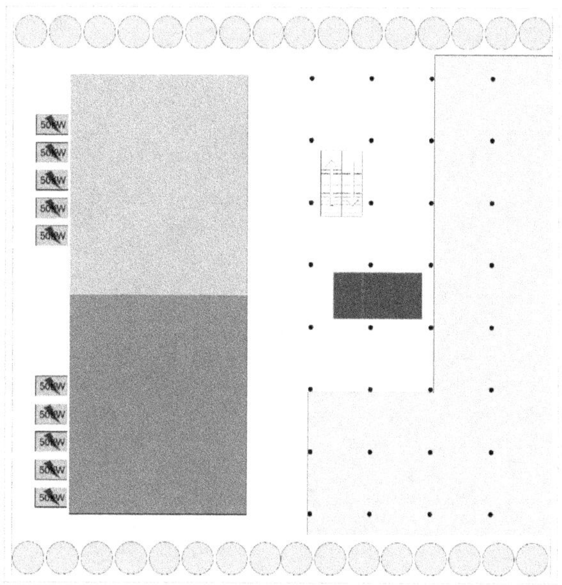

Maintenance Bunker

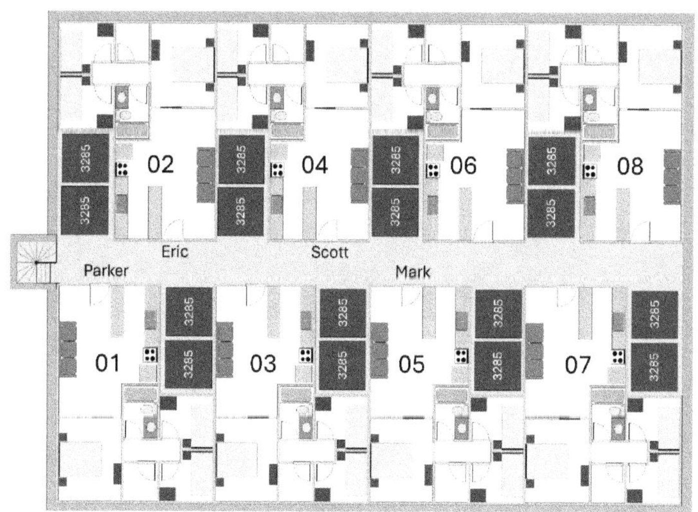

Apartment Bunker Level 1

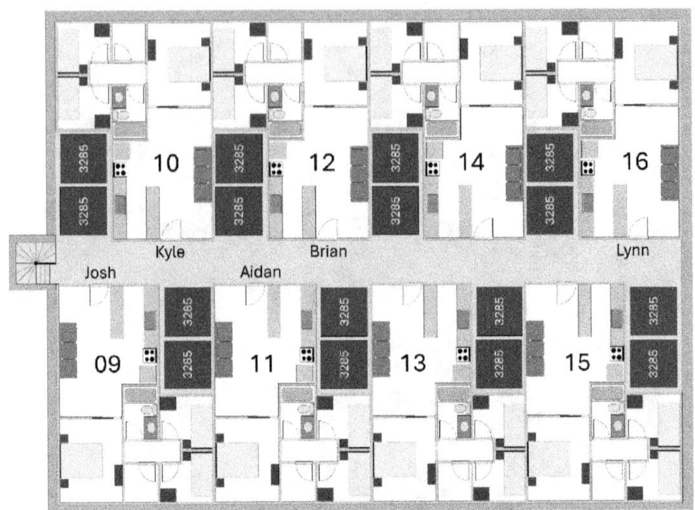

Apartment Bunker Level 2

www.ingramcontent.com/pod-product-compliance
Lightning Source LLC
Chambersburg PA
CBHW070503300726
48975CB00007B/2304